MEN ON
FIRE

Also by Susan Lyons:

Sex Drive
She's on Top
Touch Me
Hot in Here
Champagne Rules

Also by Rachelle Chase:

Sin Club
Sex Lounge

Also by Jodi Lynn Copeland:

Escape to Ecstasy
Sweet and Sinful
Handyman
Body Moves
Operation G-Spot
After Hours

MEN ON FIRE

Susan Lyons
Rachelle Chase
Jodi Lynn Copeland

A

APHRODISIA

KENSINGTON BOOKS
http://www.kensingtonbooks.com

APHRODISIA BOOKS are published by

Kensington Publishing Corp.
119 West 40th Street
New York, NY 10018

All Kensington titles, imprints and distributed lines are available at special quantity discounts for bulk purchases for sales promotions, premiums, fund-raising, and educational or institutional use.

Special book excerpts or customized printings can also be created to fit specific needs. For details, write or phone the office of the Kensington Special Sales Manager: Kensington Publishing Corp., 119 West 40th Street, New York, NY 10018. Attn: Special Sales Department. Phone: 1-800-221-2647.

Aphrodisia and the A logo Reg. U.S. Pat. & TM Off.

ISBN-13: 978-0-7582-3801-6
ISBN-10: 0-7582-3801-0

First Kensington Trade Paperback Printing: November 2009

10 9 8 7 6 5 4 3 2 1

Printed in the United States of America

CONTENTS

TOO HOT TO HANDLE

Susan Lyons

Acknowledgments

Warm thanks to my critique group for their invaluable assistance: Elizabeth Allan, Michelle Hancock, and Nazima Ali. Special thanks to my editor, Hilary Sares, for offering me the opportunity to contribute to Aphrodisia's second firefighter anthology. (I love firefighter heroes!) And thanks, too, to my wonderful agent, Emily Sylvan Kim, for her wisdom and enthusiasm.

Most especially, thanks to the brave men and women who serve as firefighters, and to the families and friends who worry about them and support them.

I invite readers to visit my Web site at www.susanlyons.ca; e-mail me at susan@susanlyons.ca; or write c/o PO Box 73523, Downtown Postal Outlet, 1014 Robson Street, Vancouver, BC, Canada V6E 4L9.

I hope you'll look for my new Wild Ride series, starting with *Sex Drive* in December.

1

"What the hell is wrong with my image?" I asked my two best friends, trusting them to tell me the truth. On this warm July evening, we were seated outside at Hapa Izakaya, a Japanese fusion restaurant on Yew Street, sipping sake martinis.

"Nothing, Jade." Kimberly's mass of blond corkscrew curls tossed as she shook her head vigorously. "You're proof that black plus Chinese equals gorgeous. You're smart, responsible, successful, not to mention trilingual. You're generous and loyal and fun. Damn, woman, you're perfect. Right, Amarjeet?"

"You truly are all those things." Amarjeet studied me, deep-set brown eyes thoughtful below perfectly shaped black brows. "This is about your job?"

"Yeah." I'd told them my boss, the CEO of the Families First Foundation, had recently had a health scare and was retiring to spend more time with his family. I was VP of Communications and truly believed I was the best person to fill his position. But today I'd had a depressing conversation with the chair of the board.

"I would guess the image problem is that you're single," Amarjeet said.

I sighed. "That's what the chair more than hinted at. But why should it matter? Not to mention, it's *illegal* to discriminate based on marital status."

"Damn right!" Kimberly said.

"Yes, of course," Amarjeet said. "But Triple-F has a mandate, a public profile, and it's all about families and children." A doctoral student in philosophy at the University of British Columbia, she always reasoned things out thoroughly. "The CEO is the figurehead. If she's a single woman . . ." She shrugged and took a soybean pod from the bowl of seasoned edamame in the middle of the table.

"If they refuse you the job because you're single, sue them." Kimberly, a fourth-grade teacher, liked to cut to the chase.

Amarjeet munched the last bean from the pod and shook her head. "How would that help? Jade loves Triple-F."

"Exactly," I said grimly. "It's not that the chair said flat out I won't get the promotion. She said there are numerous factors to consider, image is one, and Candace's—she's VP of Donor Development and my main competition—might be a better fit for Triple-F. Candace is also *gorgeous*"—I glanced at Kimberly, who made a face—"and smart, et cetera, though only *bi*lingual, I might point out. However—damn her!—she's married to a handsome lawyer and has the cutest twins. One girl, one boy. Blonde. Can you imagine how image-worthy that family is? Compared to me?"

"That sucks," Kimberly said, and Amarjeet nodded vigorously.

I downed the last of my melon sake martini as our Japanese waitress arrived with tapa-sized platters of food. She decorated the table with strikingly presented salmon sashimi, fried udon noodles with chicken and veggies, soft-shell crab tempura, and a salad of field greens with shrimp and avocado in a tangy citrus sauce. We thanked her, ordered another round of drinks, then picked up chopsticks and dove in.

As I swirled up udon noodles, I sighed. I'd devoted the last three years to Triple-F and totally believed in the work we did, funding services to families in need. I had ideas for new sources of funding, ways to cut administrative costs, all sorts of things to improve the organization. My current boss was an idealist, Candace was Ms. Practical, and I combined both qualities. "Damn it, I'd be the best CEO. So, any brilliant ideas? Aside from suing Triple-F? Or getting married?" Finally, I popped the noodles into my mouth.

Kimberly wiggled her left hand so her solitaire engagement ring sparkled in the evening sunlight. "I vote for marriage."

"I've wanted to get married since I was six," I reminded her.

"So have I." Amarjeet mixed wasabi with soy sauce. "We're twenty-seven, Jade. What are we waiting for?"

If it were that easy, I'd have been married years ago. "Duh. Prince Charming. So far all I've found are frogs."

"As have I. And I, personally, am tired of kissing frogs who remain frogs rather than transforming into princes. In fact—" She broke off as our second round of sake martinis arrived, then went on, "I may agree to let my mother look into an arranged marriage."

My jaw dropped. Her mom had been talking about arranged marriage since my friend was old enough to dress her Bride Barbie in a red silk sari. I'd never thought Westernized Amarjeet would go for it.

"Oh my God," Kimberly said, "it's so Dark Ages."

"Not in India," Amarjeet responded.

"*You* aren't in India," I said. "You were born in Vancouver, Canada. Not two miles from where we're sitting." The three of us had attended the same elementary school, where we'd become *best friends forever* long before anyone had invented that term.

"Indian families care more about tradition," Amarjeet said softly. "You know my parents. You've been to my sister's wedding here, and heard me talk about my brother's in India."

I nodded. "Not to mention all those cousins. Seems to me, every few months someone in your family is getting married."

"And a lot of them are arranged."

"But you've always resisted," I said, as Kimberly said, "It's archaic."

Amarjeet raised her shoulders, smooth and brown against the Kelly green top she was wearing, and rotated them as if to ease out tightness. "Dating hasn't worked. Perhaps too much choice is a bad thing. I've wasted time. I want to get married and start a family."

"I'm impatient too," I admitted. Good friends and a great job were all very well, but I'd always dreamed of a husband and children. It was time.

"So," Amarjeet said, "you and Triple-F want the same thing."

"True." But how to achieve it? Jokingly, I asked, "Are you suggesting we get your mom to arrange me a marriage too?"

Amarjeet's eyes sparkled with humor. "She would so love to do that."

"So would your granny, Jade." Kimberly bowed her head and spoke in a dreadful Chinese accent. "Me, ancient Chinese grandmother, say sweet innocent granddaughter marry nice respectable Chinese boy."

The three of us laughed. Yes, my mom's mother had a slight accent, but she'd been in Canada since, at 18, she married a Chinese-Canadian—in an arranged marriage. She was fluent in English, had obtained a degree in fine arts in her 40s, and now, in her mid-70s, was stylish, attractive, and anything but "ancient." The sentiments Kimberly had expressed were, however, bang on. Granny had grown to love my black Québécois papa, but she'd never quite forgiven Mom for not marrying a Chinese man. She hoped I would make up for my mom's disobedient behavior.

"Okay," I said, "let's agree my goal—for personal and work reasons—is to find Prince Charming and get married. Leaving aside arranged marriage, what's my best strategy?"

"Meet lots of men," Kimberly said promptly.

"I have. I've wasted years dating frogs."

"Hone your frog detector," Kimberly said, "so you don't waste time."

I nibbled on crab tempura. "How about this? I'll date like crazy—even let Granny fix me up—and on the first date I'll decide whether the guy has Prince Charming potential."

"What if he doesn't?" Kimberly asked.

"He's a write-off. On to the next guy."

"It's not a bad plan," Amarjeet said. "But it could take time to find the right man. What about the job promotion?"

Our conversation had helped me realize my problem. In my dating life, I had lacked the focus I brought to my work. I'd hang out with an okay guy for months, knowing we had no future. Now I had a plan and a goal, actually two goals: marriage and promotion. I was highly motivated—I'd be realizing two dreams—and when I was motivated, I could achieve great results. "I'll go on lots of dates. I'll go on a date every night. If I apply myself, how long can it take?"

"Months," Amarjeet said, "or longer. If your granny arranged a marriage, you could have a fiancé in a week. I'm sure she has men in mind."

"No, I believe in free choice." That was how my parents, who'd married against both their families' wishes, had raised me. And look at how solid and loving their relationship was.

"I have a better idea." Kimberly's blue eyes sparkled as brightly as her ring. "Have you seen the posters for 'It's Raining Men'?"

"The bachelor auction?" What woman could ignore the posters

featuring hot guys in everything from bathing suits to tuxes, all holding umbrellas? "The one that benefits the new children's wing at the hospital? What does that have to do with my problem?"

"You could buy a faux fiancé. The children's wing is a great cause, right up your alley. Bid on an amazing guy, tell him to pretend you're engaged, and trot him around to the office."

"Deceive them? I can't."

"Why not?" She stuck out her chin. "They're all set to break the law by discriminating in favor of image-perfect Candace."

"They might not. I could still get the job."

"Even the playing field a little. Candace has the Hallmark card family. Get yourself a cute, successful, devoted fiancé."

"Hmm." I glanced at Amarjeet. "What do you think?"

She frowned into her drink. "Deception is a bad thing. But you do intend to get married and have a plan for finding a husband." She glanced up. "Wait. How could you date if you tell Triple-F you're engaged?"

"Good question. Uh . . . First dates will be casual, just coffee or lunch. When a guy makes it to a second date, we'll find activities that aren't too public."

"Way to go!" Kimberly winked.

I giggled. "Dirty mind." Though the idea of sex was tantalizing. I'd gone months without.

"But," Amarjeet said, "what happens to the faux fiancé after Triple-F announces the new CEO? Or if you find a serious boyfriend before then?"

"Um . . ."

Kimberly tossed her curls. "You tell Triple-F the jerk fiancé dumped you, and they'll be sympathetic." With her chopsticks, she picked up the last piece of salmon sashimi and dunked it in dipping sauce.

I liked the people at the Families First Foundation, and I had a rep for being honest and straightforward. No one would doubt me if I said I was engaged, which in a way made it even scummier to lie. But I really, really wanted that job. I'd make a better CEO than Candace, and if she got the job, she'd dig in for years and years of unimaginative leadership.

Damn it, the position should be awarded on merits, not marriage.

I took a deep breath, then hoisted my martini glass. "Okay, ladies, we're going to a bachelor auction!"

2

From: Jade Rousseau [jade_rousseau@shaw.ca]
To: 'Amarjeet Nagra'; 'Kimberly Brock'
Subject: Write-off: Brian's cousin Peter

How shallow am I to be repelled by a potbelly? I'm not saying a guy has to be gorgeous, but how about at least moderately fit??? It's not just about looks, it's about health. (See, I'm not REALLY that shallow <g>.) No 2nd date for Peter. (Kimberly, I know he's your future cousin-in-law. He's nice, just a couch potato.)

Frog detector rule: No dates with guys who aren't in shape!

See ya at the auction!!! Let's find me a fiancé <G>.

In a room packed with 300 dressed-up women, we'd found seats with a good view of the stage. The air was filled with perfume and impatience as a distinguished silver-haired man made a rah-rah pitch for the children's wing, encouraging everyone to bid their hearts out. Viewing screens behind him projected his image for those who couldn't see the stage clearly.

We sipped the event's signature cocktail, called Raining Men. It was pink and creamy and tasted of strawberries, passion fruit, and a hint of brandy.

I rolled up the program and tapped it nervously against my thigh, above the hem of my black cocktail dress, as the man on stage thanked the bachelors, the silent auction donors, and the event sponsors. "Now please welcome radio talk show host Cara Winters, your emcee for the bachelor auction."

A brunette in a slinky red evening gown and killer stilettos embraced him and took the mike. Holding it close to her shiny red lips, her overblown image repeated on the viewing screens, she said in a sexy drawl, "Ladies, I know why you're here tonight, and I'm here for the same reason. I—" her voice rose in volume— "need a MAAAAN!" The audience chuckled.

"Say it with me, ladies," she said. "Tell me what you need." Together, voices escalating, the audience chanted, "I NEED A MAAAAN!"

Jazzed, I joined in. The rules said we could buy a man to paint the living room, do our taxes, escort us to the theater, or do almost anything our little hearts desired—except have sex. The rule was, we weren't buying sex, but despite that, the whole ambience was sexy. For example, the waiters who'd passed appies were, to a man, eye candy. My body, which had been celibate for six months, had definitely perked to attention. Tonight might be purely business, but that didn't mean I couldn't enjoy the scenery. And the company of my vibrator later tonight.

"Then that's what you're going to get," the emcee said. "Twenty-four of Vancouver's finest bachelors. So, without further ado . . ."

The lights changed to dramatic stage lighting and the song "It's Raining Men" poured out of the sound system. Men, each carrying an open umbrella, paraded onstage as the audience clapped and whistled. A few guys strutted, others danced to the music, some walked normally. They were a fine-looking bunch—some cute, some handsome; some lean, some broad; some fair, some dark. There were men in business suits, men in tuxes, men in muscle-hugging T-shirts and ripped denim, one in only board shorts, and three in firefighter garb. A true smorgasbord of attractive guys—and with luck and enough money, one of them would be my fiancé.

Kimberly pointed. "Look at the firefighters!"

I'd already focused on them. The three were clearly together and had planned what they'd wear. They were all in turnout pants, bare-chested but for suspenders. One toted an ax, one had a coil of hose, and the other held a huge torch. "They can save my life any day."

The three really were hot. Especially the dark-haired one with the ax and killer smile. That smile made all my female parts hum with sexual awareness. So did his stride, as the men circled the stage. Not a swagger, just a natural ease with his own body. The kind of walk that made a woman imagine how good he'd be in bed.

"You can buy a firefighter," Amarjeet whispered.

I shook my head. "I want a white-collar guy." A man who fit my image as—hopefully—the future CEO of Triple-F. Yet, it was hard to tear my gaze away from the firefighter and study the rest of the candidates.

When the song ended, the men left the stage to enthusiastic applause. The emcee said, "Now that your appetites are whetted, ladies, let's learn what's on the menu. Each bachelor's going to tell you a bit about himself and answer one question. They won't know the questions ahead of time. I'm choosing them at random." She waved hot-pink index cards.

"I'll call the men in the order listed in your program. After, we'll have a break so you can collect your thoughts." She winked. "Then we'll start the bidding."

I clicked open the red pen I'd been given at the door and got ready to take notes.

"First up," the emcee said, "is Justin Wong, a tax lawyer who loves fine dining."

As a sleek guy in a tux took the stage, Amarjeet leaned close. "White collar, Chinese, attractive, fit. Bachelor number one could be your man."

"He could." I listened as Justin gave his spiel. The bachelors would have been told to play to the audience and sell themselves, and he did a good job, but underlying it was a note of Chinese humility. Granny would love him. I was pretty impressed myself. This was a man I'd like to date for real. Maybe my faux fiancé could turn into my genuine one!

The next guy was the one in board shorts. Cute, but not the image I was looking for. The next was too old and too arrogant about his job. Then came the firefighter with the hose. Not being interested in a blue-collar guy, I slipped away to get a second round of Raining Mens.

For another dozen or so guys, my friends and I made admiring or snide comments and I jotted notes. A high-school teacher made it onto my list, and a doctor with a family practice.

I was scribbling madly when Kimberly said, "Ooh, another firefighter."

"He's very handsome," Amarjeet said. "And don't you love the ax?"

My head jerked up. Sure enough, it was the dark-haired man with the great smile. Quinn O'Malley, his name was. His skin was darkish, though lighter than mine. His black hair was cut short, in a style that emphasized his strong features and the dramatic slashes of cheekbone and black eyebrows. His eyes—dark brown or black—sparkled and his sensual lips curved, counterbalancing the impression of raw masculine strength.

His bare torso was strong and toned, but not in an overdone "must be on steroids" way. Even though his lower half was concealed by the turnout pants, I knew it would measure up. I wondered what, besides more toned muscles, he was hiding under those bulky pants, and felt the hot throb of arousal between my legs. With the cute waiters and some of the other bachelors I'd felt a quiver, but with Quinn O'Malley, the impact was a hundred times stronger.

He was utterly masculine and had a devil-may-care aura that reached out and grabbed a girl by the throat. And the pussy. No question which guy my body would vote for if it got a say in the matter.

"We're supposed to talk about our jobs," he said, "but you folks know what firefighters do. When I'm not at work, I sail, windsurf, ride my motorbike, hike."

Though I had no interest in bidding on him, my brain was still in evaluation mode. Humble about work: a good thing. Hazardous occupation, motorbike, dangerous hobbies: bad. Very bad. An adrenaline junkie, a man who flirted with danger. That was unacceptable. In my teens, my papa, a cop, almost lost his life on the job. It traumatized Mom and me. She'd persuaded him to give up active duty, and since then he'd taught at the Justice Institute. I would never go through that kind of horror again. Never get involved with a man who risked his life every day.

No, wait. This wasn't about whom I'd date for real, it was about finding the best faux fiancé. And it wasn't Quinn O'Malley.

His smile deepened, revealing a dimple. "And, yeah, I've been known to enjoy romantic stuff like dinners out, dancing, moonlight strolls along the beach."

Oh, God, those things were good, very good. I imagined dancing with him, feeling the coiled strength of that powerful body moving sensually against me. Or kissing in the moonlight, finding a deserted pocket of beach, making love with only the stars watching.

"Jade?" Kimberly tugged my arm. "You're gaping at him like you want to eat him up."

"Mmm." With my tongue, my lips, my entire body. And then I wanted him to eat me up. Under my skimpy dress, my nipples rubbed against the lace of my bra, and the crotch of my panties was damp with need. Oh, yes, he could eat me up this very minute, and launch me into a shuddering, screaming climax.

He was talking about his skills, mentioning carpentry and cooking. His manner was so warm and intimate, it was as if he were speaking to me individually. Of course, every other woman no doubt felt the same way.

"So," he finished, "if you win me, you can ask me to build a gazebo in your garden, barbecue you the best steak or salmon you've ever eaten, or take you out sailing and find a moonlit beach." The dimple flashed again.

Cara Winters, the emcee, fanned herself. "Ladies, our imagination can fill in the rest."

My imagination was working overtime. I had a feeling Quinn O'Malley could end my sexual dry spell with a bang. He hadn't been any more blatantly sexy than the other men, yet his easy confidence told a story of its own.

Cara held out a fan of index cards. He chose one and handed it to her. She read, "Why are you still a bachelor?"

He was quiet a moment, and when he spoke his tone was serious. "I believe in marriage and kids. They give life meaning, and they're a long-term commitment."

As he spoke, I nodded in agreement.

"Yeah," he went on, "I'd like that one day. I can see it." His expression was reflective, almost as if he'd gone inside his own head and was envisioning the future. The man was no doubt a player, but these remarks seemed genuine. Then the grin and dimple flashed again. "So I'll fall back on that old line, a guy has to wait for the right woman to come along."

When he strolled off stage, his gait was easy, powerful, totally masculine.

"Jade, you aren't writing any comments," Amarjeet said.

"He's—" I could barely speak, my throat was so dry. "He's not the kind of man I want."

"Yeah, that's why you can't peel your eyes off him," Kimberly teased, "and you've crunched up your program in your sweaty little hand."

I smoothed out the program, tried to calm my achingly aroused body, and did my best to concentrate. But my attention was shot. I made notes about one man, a lawyer who worked for a civil rights organization and was perfect, yet I couldn't summon enthusiasm.

After the last bachelor, the emcee announced a 15-minute break. The three of us rose with the rest of the audience. "Another drink?" Kimberly said.

"Sure," I said. "Bet they're mostly fruit juice."

"I will as well," Amarjeet agreed. "I'm having so much fun." As we lined up at one of the bars, she asked, "Have you chosen your man, Jade?"

3

I opened my crumpled program. "I've narrowed it to four." I pointed to the pictures of the high-school teacher, the doctor, the civil rights lawyer, and bachelor number one, Justin Wong.

"Quinn's not on the list?" Kimberly asked.

"The firefighter?" I tried to sound casual. "Blue collar isn't the right image for Triple-F."

"He's a hero," Amarjeet said. "Didn't you hear the emcee say he's got a commendation for bravery?"

"I missed that." No doubt I'd been drooling over his pecs and dimple at the time.

We'd finally reached the front of the line and ordered another three Raining Mens.

"He has a great attitude about marriage and kids," Amarjeet said.

"The guys were making a sales pitch. Half of what they said was just a line." Except, while Quinn's eyes had twinkled as he talked about sailing, cooking, and carpentry, his expression had seemed earnest when he spoke about families and commitment.

"I believed him," Amarjeet said as we moved away from the bar.

"Plus, he's sexy," Kimberly said, "and Jade's totally lusting after him. A girl should be attracted to her fiancé, even if he's only a faux one."

"Look, you two, I—"

"Jade?" A female voice behind me made me turn.

Oh, crap. It was Melinda Daniels, my boss Fred's wife, looking sophisticated in a black-and-white dress. From the day I'd started at Triple-F, she'd been nice to me, and I always enjoyed talking to her. But her being here tonight could ruin everything.

"Melinda, what a surprise." I tried to act pleased. "Is Fred here too?"

"You think I could drag him to a bachelor auction? No, I came with friends. It's such a good cause. I've bid on a couple of items in the silent auction."

I introduced her to my friends, then said to her, "It's going to be an interesting time for you and Fred, with him retiring. I guess you're looking forward to it."

"Mostly yes. But it will be an adjustment." She smiled. "Marriage goes through phases, and the transition times are interesting. But like that young man onstage said, it's about commitment and being in it for the long term."

"I believe that too."

"How about you, Jade? Is there a special man in your life these days?"

"Uh, well . . ."

Kimberly grabbed my left hand and pulled it behind my back; then I felt a ring slide on my finger. "Jade's engaged," she said brightly.

"Really? Congratulations."

I lifted my hand and flashed Kimberly's diamond. "Thanks. It just happened." Beside me, Amarjeet choked back a laugh. I told myself it wasn't a lie. I just didn't know which of my four choices he'd turn out to be.

"Guess you're not bidding on a bachelor, then?" Melinda teased.

"Me?" My voice squeaked. "Oh, no. Just to support the cause. Which reminds me, there's something I want to bid on in the silent auction. Will you excuse me?" I had to get away before she asked for details about my fiancé.

"I'll see you next week at the Triple-F picnic. I can't wait to meet your fiancé."

"Me either," I muttered under my breath as I hurried away, Kimberly and Amarjeet following me. "Why did you do that, Kimberly?"

"Impulse." She shrugged. "You were going to announce it at work Monday, right?"

"I guess." We huddled in a corner. "But, damn, now I can't bid. One of you has to do it."

"Me!" Kimberly said. "Let the engaged girl live vicariously."

Amarjeet frowned. "But Melinda's met you, Kimberly. She'll notice, and probably recognize the guy when Jade takes him to Triple-F."

"I'm so screwed," I moaned. "Do we have a plan B?"

"We can figure this out," Kimberly said. "If I buy the guy, you can tell Melinda, uh . . ."

"That your fiancé volunteered for the fund-raiser before the two of you got serious," Amarjeet said. "He didn't want to pull out and leave the organizers in the lurch. But nor was it fair that some poor woman win him under false pretenses, so you got a friend to bid. No, wait, with that story, you could bid your-self."

"I'd rather have a degree of separation. Thanks, Amarjeet, that's a good cover story."

"Oh, yay, I get to buy a guy," Kimberly said gleefully. "Brian's going to get such a laugh out of this."

We were chuckling when the loudspeaker told us to return to our seats. "Okay," I said, "let's try for the first one on my list. If the bids go too high, we'll bail and wait for the next."

"Hurry up," Kimberly said, "we want to get good seats."

"Save me one," I said. "I have to go to the ladies' room."

I hurried away, noticing that the floor swayed gently. Those Raining Mens packed more of a punch than I'd thought.

When I returned, my friends were giggling and their glasses were empty. They'd saved me a seat on the aisle, beside Amarjeet. I slipped into it as the male emcee took the stage.

He announced the winners of the silent auction, thanked the donors, then said, "If you didn't win, we hope you'll still support the children's wing. You'll find donation forms in the program, and you'll get a tax receipt."

Cara, the red-dressed emcee, took the stage. "Thanks again to all these wonderful, handsome, amazing bachelors who have participated in the auction. It's easy to give a little money to charity, but these men have gone above and beyond. They're giving their time—their brains and muscles and charm—for tonight's valuable cause. And they don't even get a tax receipt! So let's show them all how much we appreciate them."

The room exploded with cheers and applause. "I'm so nervous," I murmured to Amarjeet.

"Have faith. If it's meant to be, then it will happen." Her pronouncement was punctuated by a hiccup.

Cara reintroduced Justin and called for bids. The lights stayed on so everyone could see who was bidding. As the bids rose, I leaned past Amarjeet to whisper to Kimberly, "Shouldn't you bid?"

"I think we should pass on Justin and figure out how things work."

It wasn't like her to be cautious. Had Amarjeet been talking strategy to her?

The bidding for Justin heated up, rising to over $500, then

stopped with a flashy redhead. And then it was the next bachelor's turn. We watched until the high-school teacher came onstage. After a couple bids, I hissed at Kimberly, "Come on!"

"Right." She placed a bid and someone topped it. When I hissed again, she placed another, of $400. A young brunette raised it, another bid came in, then the brunette topped that one. Amarjeet said, "Kimberly, don't bid again. That woman's determined. It's not worth going high enough to win."

"You're right. Sorry, Jade, this isn't your guy." Her giggle told me she, too, was tipsy.

After another few bachelors, it was the doctor. "Bid on this one," I reminded Kimberly.

"Have you thought seriously about his job?"

"He's a family practitioner. What's not to like?"

"He spends a lot of time peering up women's vaginas," Kimberly said, loudly enough that we both hushed her.

"It's his job," I said.

"But isn't it kind of creepy?" She gave an exaggerated grimace. "Wouldn't you feel weird, going to bed with him after he'd spent his day doing that?"

Surely doctors viewed the female bodies they saw at work in an objective, professional way. And the female body in their personal life in a completely different manner. Didn't they?

"I heard a talk show the other day," Kimberly said, "where some doctors said they couldn't do gynecology or general practice because the vagina thing made them uncomfortable."

"Well, he's obviously not one of them."

"No, but—"

"Moot point," Amarjeet said, sounding almost smug. "While you two were arguing, someone else bought him."

"Damn." I shifted anxiously as the winner claimed a hug from the doctor. How could I have lost out on three men? "I'm down to just the civil rights lawyer. Kimberly, you have to win him." He was an excellent candidate. Sure, I hadn't felt enthusiastic when I'd seen him onstage, but that was only because the fire-fighter had me so fired up. Speaking of whom, he'd been up after the doctor . . .

And there was Quinn O'Malley, strolling across the stage with his distinctive brand of male confidence and grace.

"I wonder what the woman who wins him will make him do?" Amarjeet asked with a wicked, slightly drunken grin.

"Put out her fire?" Kimberly joked, her voice too loud again. Three drinks were obviously too much for us when all we'd eaten were a few tiny appies.

The firefighter had left his ax behind and stood easily, legs slightly apart, hands clasped behind his back. The posture emphasized his muscular chest and shoulders. Easy to imagine him hefting a woman in his arms, toting her out of a burning building and down one of those long, swaying ladders. Placing her on the ground, breathing air into her parched lungs as his sexy lips caressed hers. As, under his deft touch, her body came to life. To aroused, passionate life.

He glanced around the audience, a half smile on his lips, seeming unworried about who would win him and what she'd ask him to do. Vaguely, I was aware of women bidding, of Amarjeet whispering to Kimberly, but the man onstage was so fantasy-worthy that I barely noticed until a new voice joined the bidding. A voice I recognized.

I dragged my eyes off Quinn O'Malley to glare at Kimberly. "What are you doing?"

Amarjeet said, "You only had one man left on your list, and he's near the end. Women will be getting desperate, bids will be higher. You might not get that lawyer."

"But I don't want this guy." I stared back at the stage. Quinn O'Malley was watching us. Our gazes connected and I felt a zap of energy—sexual energy.

Kimberly giggled. "That's not what your body language says.

You're leaning forward like you want to leap out of your seat and jump him."

Quickly, I sat back, breaking that compelling eye connection, and tried to regain my sanity. "My body language is irrelevant."

"He's a hero. And he's hot," Amarjeet said as Kimberly placed another bid.

"For sure! But I want someone more conventional. White-collar job, good-looking but not so—"

"Freaking gorgeous?" Kimberly put in.

"Exactly."

"Well, that's too bad." She waved her hand in the air.

A moment later, the emcee's gavel fell and Kimberly said triumphantly, "Because this is the guy you're getting."

4

From: Jade Rousseau [jade_rousseau@shaw.ca]
To: 'Amarjeet Nagra'; 'Kimberly Brock'
Subject: Write-off: Amarjeet's new coworker, Sebastian

A compulsive exaggerator! (I'm being polite—really think-ing LIAR <g>) Said he was a gourmet chef. I don't care if a guy can cook, but if he says he can do something, he should be able to. He made a fancy French meal, said he added his "personal touches." All I can say is, BARF!! (Yeah, liter-ally. I'll spare you the disgusting details.)

Frog detector rule: No dates with liars or exaggerators! And I'm going back to the original plan: only coffees or lunches, no dinners.

I could have stayed pissed off at my friends for conspiring to buy me the firefighter, but it was done. They'd been operating under the influence of too many Raining Mens. Quinn O'Malley was so not what I needed, but it wasn't like I could exchange him for a more suitable model, so I'd make the best of the situation.

How bad could it be, playing lovey-dovey with one of the hottest men I'd ever seen?

Kimberly had told him she'd bought him for a friend and got his phone number. When I called, he'd sounded intrigued and asked what "services" I'd like him to provide. Wanting to tell him face-to-face, not in public where someone might overhear, I'd invited him to my place.

Pacing my Kitsilano condo, I resisted the urge to change clothes. Cotton pants and a T-shirt were perfect. Fancier might suggest a come-on, and work clothes were too stuffy. I left my hair loose, in a tumble of black waves that rippled past my shoulders.

After I buzzed him into the building, my heart raced as I waited for his knock on my door. I told myself it was only because this faux fiancé thing was so important to my career.

But then I opened the door and knew I'd been rationalizing. Quinn was dressed in jeans and a blue T-shirt that showcased his great body. His short black hair gleamed damply, his dark eyes twinkled, and he gave off testosterone, pheromones, and pure wicked sex appeal.

He grinned and that dimple winked. "It *is* you."

My heart was thumping in response to all that hot masculinity. "What do you mean?"

"When Kimberly said she bought me for a friend, I figured it was one of the two she'd come with."

"You noticed us?" I'd been right about our gazes connecting.

"Hard to miss the three of you. Especially you." He made a leisurely and utterly blatant appraisal that started with my face, moved down my body, heating every inch, then returned. "Oh yeah, I noticed you, Jade. I hoped you'd be the one."

"You're not here because I need flattery." My voice didn't come out as businesslike as I'd intended. His appraisal made me feel tingly, sensual, utterly feminine, and incredibly horny. Why didn't any of the men I dated make me feel like this?

"Why am I here? Now that you've got me, what do you want?" His voice was husky, curious, with an undertone of teasing innuendo.

You. Naked. Right here, right now. My body blushed all over, and I doubted my skin was dark enough to hide it. Disconcerted, I stepped back from the magnetic field he wielded. "Come in and we'll discuss it."

He kicked off his sandals and walked past me. With his left hand, he held out a bag from a wine shop. "Didn't know what you had in mind, but wine's usually a good thing."

I had to step closer again to take it. When I did, he put out his right hand. "Hi, Jade Rousseau. I'm Quinn O'Malley."

Trying to keep my own hand from trembling, I gripped his. Heat. A jolt of energy that weakened my knees and made my already racing pulse kick into overdrive. Honestly, a girl should be able to go without intercourse for six months without turning into a sex maniac.

I pulled my hand away and fussed with the wine bag, extracting a chilled Pinot Grigio. "Looks great. Should I open it?"

"Whatever you want."

"I don't drink on an empty stomach, and I haven't had much to eat today." My tummy had been sensitive after Sebastian's dinner and last night's close encounter with the toilet bowl.

"Got any snacks? We missed our last meal because we got called out."

So he'd come directly from the fire hall. From the shower. The idea of Quinn in the shower did nothing to cool my body heat. "Uh, sure." I realized I was hungry, as well as aroused. Better to concentrate on the safer craving. "Come into the kitchen and I'll find something."

He followed. "Nice apartment."

"Thanks." The condo was in a well-kept older building, and

the rooms were spacious. My one-bedroom had an actual kitchen rather than a walk-through, a rare thing in Vancouver.

When I opened the fridge to peer inside, he stood behind me, and suddenly my kitchen didn't seem so big. Though he didn't touch me, he was close enough I felt his heat. I wanted to step back and plaster my back against his front. If I did, would his arms circle me? Would he palm my breasts, rub my aching, budded nipples? Did I want him to?

"Could do some kind of stir fry," he said.

Oh right, food.

I'd been thinking cheese and crackers, and now he wanted a real meal? No way. *I* had bought *him*. He was supposed to be meeting my needs, not using his sexy charisma to get me to slave for him—a trick that no doubt worked on most women. Sweetly, I said, "I've had a long day. I don't feel like cooking."

"No sweat." He stepped past me to rummage in the fridge. "I'll whip up something."

I remembered what he'd said at the auction, that he'd cook a meal for the woman who won him. "This isn't why I bought you."

"Tell me about it when we're eating." He handed me some vegetables and a packaged chicken breast, then took out fresh ginger root and soy sauce. "Soy ginger stir fry sound okay?"

"Great." The ginger would be good for my stomach.

But then, the meal Sebastian had described last night had sounded nice too. My stomach twinged in remembrance. "No, let's have cheese and crackers. I don't want to put you to any trouble."

His eyes—dark brown, like strong espresso—gleamed. "You don't think I can cook."

I squared my shoulders. "Nothing personal, but I've recently had a bad experience."

"Trust me, firefighters can cook." His gaze and words were direct. "Where's the rice?"

Reluctantly, I took down a bag of basmati. "I'll open the wine. Uh, there are recipe books in the cupboard above the stove."

He snorted.

I couldn't bring myself to be utterly rude and tell him to stop, so soon I found myself seated at the table while Quinn moved comfortably around my kitchen. I took tiny sips of wine as we made superficial getting-to-know-you chitchat about my apartment and neighborhood. He chopped, sautéed, and stirred, while I kept an eagle eye on him to make sure he didn't throw in any weird ingredients, like Sebastian's "personal touches."

Whatever the result might turn out to be, Quinn looked awfully sexy as he prepared the meal, each movement stretching his muscles in an intriguing way. Mostly, I saw his rear view, which gave me ample time to appreciate his amazing butt. Butts were great, but if I was going to ogle, I'd prefer the front view. From what I'd seen so far, his package filled out his jeans pretty damned well, but I was looking forward to an opportunity to verify that fact.

He swung around. Yup. Very nicely, indeed. "How hot do you like it?" he asked.

As hot and hard as you can dish it out, babe. "Uh, hot?" My voice squeaked.

His lips curved into that dimple-flashing grin. "You look like a woman who likes it hot."

"I . . ." The stir fry. He meant the stir fry. "Normally I'm good with spicy, but my stomach's sensitive today." Great. Now he'd probably figure I had menstrual cramps.

"I'll keep it gentle."

Dinner. He really did mean dinner. Not his strong hands caressing my body, awakening every nerve ending. His big cock sliding back and forth in slow, seductive motions.

Watching as he added a tiny amount of crushed red chili pepper, I wondered what was going on with me. I was a healthy woman with a normal sexual appetite, but I'd never reacted so strongly to a man before. How could I take him to a work event when all I could think about was stripping him naked and having my way with him?

He dished up the meal and sat across from me. "Okay. Why did you buy me, Jade? And why get your friend to bid for you?"

I took a quick gulp of wine for courage. "I need you to pretend to be my fiancé."

Quinn gaped, then burst out laughing. "Seriously?"

"I need a fiancé to take to two or three work events. And I asked Kimberly to bid because my boss's wife was at the auction." He was still chuckling. "I'm glad you find this so amusing."

"Well, it's pretty weird." He picked up his fork. "Could've been worse, though. Know what my buds got bought for?"

"The two other firefighters? What?"

"One has to rent a tux and escort a woman to the opera. And he's a hockey guy."

Cautiously, I tasted the food. Wow, the man really could cook. "This is wonderful. Thank you. How about your other friend?"

"Salsa lessons. She wants to take salsa lessons and needs a partner."

"That could be fun."

"She weighs a couple hundred pounds, and it's definitely not muscle."

"It's wrong to discriminate against someone because they're a little heavy." I thought about my write-off date, potbellied Peter, and felt like a hypocrite.

"See if you say that when it's your toes she's tromping on."

"I thought you firefighters were supposed to be tough."

He chuckled and refilled our wineglasses. "Yeah, my buds'll suck it up. The children's wing's a good cause. We see kids injured every day, and the facility's really needed. When we volunteered, we knew we might get stuck with some weird stuff."

What generous men, Quinn and his friends. "Please don't tell them about our arrangement. It has to be a secret. Tell them . . . I got you to cook me dinner."

"They'll think I got off easy." He ran his fingers lightly over the back of my hand. "And I did." He stroked up my bare forearm, igniting sparks. His tone altered, took on that husky, seductive note. "It's not exactly a hardship being with you, Jade." The heat in his dark eyes matched up with his voice, like sinfully rich and tempting dark chocolate.

As I'd figured, he was a player. All the same, his touch, his voice, those sexy eyes were so tempting that I said, "You either, Quinn," before I realized what I was doing.

He gave a satisfied grin. "If we're engaged, we need to get to know each other."

Right. Business. The man was so distracting it was hard to keep focused. "I've typed up a biography you can study. And I'll need to know things about you, the things a fiancée would know."

His eyes danced. "She'd know if I'm a good kisser."

5

She'd know if I'm a good kisser? "I . . . uh . . ." I gaped at Quinn.

"And I am. But you shouldn't take my word on it. You need to check it out yourself."

A horrible suspicion crossed my mind. "I didn't buy you for sex."

He chuckled. "I know. I'm just saying, it'll be easier to pretend we're engaged if we've kissed." His lips said "kissed," but his dark, gleaming eyes suggested a whole lot more.

I jumped up and crossed the kitchen, needing distance. Yeah, I'd bet he was a good kisser. My body lusted to find out. But kissing Quinn—a kiss that, given the gleam in his eyes and my own arousal, could easily go further—didn't fit anywhere in my game plan.

Either game plan.

I had two goals, each with a distinct strategy. One was short term and work oriented: to find a faux fiancé and win the promotion on my merits, not my marital status. The other was long term: to find my Prince Charming, get engaged and married for real, and live happily ever after. Two separate boxes on my "to-do list," and I was eager to put tick marks in both.

Quinn definitely didn't fit box number two, yet his body language said he didn't want to stick within the confines of box number one. Would it be crazy to create a third box, just for him? A box that had nothing to do with long term and everything to do with satisfying the overpowering sexual hunger he kindled in me?

"D'you agonize this way over every decision?" He cocked an eyebrow, rose, and strode determinedly toward me.

"No." I evaded him, darting back to the table to gather plates. "Well, yes, if it's important." I walked to the counter and turned, the plates in front of me serving as a barrier. I needed to think clearly, and when he touched me, I couldn't.

"Man, woman, attraction. It's not that complicated."

"Isn't that what Tarzan said to Jane?" But I wasn't in a jungle inhabited by a sole male, and I'd set my priorities. "I can't waste time on a relationship that isn't going anywhere." That had been my mistake in the past.

Both brows rose. "Not that I was going to go down on one knee and propose, but out of curiosity, how did you reach the snap decision we weren't going anywhere?"

"I don't date men who have dangerous jobs. Or who do crazy things like ride a motorbike."

Quinn looked a little stunned, then took the plates from me and set them on the counter. He rested his hands on the counter on either side of me, trapping me. Our bodies were only inches apart, and again I felt his sizzling energy. "Jade, did I ask you on a date?"

"Uh, no."

"I said a kiss. How can we convince people we're engaged if we've never even kissed?"

"Uh . . ." There was a flaw to his logic, but my brain had shut down, except to echo *a kiss, a kiss, a kiss.* Every cell in my body urged me to hurl myself against him, twine around him, and kiss him until I melted into a puddle.

Perhaps he read it on my face. His grin turned into something intense and knowing.

Standing in the cage of his arms, a hot surge of need and anticipation rushed through me. It wasn't that I hadn't dated sexy guys before, but never one so purely masculine, so confident. Never one who gave off that crazy energy, who made me so hungry for his touch.

His head dipped toward me and I stared, fascinated. His expression was appreciative and predatory, like the way I felt when I reached for my favorite treat, a rich chocolate Nanaimo bar.

His lips brushed mine, soft but not the least bit tentative. Leisurely, yet not casually. Almost chaste, yet definitely not innocent. His touch was skilled, deliberate, as he traced the outline of my lips with the tip of his tongue, then nibbled and sucked my bottom lip. Small caresses, yet each brushed fire across my skin, darted arousal through my body, and made me tremble.

Box number three was looking *so* appealing. Oh, God, I could no more *not* kiss him back than I could resist a Nanaimo bar. With a moan of surrender, I returned his gentle pressure.

He made a sound in the back of his throat, a big male cat sound like a growly purr. A sound of satisfaction, not of surprise. He'd known I couldn't resist.

Fine. He was cocky. But damn, he had reason to be.

His tongue flicked against the seam of my lips and I parted, eager for more of this blissfully sensual, erotic experience. He tasted of wine and spice, his tongue was talented but willing to yield to my own explorations, and somehow, without me realizing, we'd stepped into each other's arms. He plunged his hands through my hair, holding my head at the angle he wanted, and my arms circled his powerful torso as I explored the muscular lines of his back. The fronts of our bodies were plastered together.

Under the jeans, he was unmistakably erect. Beneath my own pants, the crotch of my panties was soaked, my sex swollen and throbbing. His mouth and mine melded as if they'd been designed to mate. Now, *this* was what kissing should be like. Kisses were often disappointing, but with Quinn, I realized kissing could be an art form. Skillful, beautiful, passionate, emotional.

No, wait, not emotional. We were strangers. We didn't care about each other. And never would, because we'd never have a relationship.

His mouth broke from mine. "Jade? Where did you go?"

I stared up at him, realizing I'd disengaged from the kiss and seeing the puzzlement in his dark eyes. "What are we doing?" I forced my hands to let go of him and took a step back.

"Thought that was obvious." The uncertainty in his voice belied his words.

"Okay, we've kissed. Now we know what it's like. We should . . . call it quits." I had to force the last words out.

He scrubbed his hands over his face. "The way we were kissing . . . That didn't feel like you wanted to quit."

"No, but . . ." The truth was, I didn't.

Perhaps he read it on my face. He put his arms around me, slipped his hands into the back pockets of my pants, cupped my ass, and pulled me close again. "You don't want to quit."

"This doesn't make sense. It could complicate things."

"Not if we don't let it. We're grown up, know what we want. Let's go for it." His pelvis flirted with mine, the press of his arousal arguing his case.

I didn't make a practice of sleeping with guys on a first date, or even a second or third one. But tonight I wanted to. It had been so long since a man had held me, satisfied me, and Quinn was . . . smoking hot. Powerfully arousing.

He must do this sort of thing all the time. That thought actually reassured me. He was right: We could have great sex and not let it complicate our lives, much less my faux fiancé plan. I could enjoy box number three as a treat on the side and remain committed to my real priorities.

"Oh, wait," he said softly, his mouth an inch from mine, a mischievous glint in his eyes. "I forgot. You said you didn't have time to waste on, what was it?"

How could I think when he was invading all my senses? "Uh, a relationship that wasn't going anywhere. But you have a point about the role-play thing. If we had sex and were, you know, attuned to each other that way, it would be easier to act engaged." Was lust making me rationalize, or did I have a valid point?

His quick "Absolutely" broke my train of thought.

I chuckled. "You'd agree to anything if it got me into bed with you."

"Pretty much." That dimple flashed.

He was irresistible. A player, a sexy bad boy, whatever he might be, I wanted him. "Of course, if we're not sexually compatible," I teased, "that could mess up the role-play."

"Not going to be a problem." He lifted my shirt to caress the skin above the low waistband of my pants. The pads of his fingers were slightly rough, a reminder he wasn't my usual white-collar date. I'd have thought the abrasiveness would be unpleasant, but it was stimulating. He stroked my skin to a level of sensitivity I'd never experienced before.

I wondered what those fingers would feel like on my nipples. My clit. Oh, God. "You're right." Need made me breathless. "Let's go someplace where we can get comfortable."

"Oh, yeah." He hoisted me in his arms, making me gasp with surprise. "Where?"

"Down the hall." My bedroom. Maybe I should have chosen the living room couch as being less intimate, but I wanted to make the most of this experience.

He carried me easily—and I am by no means tiny—then, in the bedroom, let me slide down until I stood at the foot of the bed. I hurried to light a couple candles; then he tugged the hem of my T-shirt. "I want to see you, Jade Rousseau. All of you."

"I want to see you too." From the first time I'd set eyes on him. And now that I'd made my decision, I was totally into it.

Dark eyes gleaming, Quinn peeled my shirt over my head. A big, smug grin curved his lips. "Talk about pretty."

I hadn't worn the champagne-colored lace bra and matching thong for him, honestly. I'd always loved sexy, feminine underwear, ever since I'd got over my adolescent embarrassment over my curviness. To put it bluntly, as Kimberly did, I had boobs and booty—and everything was toned and in the right place.

From the expression on his face, Quinn agreed. He flipped open the button at my waist and undid the zipper; then I took over and tugged my pants down.

My nipples were taut, thrusting against flimsy lace. My inner thighs and the crotch of my thong were damp. Knowing I made a sexy picture, a portrait of arousal, I thrust back my shoulders and stood proudly as his gaze roamed my body. When he reached out, I took a step backward. "Uh-uh. Not until you lose some clothes, mister."

"Want to help?"

"No, I want to watch." Perhaps because I'd first seen him onstage, I had the crazy notion I'd like to see him do a striptease. With music. The whole bump and grind thing. Not that I had the nerve to tell him that.

He stretched, flexing and flaunting the muscles that pressed against his blue tee, then pulled the hem free from his jeans. His fingers grazed the fly, drawing my attention, and I gaped hungrily at the imposing bulge. Slowly, he raised his shirt and my gaze tracked up his body as the T-shirt rose, revealing six-pack abs and muscular pecs with a scattering of dark hair. Yes, I'd seen his naked torso the night of the auction, but this time I was up close and personal with all this beautiful masculinity, and his body was gilded by flickering light.

When he pulled the shirt over his head and tossed it aside, I sucked in a breath. Never had I been with a man who was built like this. How was any other guy ever going to measure up?

He unbuckled his leather belt, then unbuttoned his jeans, movements relaxed and confident. Not arrogant, just sure of himself, and of his effect on women.

Well, I wasn't exactly chopped liver myself. Casually, I raised my right hand and flicked my thumbnail slowly across my nipple through the lace, a soft, warm prickle of sensation that made the taut bud even harder.

His heated gaze followed the motion and his hands paused in the act of unzipping his fly.

"Don't let me stop you," I said.

The zipper rasped and the jeans drifted down an inch, revealing his lean belly, the waistband of his underwear and—oh, God—the crown of his erect cock thrusting out the top. "In a rush, are you?" he teased back.

I had to swallow before I could speak. "To see what you have to offer? You bet."

He stuck his thumbs in the waist of his jeans on both sides and eased them down farther, over bulging navy boxer briefs. The jeans hit the floor. Oh yeah, I was going to have trouble finding another guy who measured up.

Not that I was all about size. It was how the man handled the equipment that mattered.

I had a feeling firefighter O'Malley had a pretty good idea of how to handle equipment.

He tucked his thumbs in the waistband of his briefs, hands framing his package. "On or off?"

I really wanted to see him, and this was no time to play shy. "Off."

He slid down his underwear and his cock sprang from a nest of dark curls, and rose full and proud up his belly. I almost whimpered as a surge of pure naked lust shot through me. I realized I was fondling my nipple through my bra, breathing fast and shallow, squeezing my thighs together against a needy ache that urged me to spread my legs and offer myself to him.

Quinn stepped toward me, took my hand from my breast, and cupped both my lace-clad breasts in his own big hands. Low in his throat, he hummed satisfaction as he explored me through the lace, teasing my nipples to buds so hard they hurt. Then he flicked open the front clasp and my breasts spilled free, into his hands. "Let's lie down, so I can do these justice."

Stunned from the suddenness of this intimacy, the intensity of the way I responded to this almost-stranger, I let him tug me to the bed. I eased free of my bra, then pulled off the duvet and lay down, the cool cotton of the sheet a pleasant contrast to the heat of my skin.

Quinn followed me down, lying beside me and stretching over to claim my lips in a slow, sexy kiss. My breasts hungered for his touch, and so did my pussy, but he was in no hurry. As our tongues and lips played sexy games, I ran my hands through his short hair, then down his neck to his shoulders, feeling soft heat over solid muscle and bone. The man felt as good as he looked.

My fingers drifted through chest hair, found a nipple, and squeezed it between thumb and index finger. His chest tensed under my hand.

My breasts were full and throbbing, crying out for his attention. Finally, he broke the kiss and eased back. He stroked down my neck, circled the hollow at the base of my throat with a finger, then moved across my chest. His touch, with those roughened fingertips, was firm, not a drifting caress but harder, as if he was recognizing and appreciating my own strength. Quinn didn't touch me as if I were a porcelain doll, but like I was a healthy, vital woman.

When he reached my breast, he lightened the touch, caressing my flesh with the gentlest of abrasion, tweaking my nipple.

Then he lowered his head and sucked that hard bud into his mouth. Exquisite sensation rushed through me and I cried out. He licked, flicked, sucked, squeezed, learning exactly how to touch me to give me the maximum pleasure.

The way he was sitting on the bed, I couldn't touch him, except to cup the back of his head, feel the springy thickness of his hair, explore the strong shape of his head.

He was deft, experienced. A patient lover, not one who rushed single-mindedly toward his own gratification. And I reaped the benefit. Perversely, I almost wished he'd lose control.

When my breasts were so sensitive they trembled at his touch, he moved down my body at a leisurely pace, his head pulling free of my grip. Now all I could do was lie there and let him bring my body to throbbing, erotic life, inch by inch.

"Pretty skin, Jade. Like rich, creamy coffee." His finger circled my navel, making my belly quiver.

"And you smell like flowers and spice," he said. That big finger traced the top band of the front of my thong, then followed the diagonal line of the edge down to my crotch, rough against my smooth skin. Gently, he spread my legs and stroked over the soaking crotch of my thong, pressing hard enough to stimulate the swollen flesh underneath.

I whimpered. "Quinn, I want more."

6

Quinn peeled off my tiny panties and studied me. His eyes gleamed, and there was a flush across his chiseled cheekbones. "No prettier sight," he said, his voice husky.

Stop looking and touch! my body screamed silently.

He must've got the message because he ran his fingers lightly over me, playing with the short curls of pubic hair, stroking my labia and the wet slit between, drifting over my clit. As if he was learning the lay of the land.

With each touch, my body quickened, skin becoming sensitized, arousal building inside me. Then he buried his face between my legs and retraced the same path with his tongue. He licked my folds with firm, sure strokes that had me pushing shamelessly against his tongue, craving more. And he gave it to me. A finger, then another, slipped inside me.

Gently, he pumped in and out, circled inside, explored all the sensitive spots and then—oh, God!—found my G-spot. "Yes, oh yes," I panted as a calloused fingertip stroked that super-sensitive flesh. I squeezed my eyes shut, saw a haze of rich, fiery scarlet behind my lids, felt my body imploding so my entire being focused on that one exquisite touch.

And then I exploded in a forceful surge of orgasm that made me cry out with pleasure.

I was still riding the tremors of aftershock when the rough pad of his thumb smoothed my juices over my clit and stroked. A second, less powerful climax rushed through me.

When I finally began to regain my breath, I gasped, "What do you do for an encore?"

"I'll show you. Soon as I get a condom out of my wallet."

"Bedside table. But, Quinn, I want to touch you too." I'd barely had a chance to explore that fabulous body.

"Next time." His voice rasped and his movements were urgent as he found a condom package, ripped it open, and sheathed that stunning erection. Then he was between my legs.

My knees came up, I lifted my hips, tilted my pelvis, offered myself to him. Yes, I wanted to touch him all over, take him in my mouth, yet I loved that he now felt some of the same desperate need I'd felt earlier.

The head of his cock probed swollen, sensitive flesh, then slipped inside. Just a little, then more, as my body softened and melted and took him in. "Mmm, you feel good," I murmured. He stretched me, filled me, stroked the walls of my channel.

I'd always enjoyed sex, been responsive and fairly easy to satisfy. But this act, with Quinn, felt different—fuller, richer, more sensual, more erotic. My body was more aware, more receptive, more attuned to his. Perhaps because he'd turned me on from the moment I first saw him. Perhaps because he'd just given me two sensational orgasms.

The reason didn't matter. His cock was inside me, his firm butt tensed under my hands, that fabulous torso glinted in the golden light, and his strong, handsome face wore an intense, impassioned expression. "Christ, Jade, you feel good."

"You too."

He stroked slowly, deliberately, occasionally speeding and changing the angle so the base of his penis rubbed my clit. So the coil of sexual tension inside me wound tight, my heart racing as I gasped for air. Then, each time I neared climax, he backed off, cooling things a little.

With some men, I'd have figured they didn't know what they were doing and I'd have taken charge, moving in a way that would bring my orgasm. But with Quinn, I sensed he was deliberately prolonging the moment when we both climaxed. And I was confident he'd make it happen, and that it would be better for the anticipation and sensual buildup.

He leaned forward, his curly chest hairs tickling my breasts, and kissed me—a deep, long, thorough kiss—while his hips continued to pump. "Let me in deeper."

Deeper? Could he go deeper?

He lifted his upper body and, still inside me, raised my lower body and stuffed a pillow under me so my hips and pelvis were lifted toward him. He rose so he was kneeling between my bent legs, hands gripping my butt. I grabbed his muscular thighs to hold myself in place, tight against him, as he began to thrust again, faster now.

"Oh my God, Quinn." His cock not only rubbed my clit with each stroke, but inside me it rubbed my sweet spot. Each long, deep slide notched up the tension, and he increased the pace, his breath coming in harsh pants now. His control, his finesse, were slipping away, which heightened my excitement. I panted, whimpered, hovering on the fine edge of climax, and this time I wanted it so badly, needed it, I'd kill him if he backed off again.

But he didn't. He plunged deep, filling me completely, tipping me over the edge until all I could do was spasm and shudder around him, crying out his name.

Seconds later, I heard his deep cry as he thrust hard and jerkily in his own orgasm.

Our bodies locked together, shuddering and quivering, for long minutes. Then he collapsed downward so he was lying atop me. He managed to pull the pillow out from under me and I sank deeper into the bed.

Resting on his elbows, he studied my face. "Christ, that was something. The first time I saw you, I thought you were hot, but damn, woman, you're . . ."

"What?"

"Fire."

"You fight fire."

"Only the dangerous kind." Slowly, his mouth curved into the smile that created a dimple. "Are you the dangerous kind?"

I wasn't entirely sure what he meant, but I smiled back and shook my head. "No, you know exactly what I want from you. Two or three dates as my faux fiancé. That's it."

"No more of this?" A frown creased his face. "We're so good together."

"I don't know." I bit my lip, rational side taking over again. "Yes, this was wonderful, but, Quinn, sex is *not* my priority in life right now." I shouldn't let myself be distracted.

He eased away to deal with the condom and grumbled, "Seems to me, sex this great should always be a priority."

I had to chuckle. "You're a guy. Of course it is, for you."

We stared at each other for a long moment; then his dimple flashed. "I warn you, when I want something, I go after it."

I smiled. "And I warn you, I'm no pushover." Before he tried to get more persuasive, I hopped out of bed. "Let's go to the living room. We should discuss my bio."

"Can do that here." He sprawled on the bed, naked and very, very tempting.

"No, we can't. But if you behave and learn your lessons, maybe we'll come back."

He groaned. "Jeez, woman, you're hard." With exaggerated reluctance, he climbed out of bed as I headed into the bathroom.

There, I studied my reflection, liking what I saw. Madly tousled hair and a gleam of satisfaction and deviltry in my eyes.

Sexy, but definitely not businesslike. I eased a large-tooth comb through my hair, splashed water on my face, and gently sponged my sticky crotch. The silky kimono wrap hanging on the back of the bathroom door was tempting but not a good idea. I opened the door a crack to make sure he'd left the bedroom, then dressed again in my pants and tee.

The man had proved himself in my kitchen and in my bedroom. But how would he do in my work environment? Would he take his task seriously?

In the living room, he had turned the lights off and lit a couple of jasmine-scented candles, and one of my favorite Diana Krall CDs was playing. He knew how to set a mood. One that I wished I could succumb to.

When he began to pour wine into our glasses, I said, "Just half a glass for me. I'm going to make coffee. Or would you prefer tea?"

He gave a resigned sigh. "Coffee's good. Black."

I flicked on the lights, blew out the candles, turned down the music, and handed him my bio and Triple-F's last annual report. "You can start reading these."

His groan followed me into the kitchen, where I made coffee using my personal blend: two-thirds dark Jamaican roast, one-third chocolate flavored, and a dash of cinnamon.

When I returned to the living room with coffee mugs, Quinn was sprawled on the couch, my bio in his hands. He was a very male presence in my room with its soft furniture, earth tones, and plants, yet he seemed to fit. I handed him a mug and, deciding it wasn't wise to sit beside him, took my reading chair and picked up my wineglass.

"Thanks." He sipped. "Nice coffee."

"Thank you. Any questions so far?"

"Yeah. Why are you doing this? Why do you need a pretend fiancé?"

I explained about the promotion and why I wanted it so badly, and my competitor with the Hallmark family.

"You're lying to the board to get a promotion?" He frowned.

I winced. "I know. But it's a small lie. I really do intend to get married soon."

"Whoa." His eyes widened and he put the mug down. "You're engaged for real? Look, I don't screw around with—"

"I'm not engaged. I'm not dating. Well, I am, but only one date each, so far."

"You're a serial first-dater? Jade, you've lost me."

"I want to get married, and soon." I traded my unfinished wine for coffee. "So, on each first date, I evaluate the guy and assess our potential as a couple. If there's no potential, I won't waste time on a second date."

"Good God." He shook his head. "You're one strange woman, you know that?"

"I'm one practical, organized woman. I decide on my goal, then develop a realistic plan for achieving it. Don't you do that?"

"Nah, I'm more impulsive."

"But, in your work? When you go out on a call, a fire or an accident, don't you all have a goal and a plan?"

"Sort of. But if the plan doesn't make sense . . ." He shrugged.

"Then what?"

"I improvise."

"Quinn? At the Triple-F events, don't improvise, okay?"

A teasing glint lit his dark eyes. "Might have to. What if someone asks a question we haven't rehearsed?"

"Let me answer it," I said sternly. If this man blew my chance at the promotion . . . . "Damn. If only Kimberly had got me the kind of man I wanted," I muttered to myself, but not softly enough because he overheard.

"I wasn't your first pick?" He looked shocked and offended.

"No, but—"

"Who the hell was?"

"Well, there was the Chinese tax lawyer, a high-school teacher, and—"

"Stop." He held up his hand, scowling. "I don't need the list. How did you get stuck with me? Your friend screwed up?"

"My friends conspired against me when they realized I was attracted to you."

He huffed. "You lost me again. You were attracted to me but didn't want to win me?"

"Sorry, but I wanted a white-collar man like I normally date. Someone the board would approve of."

"You're too damned good for a blue-collar guy?" Now he was glaring.

"No, I'm not," I shot back. "My father was a cop, and men don't come any better than him. But when I've dated blue-collar guys, we don't have a lot in common."

He folded his arms across his powerful chest. "Seems we proved that one wrong."

"I mean, outside of bed. Look, I'm not being snobby, just realistic. You're into . . . What did you say at the auction? Your motorbike, sailing, carpentry, cooking."

"Didn't see you complain about my cooking." Then he scraped a hand across his jaw. "Shit, what'm I doing? Doesn't matter if we're compatible for real. This is all about a fake relationship." He picked up my bio. "You want me to memorize this? Fine."

He was being businesslike, as I'd wanted, but there was a coolness in his manner that I regretted. Had I actually hurt his feelings? "Look, I'm sorry—"

He hefted the annual report. "Tell me I don't have to learn these statistics."

I missed his sexy teasing. But that was silly. There was one thing, and one thing only, I needed from this man. "No statistics," I said evenly. "Just the kind of things I'd have told my fiancé about."

He sighed. "The dates my buds got stuck with are starting to look awfully good."

7

From: Jade Rousseau [jade_rousseau@shaw.ca]
To: 'Amarjeet Nagra'; 'Kimberly Brock'
Subject: My pathetic dating life: Granny's friend's nephew
          George

A high-powered accountant who nickels-and-dimes life to death! I asked why he drove 3 blocks to lunch. He said it saved him 9 minutes' time, which could be billed at .2 hr, and he had an exact dollar value for that. LOL! (Which I almost did, in his face!) When I said I work for a charity, he said charitable contributions are good as long as they're effective tax deductions. Ack!!! (Frog detector rule: Don't date a guy who isn't generous about supporting good causes.)

Now to the HOT (steamy, sizzling!) news. I had mind-blowing sex with Quinn!!!! It was FABULOUS. And before any I told

you so's, it was JUST SEX. Nothing serious. (Frog detector rule: No dates with risk-takers!)

PS—No, I'm not DATING Q.

PPS—Did I mention the sex was SPECTACULAR!!! <G>

Saturday, I dressed in white cotton pants and a sleeveless top
of cinnamon-colored silk, and added simple copper jewelry. I
pulled my hair back into a loose knot, applied minimal makeup,
and slipped my feet into braided leather sandals.

I had told Quinn I'd pick him up, and I'd instructed him to
dress along the lines of khakis and a short-sleeved cotton shirt
or golf shirt. By that point in the evening, his eyes had been glazed
from information, instructions, and barely contained annoyance.

No question of there being a second round in the bedroom,
which my brain said was a good thing. Maybe I shouldn't have
indulged in the first round, but breaking my dry spell had sure
felt damned fine. All the same, best to keep things between us
businesslike from here on. I only hoped he didn't screw up the
afternoon, particularly if he was still pissed off at me.

Top down on my chili red Mini Cooper, I drove toward
West 6th and Oak, where Quinn had said he'd meet me. There
he was, leaning against a telephone pole, in tan khakis and a black
golf shirt. No real-life golfer, not even Tiger Woods or that guy
Adam Scott from Australia, had ever made a golf shirt look so
sexy.

And I'd had sex with this man. Superlative sex. Despite my
anxiety, my body hummed with arousal. As I pulled over to the
curb, I tried to remember this was business.

Quinn slid into the passenger seat flashing that sexy smile
with the dimple. "A pretty lady in a cute convertible." He
pressed a kiss to my cheek. A slow one.

Arousal turned to pure lust. Hurriedly, I pulled away from the curb. "You're in a better mood than when you left the other night."

He shrugged. "Strange evening. Great sex, then that weird conversation about compatibility, then you snowed me under with details."

"And now?"

"When I volunteered for the auction, I took my chances. The downside was having my ego kicked in the balls and having to study all the info you gave me. But the upside's just fine." His hand settled on my thigh, burning through my pants.

"What upside?" I asked warily.

"Compatibility where it counts."

"In bed." The words slipped out. Damn, this wasn't supposed to happen again. It was easier when he'd been grumpy.

His hand moved higher, inches from my crotch. "When I was inside you, you promised me a next time."

Had I? "Wasn't that you who said something about next time?"

"We both know it's going to happen."

"It shouldn't. We need to focus on the role-play."

"Okay." He slipped on dark glasses. "I'm role-playing a patient fiancé who got dragged along to his girl's work thing, and can't wait to get her home and in bed."

Despite myself, I laughed. But I was torn. Why resist another plunge into box number three? Besides, his improved mood would make things easier this afternoon, so I'd best not shatter it. "Let's see how we feel later. In the meantime, please, please be on your best behavior. Now, let's do a quick brushup on this event."

"It's a picnic, but not a shorts and baseball caps one."

"Right. It's a fund-raiser—"

"Put on by the Families First Foundation—Triple-F—for donors and prospective donors. Low-key, because funds should go to programs rather than glitzy fund-raisers."

"Very good." Despite his frustration, he had been listening.

"And you said something about showcasing some funded programs?"

"Yes, for example, there's one for abused women and their kids. Shelter, counseling, job skills for the women and the older kids, clothing and basic necessities, help finding accommodation, and a Big Sibs system for kids who've basically lost their fathers."

"As in, big brother or sister?" At my nod, he said, "Cool."

"Yeah. Anyhow, the women have prepared the food and it'll be served by the older kids, assisted by Big Sibs volunteers." I filled him in on more details as we drove toward ritzy Shaughnessy, where one of the board members had a giant house with a huge yard.

When we arrived, it didn't help my anxiety that my boss's wife, who'd been at the bachelor auction, was first to greet us. "Hello, Jade. This is your fiancé?"

"Yes, Melinda, this is Quinn O'Malley. Quinn, this is Melinda Daniels. She's—"

"Married to your boss, Fred." He held out a hand and gave an easy smile. "It's a pleasure."

She took his hand with a baffled smile. "You were at the auction. The firefighter who said you were a bachelor because you hadn't found the right girl."

Quinn flashed his dimple. "No, I said a man has to wait for the right woman to come along. Never said mine hadn't."

I breathed a sigh of relief, glad I'd prepared him.

"But . . ." She shook her head. "I'm confused."

I took over. "Quinn volunteered for the auction because he supports the cause. And then he and I got serious. They'd printed the catalogs and he didn't want to leave them in the lurch. I got a friend to bid on him so the auction would still raise the money, but no other bidder would be disappointed at getting a man who wasn't really a bachelor."

"Well, good for both of you for supporting such a worthwhile cause. And, Jade, I'm delighted to meet your fiancé. You have excellent taste in men."

Quinn put his arm around me. "And I have great taste in women." For a moment our gazes held and I felt a twinge of longing. Almost as if I wished this was real. Him and me.

No, surely it was just a longing to be engaged for real. To Prince Charming, not the daredevil firefighter.

Melinda beamed. "You're a beautiful couple. Let's find Fred. He'll want to meet Quinn."

For the next hour, Quinn and I wandered around the manicured yard hand in hand, chatting with people. To my surprise, he fell easily into character. He got along equally well with board members, wealthy donors, and the nervous kids who were serving delicious snacks.

As my faux fiancé, he was considerate, affectionate, demonstrative, but not inappropriately so. All the same, the constant touches, smiles, and kisses on the cheek took their toll on me. If he'd been fondling my breasts, I couldn't have got much more turned on.

When we were alone for a moment, I murmured, "You're doing a wonderful job."

He shrugged. "I have some experience."

"From firefighter open houses and fund-raisers?"

"Yeah." He gave a wry smile. "Plus the fact that my dad was an oncologist, my mom a gynecologist, and my grandfather one of the leading cardiothoracic surgeons in the city. I grew up with people like this."

"Wow. Sorry for making assumptions." I'd been so busy briefing him about me and Triple-F, I hadn't asked much about him. Some faux fiancée I was.

We accepted mini-quiches from a shy serving girl, talked to another board member, then went to the bar for fresh drinks. I was playing it safe with Aranciata, a nonalcoholic orange drink, needing no Raining Mens–type loss of judgment. Quinn was drinking Corona with lime, but had only gone through one in an hour. As we waited behind an older woman who was having a long chat with the bartender, Quinn stood slightly behind me, rested his hand on my hip, and squeezed gently. "Can't wait to get my fiancée alone."

I leaned back against him, feeling the press of his firm chest against my back, resting my head against his shoulder. "I'm feeling tempted."

He gave a sexy chuckle, his breath brushing my hair. "I'm being good. I deserve a reward."

Male throat-clearing from behind us made us both start.

Bert Masterson, a board member, had an amused expression on his face. "Sorry to interrupt, but, Jade, can I steal you away to talk to a prospective donor? He has some questions I think you're best equipped to answer."

"Of course. Quinn, you'll—"

"Find something to do. Go ahead."

Could he keep up the act when he was on his own? It wasn't his personality I was worried about, but the minimal time I'd had to brief him. Candace, my main competition, was bearing down on him, and I had no choice but to follow Bert.

As I spoke to the donor, I kept an eye on Quinn. He and Candace got drinks—he switched from beer to something dark brown served in a highball glass—and were chatting like old friends. One of the serving boys, a lanky redhead who looked about twelve, went over, carefully balancing a platter of snacks, and got drawn into the conversation. Then Candace left Quinn alone with the boy.

When I'd finished with the donor, I joined them. They were discussing baseball. "Okay," Quinn said, "I'll check into those tickets." He grinned at me. "Jade, meet Timothy. D'you have a pen and paper in your bag?"

"Hi, Timothy." I rooted around in my purse, finding a pen and the small notebook I always carried. "What's up?" I handed them to Quinn and he gave me his glass to hold.

"Quinn's going to get me and my mom box seats for a Vancouver Canadians game at Nat Bailey Stadium!" The boy's blue eyes sparkled.

"You are?" I glanced at Quinn.

He winked. "I know a guy who knows a guy."

"Sweet!" Timothy said, then told Quinn his phone number. Quinn noted it, then wrote his own name and phone number on another sheet and tucked it in the boy's shirt pocket.

Timothy grinned. "Thanks. I'd better get back to work." He took off across the lawn.

Thirsty, I sipped from Quinn's glass before handing it back. The drink tasted like straight Coca-Cola. "What's up with Timothy?"

"He and his mom are having a rough time, and Big Sibs hasn't paired him up with anyone yet. He likes baseball..." He paused. "Maybe I could use a little brother." A shadow crossed his face, and I remembered him saying, during our briefing, that his only close relative was his grandfather. "How do I get involved in the Big Sibs program?"

I stared at him. "You want to be Timothy's big brother?"

He shrugged, and for the first time since I'd met him he looked awkward. "He's a good kid."

"I'm sure. But..." Did Quinn have any idea what was involved?

His eyebrows went up. "You think I don't mean it."

"You just met him. It's a long-term commitment."

"Yeah."

"How could you leap into a decision like that so quickly?"

"Told you I'm impulsive." He glanced down, shuffled his feet. "He reminds me of my brother."

"I thought you didn't have any siblings."

"Not now."

"What?" He had me totally confused.

His mouth tightened. "I had a brother. Patrick. Three years younger. I got the black Irish looks; he got the red hair and freckles. Like Timothy."

Softly, I asked, "What happened to Patrick?"

"Died. Along with Mom and Dad when I was fifteen."

"Oh my God." I gripped his arm, as much for my own comfort as his. "What happened?" And then I knew. "A fire."

He nodded, throat working, then took a long swallow of Coke. "Heritage house. Electrical problem."

"How did you . . . ?"

"Survive? Somehow I walked through the smoke, the flames, and made it out safely. It seemed natural, automatic. I never thought . . . just assumed my parents and Patrick had done the same. When I got outside, I saw the engine, the ladder truck, firefighters rushing around with hoses and axes. It was exciting." He closed his eyes. Swallowed. "I was actually excited. Until I started looking around for my family."

And they weren't there. My heart ached for him. "You became a firefighter."

"I didn't rescue them." His dark gaze was fierce. "Fire's not going to claim any more lives if I have anything to do with it."

Each time he went into a fire, did he think about his parents and brother? I couldn't ask. "Quinn, about Timothy . . . If he reminds you of Patrick, wouldn't it be hard to be with him?"

"Maybe." He sighed and gazed at me, eyes troubled. "But it feels right. Like maybe he and I can . . ."

What? Help each other? "You are serious." I had a habit of underestimating this man.

One corner of his mouth lifted. "Yeah."

A rush of emotion dampened my eyes and I blinked quickly.

"On Monday, I'll put you in touch with the Big Sibs people. There'll be paperwork to do."

"Hate that stuff. You ever think how much would get done if it wasn't for paperwork?"

I stared him in the eye. "You ever think how many kids would be abused if that paperwork wasn't done properly?"

He winced. "Sorry. Yeah, there's a point to it in this case. Besides, I've probably gone through most of it anyhow, to be a firefighter."

A man who could admit he was wrong. I was liking my faux fiancé more and more. "I'm sorry for misjudging you. I'm not used to people being so impulsive."

His face lightened and he stepped closer, into my personal space, so I could feel that energy he gave off. "I have good impulses. As a matter of fact, right now I'm having an impulse to take you inside and find a room with a door that locks and—" He reached for my waist.

I stepped backward. "Quinn!" There were kids around, not to mention colleagues. I wasn't going to jeopardize my job for the sake of sex. Even spectacular sex with a man who was handsome, warmhearted, complex, and damned near irresistible.

"Relax, I'm teasing. I'm just saying, I can't wait until we're alone."

"Nor can I." I no longer had any second thoughts about enjoying another round in bed. The more I saw Quinn, the more I wanted him. He'd behaved perfectly today, saving his teasing for when we were alone. He had a generosity of spirit and an ability to get along with almost anyone. Even the dark side—the death of his brother and parents and his own fierce commitment to fighting fire—added to his appeal.

He made his dimple flash. "How much longer?"

"Can you be good for another hour?"

"Yeah, but I'm going to be even better when that hour is up."

8

We walked down the quiet street toward my car, decorously hand in hand, but the sexual tension between us was like the electrical energy in the air during a thunderstorm: building, ready to explode. Quinn opened the driver's door for me; then as I started to swing in, he yanked me roughly into his arms. "Crap, I can't stand it any longer."

We kissed with all the pent-up fervor of an afternoon of watching, touching, teasing. Our hands roamed greedily, tongues thrust with more passion than finesse, and both of us panted for breath. His erection rubbed demandingly against my belly, and my pussy tingled with moist heat.

"Damn it, Jade, I have to—"

"Way to go, man!" "Get a room!" The taunts came from a couple teenaged boys on bikes.

I jumped away from Quinn, cheeks burning, and slid into the car. "How embarrassing."

Quinn climbed in beside me. "They'll have wet dreams tonight."

"Eeyew!"

He chuckled. "Girls don't get it."

"Thank God. I can't imagine what it's like to have a penis. Especially at their age, when it's so uncontrollable."

He grabbed my hand and placed it on his distended fly. "Mine's not so controllable when I'm around you." Then the humor left his face. "I want you, Jade."

"I want you too. Let's go to my place."

"How about mine this time?" His eyes glinted as if he had a secret.

Curiosity made me agree. I headed back to Fairview Slopes where I'd picked him up, a condo-intensive area that lined the south shore of False Creek. It was late afternoon, not far past the longest day of the year, and the sun was high in the sky as my little convertible buzzed along. Lots of people were out, most in shorts. Even in summer, Vancouver's weather was erratic, so when the sun blessed us, we made the most of the gift.

"Thanks for this afternoon, Quinn. You were wonderful."

"Blue-collar guy didn't totally embarrass you?"

Though his tone was teasing, not accusatory, I felt guilty. "I'm sorry. I was wrong about that. Wrong about a lot of things."

"Got that right. But it's okay. I don't hold a grudge."

"So, was this afternoon worse than the opera or salsa lessons with a foot-stomper?"

"Nope. Meeting Timothy was good. The other folks were mostly nice. Interesting. The only bad part was being with you."

"What?" I glared at him.

"Wanting you, and not being able to have you. Drove me crazy." He squeezed my thigh.

The heat in his voice gave me sexy shivers. "Me too."

He pointed ahead. "Turn left at the next light." We took a left, a right, another left, heading into the False Creek area and closer to the ocean. Did he own or rent? Would his place be tidy or a mess? Comfortable or a black leather "bachelor pad," to use one of Mom's old-fashioned expressions? I imagined all the possibilities.

Or at least, I thought I had. What I hadn't imagined was walking toward the locked gate of a marina. I remembered Quinn saying he liked to sail. "You have a boat?" When he'd invited me to his place, he'd meant his sailboat, not his home. Foolishly, I felt a little hurt.

Holding my hand, he guided me down a steep nonskid ramp and along wooden fingers of dock. We passed sailboats and power boats of all description, some hardly more than ten feet long, others large enough to live on comfortably.

He paused beside one of the latter, an immaculate sailboat with gleaming white paint, glossy wood trim, and navy sail covers. Then I saw the name on the side: *Padraig O'Malley*. "Quinn! This is yours?" He'd named the boat after his brother.

"Used to belong to my gramps, the surgeon. I lived with him after the fire. He had a house in Kerrisdale and this boat. Patrick and I had done a lot of sailing with him, and Gramps and I decided to change the boat's name so, you know . . ."

So in a sense Patrick would still be with them. I nodded.

"When Gramps hit seventy-five, he sold me the boat. He's in his eighties now and we still go out sailing together regularly."

I thought about the 15-year-old boy who'd lost his parents and brother going to live with his grandfather. An old man and a young man. It must've been a challenge for both of them. How wonderful that they were still close.

This was so strange. We'd come here because we were both lust driven, aching for sex. Yet, the drive, the walk along the docks, the thoughts of his family had changed my perspective. It wasn't that I wanted him any less—God, maybe more—but it wasn't so much that "take me" need as something . . . Less immediate? More complex?

"Come aboard." With a flourish, Quinn offered me an arm and I stepped up to the deck.

He unlocked the wooden door to the cabin and I saw narrow ladderlike steps. When I started down, he said, "Go backward. Let me guess. You don't spend much time on boats."

"Only the BC ferries to Victoria or Nanaimo. I've never known anyone who had a boat."

At the bottom of the ladder, I turned and gazed in wonder at the little kitchen, dinette, comfortable couch, TV and sound system. "Oh my gosh, this is amazing." It was an adult dollhouse, though big tough Quinn probably wouldn't appreciate me saying so. The place was neat and clean, but with a lived-in look: a thriller open and facedown on the table, a CD case by the player, a jar of peanuts on the kitchen counter.

"Thanks. I like sailing, so I figure, why not have a comfortable boat and live on her. And being on the ocean's good for getting the scent of fire out of my nostrils."

My gosh, he lived here. He really had taken me to his home. "That makes sense." I wondered, too, if having his family's home burn down had made him wary of owning another. "But don't you get claustrophobic?" Though the boat must be forty feet long, that was nowhere near as spacious as an apartment, and Quinn was a big man.

"Nah. When I'm inside, it's cozy. Or I'll be out sailing, or working on something on deck. On a boat, especially a wooden one, there's always work to do. Or I go biking, windsurfing, hiking." He opened the small fridge. "You've been a teetotaler all afternoon. Want a glass of wine? Beer?"

"White wine if you have it." Half an hour ago, all I'd had on my mind was sex. Now, he'd given me so much more to intrigue me. I knew, from the still-present simmer of sexual awareness between us, that we'd end up in bed, but right now, getting to know him and his home was a kind of seductive foreplay. "Can I explore?"

"Help yourself."

I accepted his invitation, aware of the boat moving gently, a reminder that below us, around us, was water, not dry land. It wasn't unpleasant, just different. I discovered a cute little bathroom with a shower, and a V-shaped front cabin that was mostly bed. A bed big enough for the two of us, though there wasn't much head room. "Is this where you sleep?"

"No, I'm in the aft cabin."

"Aft?"

"Back. The master cabin. Though I use the V-berth when Gramps is on the boat. If things work out with Timothy, he'll get the V-berth when we go out."

"You'd take that boy sailing? Quinn, it's too dangerous."

"I'll make sure he wears a life vest, learns the rules. Jade, I grew up on this boat."

"Be sure you check with his mom first."

" 'Course I will. I'll take her out, too, so she sees what's involved."

A twinge of jealousy made me hope Timothy's mom was plain and boring, and wouldn't be staying overnight on the *Padraig O'Malley*.

I walked from the front cabin to the aft one, fewer than ten steps, and opened the door. The room consisted mostly of a queen-size bed, along with built-in wooden cupboards and drawers. The ceiling was low but higher than Quinn's head.

The whole boat was adorable yet somehow very masculine. I grinned at him as he handed me a chunky, blue-banded wine-glass that looked Mexican. "Your boat is gorgeous. And suspiciously tidy. You knew I'd come back with you."

"Let's say hoped." His dimple winked. "But it's always pretty tidy. Small space like this, you have to keep things ship-shape." He raised a can of Coke and tapped it against my glass. "Glad you're here."

"Me too." I took a sip of crisp white wine. "Aren't you drinking?"

"I'm on shift tonight at eight."

A couple hours from now. We wouldn't spend the evening together. Just as well. This interlude was threatening to slip the confines of box number three, the sexy box, and I really should refocus on my priorities. Later. After we had sex.

His dark eyes smoldered as he studied my face, igniting sparks of arousal. He stroked my hair, then tugged out the pins that secured it. "Great hair. I wanted to do this all afternoon."

I shook my head so my hair tumbled over my shoulders. "It was hard to focus on business. All I wanted was to touch you. And feel you touch me."

"Then let's get naked. Now."

"Naked would be very good."

He ushered me into the back bedroom. "Not as big as yours, but it'll serve the purpose." Small windows let in bright drifts of sunshine that fell across the navy duvet, and one was open to a soft sea breeze. He pulled a cord and mini-blinds clattered down over the window on the dock side of the boat.

Without further ado, he unbuttoned my top, unzipped my pants, and stripped both garments off me. Today's undies were white, a lacy thong and demi-bra. His lips curved. "Hmm, maybe I'm changing my mind about naked. Damn, Jade, you look hot."

"While you're deliberating . . ." I tugged his golf shirt free from his pants and pulled it up. He took over, and yanked it off while I went to work on his belt and zipper. Then I shoved his pants down to reveal black boxer briefs that barely confined his erection.

He looked hot, too, but for me there was no debate: naked was best.

When I'd removed all his clothing, the pent-up lust and every-thing else—the way he'd mingled at the picnic, the boy Timothy, his brother Patrick, his grandfather—flooded through me. I launched myself at him, toppling him onto the bed with me atop him. He grabbed my butt with one hand, pulling me against his groin. His other hand tangled in my hair, brought my head down to his; then his mouth captured mine in a long, breathless kiss.

Mindlessly, frantically, our lips and tongues meshed, our bodies ground against each other. I tasted passion, Coke, a bright copper nip of blood where a tooth had broken skin. His, mine, it didn't matter.

One-handed, he released the back clasp of my bra and pulled the garment from between our heated chests. I moaned into his mouth as my sensitive breasts rubbed against his firm pecs, taut nipples, curls of hair, and my nipples tightened.

The last time we'd had sex, I hadn't had an opportunity to explore his body. This time would be different. Despite the seductive press of his rigid cock against my belly, I eased away from him, breaking the kiss, and went up on my hands and knees as I straddled him. I blew warm breath across his chest, circled a nipple with my tongue, teased it between my lips, then did the same to the other one. Touching him turned me on, and I felt moisture trickle down my thighs.

"Turn around," he said. "Let me get in on the action."

He'd get no argument from me. I swung around on the bed and he shifted down so his legs hung off the end, giving me room to straddle him in the opposite direction. When I returned my attention to his nipple, my breasts hung down in his face.

He gathered them in his hands, then buried his face in them with a muffled, "Oh, Christ." When he sucked my already budded nipple into his mouth, I moaned approval. This man knew exactly how to touch me. How to stoke the sparky fire of arousal.

As I worked my way down his body, he lavished attention on my breasts until he could no longer reach them. But I didn't care, because now I was focused on his cock. It rose up his belly, full and heavy, the epitome of male virility. The heady, musky scent of his arousal filled my nostrils as I explored the crown with my tongue, lapping the resilient velvety skin.

The sight and scent of him was so erotic, my pussy pulsed with the need to feel him.

Instead, I gave my mouth that pleasure. Opening wide, I wrapped my lips around him, took him in, and bathed him in wet heat. He groaned as I alternately sucked on him and ran my tongue around his crown. Bracing myself on one arm, I slicked saliva down his shaft, circled him with my fingers, stroked gently, all the time keeping up the mouth action.

"Oh, yeah, Jade." His hips rose, encouraging me but not forcing himself deeper than I could take him. I pumped harder, watching my hand at work. His skin was a couple shades lighter than mine; his thick pubic hair was shiny and black in the sunlight.

The sunshine, the fresh breeze through the open window, the occasional gentle rocking of the boat all intensified the sensuality and immediacy of the experience.

Then Quinn grasped my hips and pulled me down to his face. My sex was soaked with the dew of arousal and he lapped it up, tongue firm against my tender flesh, each stroke building the need that was coiling inside me, so I quivered and pressed myself against him.

He gave me what I craved, sliding a couple of fingers inside me, then a third. It was so sexy, having his cock in my mouth and hands while fingers stroked me deep inside, his tongue teased my swollen flesh, his thumb—oh, God—toyed with my clit. So many blissful sensations, I couldn't separate them, they mixed together in one giant spiral of arousal, of cresting climax.

As my own excitement built, I pumped him harder, squeezed the head of his cock between my lips, licked up pre-come even as I panted with excitement. The feel and taste of him made something deep inside me clutch with primal recognition.

His cock jerked, his rough finger stroked my G-spot, my body clutched again and then orgasm surged through me, making my whole body shudder and quake.

Quinn let go, too, in spasms of salty come that I swallowed one after the other.

When he was done, when I was done, I eased away from him, body trembling, and collapsed on the bed. "Oh my God."

"Yeah." He pushed himself up the bed to lie beside me. "Christ, that was good."

Neither of us moved or said another word for a few minutes. Then he shoved pillows behind his back, sat up, and took a long swallow of Coke. "Maybe an afternoon of frustration is worth it, if that's the payoff." He held my wineglass out.

I sat up, too, and sipped wine. "Anticipation's not a bad thing."

He tucked his arm around my shoulders and I moved into the curve of his body. Sunlight fell across our legs, the soft breeze brought the scent of ocean to mingle with the musk of sex, and I felt sublimely content. We chatted about his gramps, my family, his boat, my job, getting to know each other. Not a single write-off flag arose. As I basked in the glow of great sex and easy conversation, I felt an affection and intimacy that were new to me.

The sun slipped away and Quinn glanced at his alarm clock. "Damn, it's later than I thought. I have to get ready for work." He dropped a kiss on my lips, then slid out of bed.

Reality rushed back and I jerked upright. What had I been thinking? There was one very good reason Quinn was a write-off: he was a firefighter, an adrenaline junkie. I couldn't get dreamy about a man who put his life at risk, who could cause me the kind of heartache I'd suffered when Papa almost died.

Back to my priorities, and our business. He'd left the cabin, giving me a brief but tantalizing rear view, and water ran in the little bathroom. "We should talk about which Triple-F event you can attend next," I called out.

His head popped round the door. "Come sailing with me."

"Sailing? What does that have to do with Triple-F?" I climbed out of bed and sorted out the tangle of discarded clothing.

He returned and opened a cupboard. "We can talk about the event when we're sailing." Underwear, jeans, and a gray T-shirt landed on the bed.

"I've never sailed. It's dangerous."

"Driving a car is dangerous. Unless you know what you're doing."

"Everyone drives. Not everyone sails. Look, I'm not into doing risky things."

"Huh?" He paused in the act of pulling on jeans.

"You and I are different." I pulled my shirt over my head and crossed my arms. "I'm cautious, and you're an adrenaline junkie who like things like sailing and windsurfing, and you're a firefighter."

"You're dumping on my hobbies *and* my job?"

"I'm not dumping. Just saying—"

"What?"

I bit my lip. "It was silly. I was going to say, I'd never get involved with a guy who did dangerous things. But of course we're not *involved*, it's just the Triple-F thing and the, uh, sex." And despite my postsex daydreaming, that's all I'd ever let it be.

He was pulling on his T-shirt. When his head emerged, he said, "We're doing your work thing and we're having sex, but we're not *involved*? Look, like I said before, I'm not going down on one knee and proposing, but d'you have to categorize things so strictly? Can't we just hang out, date, see where things go?"

"No." I ran my hands through my mass of unruly hair and wondered where he'd tossed the pins he'd removed. "That's what I was doing before, with guys. Now I want to get married. I need to focus and not waste time."

"Oh, yeah. That serial first date thing." He shook his head. "Which I totally don't get."

"Because you're impulsive and you, uh, go with the flow. I don't."

He gave a wicked grin. "Seems to me you do in bed."

"I, uh . . ."

"Do you have a serial date every day?"

"No, and I only meet them for coffee or lunch. If we had dinner, someone might see and think I was cheating on my fiancé. Coffee and lunch are more casual."

He gave a snort of laughter. "Christ, woman, you lead a complicated life. Okay, here's the deal. The next afternoon we both have free, you're coming sailing with me and you can brief me about the next Triple-F function."

"I already said, sailing's too dangerous."

"Life vest. Calm water." His eyes glinted with humor and his dimple flashed. "Haven't you heard of compromise?"

He had a point. Sometimes I got so hung up on planning, I could be inflexible. "I'll visit you on the boat again, and we'll discuss compromise then."

9

_____

From: Jade Rousseau [jade_rousseau@shaw.ca]
To: 'Amarjeet Nagra'; 'Kimberly Brock'
Subject: What's up with guys and their families?

Case in point: Harry, a Granny fix up. 28 and lives at home, but OK, a good Chinese boy. No biggie. Then I find out Mommy does his laundry, makes his lunch. He can't express an opinion of his own, it's, like, Mom says this and Mom says that. Well, Jade says, WRITE-OFF!!!

Case #2: Jefferson, a corporate lawyer I met through work. Wary after Harry <g>, I asked about his parents. Get this, he never sees them because he LEFT THEM BEHIND when he went to law school. Snotty, pretentious. Yuck!

Frog detector rule: No guys who are squirmily close to or obnoxiously distant from their folks.

Look at Quinn. He lost his folks and brother and that's tragic, but he's got a great relationship with his granddad.

BTW, Q thinks he's taking me sailing. (Scary!) My plan? Distract him with sex <G>.

Quinn had said to wear jeans, a long-sleeved top, and soft-soled shoes, and to bring shorts, a lighter top, and a bathing suit. Though I planned on spending the afternoon in bed, focusing on sex and Triple-F planning, I'd obeyed. I'd also made a pan of Nanaimo bars to contribute to our picnic lunch.

At eleven Saturday morning, I was downstairs, backpack slung over one shoulder. He'd said he would pick me up, and I was curious what kind of vehicle he drove. Was he a muscle truck kind of guy or a sports car one?

When a big black motorbike cruised down my street, I ignored it. Until it pulled to a stop beside me, the engine died, and the rider, clad in jeans and a white T-shirt, took off his helmet. Quinn gave me a heart-stoppingly sexy dimpled grin. "Hey, Jade."

I tried to ignore the heart-stopping effect because, mostly, I was pissed off. "Quinn! You never said you were bringing your motorbike." What was he thinking? I wasn't about to climb onto one of those scary machines.

He put it on a stand and came over to give me a quick, firm kiss that made me want more, despite my general pissed-offedness. "That's my ride. Don't have a car."

No car, only a bike. No house, just a boat. He clearly believed in simplifying his life. I, on the other hand, believed in prolonging mine. "I'll get my car and follow you."

He frowned. "Are you doing that 'it's dangerous' thing again?"

"Don't joke about it. I don't believe in taking needless risks."

"I don't take needless risks." His annoyed tone told me I'd

insulted him. He held out a helmet, and said, more patiently, "This is a top-notch helmet. I'll stick to the speed limit and avoid the busiest streets. This bike's been down to California and up to Prince Rupert, and I've never had an accident."

"Wow. Really?" I imagined him on a coastal road in California, cruising along in the sunshine, a woman—me?—straddling the bike behind him, hugging his waist as . . .

Somehow, the helmet was now in my hands.

"I like bike touring. Riding scenic roads, sleeping under the stars." He touched my cheek. "Jade, the last thing I want is for you to get hurt. Trust me."

The helmet was heavy. Sturdy. Kimberly and Amarjeet always chided me for being too cautious and letting fear stop me from having fun. Battling nerves, I took a deep breath. "Okay, just please be careful." I put the helmet on and he tugged it forward to fit snugly and tightened the strap. When he tucked my bag into a storage container, I noticed a BMW logo on the body of the bike. That was comforting. Presumably the bikes were as high quality as the cars.

He climbed aboard and I became the woman in my fantasy as I slid into place behind him, spreading my legs to hug his butt and thighs, putting my feet where he told me, wrapping my arms around his waist.

Okay, this part was as good as I'd imagined. I was pressed so tight to him, I felt his muscles shift as he put on his own helmet, started the bike, and pulled slowly away.

Feeling totally vulnerable without the comforting shell of a car around me, I clung tight. It felt like we were racing, but when he turned onto Cornwall where there was more traffic, I realized we were going no faster than anyone else. Air rushing past us gave the illusion of speed.

Quinn's solid strength was reassuring, and anxiety slowly gave way to excitement. With the sun beaming down, my body cuddled up close against his as we cruised past Kits Beach where dozens of people strolled around in shorts, it felt pretty cool. I loosened my death grip.

When we stopped at a light, he took his hand off one of the handlebars and squeezed my arm. "You okay?"

I raised my voice the way he'd done, to be heard over the engine. "So far, so good."

"I'll get you out on the highway yet."

"No, you—"

He revved the engine and pulled away, the noise drowning out my denial.

As we rode to False Creek, I savored new sensations. The padded seat was comfortable, and there was definitely something sexy about the spread of my legs as they hugged Quinn's, the bike's throbbing beat against my denim-clad crotch. The in-and-out motion of his warm chest as he breathed, and the intriguing knowledge that my hands were only inches from his cock. I could see why biker groupies got into this. Riding with a man like Quinn was a turn-on.

All the same, when he parked in the marina lot, I was relieved to climb off the bike in one piece. Albeit an aroused piece.

He helped me undo the helmet and take it off. "Felt good, having you behind me." He pulled me into his arms, and the hardness of his cock under the fly of his jeans told me just how good it had felt. Our lips met in a long, searing kiss that was only the prelude to what my revved-up body really craved.

I whimpered with need and ground against him as he gripped my butt, intensifying the tantalizing pressure. God, I needed more. Now. Just down a ramp and along a dock, there was a queen-sized bed. "Quinn, let's go to the boat. I want to get you into bed."

His dark eyes, glazed with passion, slowly focused. "The boat. Right, the boat." He blew out a long breath, then put his hands on my hips and eased me away. "Time to cool down."

He busied himself with the bike, retrieving my pack and some grocery bags. "You were okay on the bike?"

"It was sexy," I admitted as he opened the marina gate and ushered me through. "But I'm still wary about going too fast."

"The more you do it, the more comfortable you'll get."

Why were we talking about motorbikes rather than sex? Likely he was trying to tame his hard-on as we walked along the dock.

"Same with sailing," he added.

We'd see about that. I still hoped to persuade him to spend the afternoon in bed.

When we reached the *Padraig O'Malley*, I caught him by the arm, stopping him. Putting my hands on his shoulders, I raised up on my toes so my lips were only an inch or two from his. "There's one thing I definitely want to do more of."

"Oh, yeah?" His eyes sparkled.

"And I won't need any of those wardrobe changes you told me to bring."

A slight grimace crossed his face. "Look, there's something I—"

"Well, there you are." A hearty male voice cut him off.

I jerked around to see a lean, white-haired man in shorts and a cotton shirt. He had a deep tan, a face creased with wrinkles, and a big smile.

As I sank back on my heels, flustered, Quinn said, "Jade, this is my gramps, Aidan O'Malley."

His grandfather? What was his grandfather doing here?

And had the older man overheard what I'd said? Cheeks burning, I took the hand Mr. O'Malley extended over the side of the boat and let him help me aboard. "I'm pleased to meet you." I shot a questioning glance at Quinn, who also looked flustered. His grandfather's visit must have surprised him too. It wasn't as if our relationship was the "meet the folks" type.

"The pleasure's mine," Mr. O'Malley said. "Quinn's been talking about you, Jade. And aren't you as lovely as he said."

He didn't exactly have an accent, but there was a cadence, a soft lilt to his voice, that spoke of his Irish roots and was as charming as his grandson's dimple.

"Uh, Quinn didn't mention you'd be here."

"He didn't? Now, that was remiss of him." His eyes had the same mischievous sparkle Quinn's often held.

So, Quinn had known. The rat. Why hadn't he . . . ?

Oh, wait. My strategy to get out of sailing had been to distract him with sex. Maybe he'd had a strategy, too, like asking his grandfather to go with us so I couldn't back out.

I scowled at him, then turned back to the older man with a sweet smile. "Did Quinn invite you to come sailing with us, Mr. O'Malley?"

"Call me Aidan. And, no, we just returned. His shifts gave him a couple days off and we went up to Smuggler's Cove and Buccaneer Bay."

I'd misjudged Quinn. Now I shot him an apologetic look. "You had wonderful weather for it," I said to Aidan.

"Grand weather. Now, how about some lunch?" He popped down the steps into the cabin, taking the grocery bags.

"Quinn," I said softly, "I—"

From below, Aidan called, "What would you like to drink, Jade? No alcohol when you're sailing, but Quinn has Coke, tea and coffee, apple juice, and Aranciata."

The last was the drink I'd ordered at the picnic. "Aranciata, please." To Quinn, I said, "Did you get that just for me?"

He winked. "Call it a bribe."

Or a considerate gesture.

Aidan handed our drinks up to Quinn, who said, "Have a seat. Or d'you want to change into shorts?"

Despite the slight breeze, the sun was hot, so I went below to change and put the Nanaimo bars in the fridge. If Aidan left after lunch, I could try my seduction strategy then. For now, I might as well relax.

I came up to find both men on deck, Quinn now wearing khaki shorts that showed off his strong, lightly haired brown legs. A platter of smoked salmon, cold meat, cheeses, and crackers sat on a folding table. A bowl held olives, celery, and carrot sticks, and another held red grapes.

When we'd served ourselves, Aidan said, "Quinn says you've never been sailing and you're a wee bit nervous."

"Yes."

"Oh, it's a grand thing, being out on the water with the wind in your sails, skimming along like a bird." He proceeded to tell stories, with Quinn chipping in. I saw what the older man was doing, slipping in comments about safety precautions and praise for his grandson's abilities. I knew Aidan had been a cardiothoracic surgeon, and suspected his lilting voice, his charm and his gently persuasive manner had been used to good effect in calming nervous patients and families. Had he not been a surgeon, he could have been a killer salesman.

It was great to see the easy way the two men related, as if they were good buddies.

I brought up the Nanaimo bars, and both men complimented me on the rich, chocolaty treats and went back for seconds. When we were finished, Quinn said, "Jade, d'you have any problems with motion sickness? I've got wrist bands, ginger, anti-nausea pills."

"Not that I know of." Of course I'd never been on the ocean in a boat smaller than a ferry. With any luck, I wouldn't today either.

The men tidied away lunch, refusing my offer of help and leaving me on deck. The marina was a busy place with people taking wheelbarrow loads of supplies on and off boats. The docks were like a single-level parkade lined with boats, and the boats came in as many sizes and shapes as the people who moved easily around them. It was rather like sitting at a sidewalk café on Yew or Robson, except the world going by was a quite different one.

This was a side of Vancouver I'd never seen before, and it was colorful and engaging.

Quinn came from below, carrying a duffel bag, which he slung onto the dock. Aidan followed. "I'll be heading home now."

My nerves kicked back into gear. Decision time was coming. "It's been a pleasure."

"You, too, Jade." He stepped down to the dock. "I'll untie the lines and see you off."

"There's no need," I said quickly.

"Would you like to do it yourself, then?" The twinkle in his eye suggested the men had been plotting. "There's a wee trick to it, but you seem like a capable lass."

I'd survived, even enjoyed, the motorbike. With a sigh, I surrendered to being finessed. "That's all right. You do it."

"There's a life vest under your seat," Quinn told me. "But you won't need it unless you want to go up on the bow."

Up on the bow? Not in this lifetime. And, yes, I was wearing a vest. I secured it over my T-shirt as he and his grandfather dealt with engines and ropes and whatever all else. Then the *Padraig O'Malley* was moving away from the dock. I gripped the boat railing with one hand and with the other hugged the vest close to my body in an effort to calm my nerves.

Aidan waved. "Have a grand afternoon. Quinn will look after you, Jade."

"Bye," I called grimly. Then, to Quinn, "That was slick."

His dimple flashed. "A little gentle persuasion to get you past your prejudice against sailing."

Prejudice. Hmm. Had I unfairly prejudged sailing as being more risky than it really was?

The engine purred as we left the marina, and Quinn, tanned and relaxed at the wheel, made no move to raise the sails. We passed under the Granville Street Bridge, then the Burrard Street Bridge, my route to and from work every day. How many times had I driven over those bridges, giving no thought to the boats below?

Cars and boats, both self-contained units as they made their journeys, but dry land seemed much safer than the ocean. Little speedboats buzzed around, kayakers paddled lazily, a couple of big boats motored past. No lanes, no dotted lines, no apparent rules of the road. I fisted the railing. "How do boats keep from crashing into each other?"

"Right of way. At least in theory. Some amateurs don't get it."

I shuddered. "Have you ever had a collision?"

"Not a one. A good boater always keeps an eye out for other boats, deadheads, floating logs. It's like defensive driving. Not taking anything for granted."

That made a lot of sense, and was reassuring.

"How you doing?" he asked.

"Okay." The motion wasn't unpleasant, and it was fun looking at the other boats and the people aboard, most of whom waved and smiled—something you sure never saw on the road. Quinn waved back, and I let go of the life vest and did the same.

The scenery on shore was interesting too. On the south side, the deck at Bridges Restaurant was crowded with diners; then the red-and-white tents for Bard on the Beach reminded me that Amarjeet, Kimberly, and I had talked about getting tickets for *A Midsummer Night's Dream*. On the downtown shore, the seawall walk wound between the beach and the strip of condos and trendy restaurants. English Bay was a mass of people, and when a few waved, I waved back. "It's different seeing everything from this side."

"Being on the ocean gives you a different perspective on a lot of things."

"Where are we going?" I finally thought to ask.

"Over to Bowen Island. There's a place we can anchor, have a picnic dinner."

He steered the boat toward West Vancouver. Crossing First Narrows, the breeze sharpened, pricking my skin to goose bumps. "I'm going to change into warmer clothes."

"Make yourself at home." Quinn's smile flashed, white against his tanned skin. He looked so happy behind the wheel of his boat. So handsome, strong, vital.

Now I was glad for this opportunity to share something he loved. Boating was growing on me. Or it would, once I was warm again. Carefully hanging on to bits of the boat, I made my way below, where I put on jeans and a sweater, and pulled my hair into a knot. Gazing out the window, I marveled at being in a little house that was cutting through the ocean.

From up on deck, I heard a snapping sound and realized I could no longer hear the motor. Anxiously, I called, "Is everything all right?"

"It's great. Can you get me an apple from the fridge?"

I found one, polished it, then, life vest secure again, carefully made my way up the steps.

To find we were sailing.

10

At the sight of the big white sail bellied out in the wind, I gasped, "Oh my God." Hurriedly, I sat and gripped the railing.

Quinn reached over for his apple and calmly began to munch.

Tendrils of my hair tugged free from the knot. "Can we slow down?"

He chuckled. "How fast d'you think we're going?"

"Fast."

"Like, six miles an hour?"

"*Six?*" I stared at him but didn't see that familiar teasing expression. "Seriously?"

"You could jog this fast."

"Maybe you could." But he'd made his point. Going six miles an hour wasn't all that scary, and there was something free and exciting about moving across the ocean powered only by the wind.

Quinn put up another sail, made adjustments, steered a course that clearly made sense to him, and exuded an aura of confidence and pleasure that was contagious. I relaxed again, though not enough to let go of the railing.

We chatted about places he'd been with his boat and motor-bike, and holidays I'd taken—to France and China with my parents, and to Mexico and Hawaii with Amarjeet and Kimberly. He was easy to talk to, and even easier on the eyes. Watching him in his element was a turn-on.

This afternoon was such a contrast to all those coffee shop first-and-only dates. It was a constant battle to remind myself that Quinn and I could never have a *relationship*.

As we approached Bowen Island, where rustic cottages and expansive waterfront homes dotted the rocky, tree-lined shore, I checked my watch. Three thirty. I hadn't looked when we left the marina and had no sense of whether we'd been on the water for an hour, two, or more.

He lowered the sails and, under power, we puttered into a peaceful cove where he dropped anchor. I was almost sorry the excitement was over.

Then he stripped off his T-shirt and my mouth watered at the sight of his brown, muscled torso. Oh, no, the excitement wasn't over.

I was all set to go below and get naked, when he said, "Want to put on your bathing suit and lie out on the bow?"

Wasn't he as horny as I was? If not, just wait until he saw me in my chocolate bikini. I changed and freed my hair so it was tousled and sexy. No sunscreen, because I planned to get him into bed before I needed it.

When he saw me, his grin was satisfyingly wolfish. "Nice suit."

I walked carefully along the side of the boat to the front, hanging on to the railing and very glad the ocean here was calm. Quinn had laid down cushiony mats and I sank onto one. "We're not going to roll off?"

"Not unless you really go wild," he teased, sprawling beside me.

"Go wild?" I found out what he meant when he pulled me

close and kissed me hungrily, as if he'd been anticipating this forever and couldn't wait any longer. Oh yes, this was what I'd wanted. His body was hard and hot, totally enticing. Arousal flared in me.

When we broke for air, he said, "Can't beat this. You in my arms out on the ocean. But let's scrap the clothes." He reached for the hook at the back of my strapless bikini top.

"Not here!"

"Live dangerously, Jade. There's no one around."

"Yeah, right. Unless someone in that house on the hill has a telescope, or one of those little seaplanes flies low, or another boat comes along."

"Then they get an eyeful, and they're envious as hell." He flicked the clasp.

Oh, what the hell. I let my top fall free. And I let him peel off the bottom of my suit, and I helped him get rid of his shorts and release his erection. How wickedly delicious to be naked outdoors, to take the risk someone might see us. Apparently, I had an adventurous, naughty side I'd never known about, because I was incredibly turned on.

I lay back on the mat, hair fanned out, a nature goddess displaying her body to the sunny sky and the handsome man beside me. *Worship me.*

He did exactly that. He leaned over me, and despite the fact that he was hard with arousal, this time his kiss was slow and seductive as he caressed, explored, teased my lips, my tongue, the inside of my mouth. I felt sun-dazed, intoxicated, willing to let him take the lead and to answer him back with the same lazy sensuality. My body smoldered, a slow burn coursing through every cell, tightening my nipples and making my thighs quiver, my sex pulse and ache.

Still kissing me, he stroked down my body with those slightly rough fingertips, a touch light as the ocean breeze yet intensely stimulating, sparking me to trembling awareness. Then his finger unerringly found my clit, brushed it lightly, and I whimpered as need suddenly became urgent. He brushed it again, with just the right degree of firmness, and again, and the sparks burst into fire and a slow, deep orgasm pulsed through me.

I cried out, arched into his hand, and he kept touching me, more gently now, but enough that my body surged again, the climax going on and on until finally the pleasure edged too close to pain. I twisted away from his hand, gasping. "Oh my God, Quinn. That was amazing. An endless wave of orgasm."

"The ocean's good for you." He bent again, brushing my mouth with a kiss, then continuing down my body, paying attention to every inch of me. Warm breath, a wet tongue, then he'd draw away an inch so the ocean air brushed the damp skin, intensifying the sensation. I closed my eyes against the sun's brightness. Behind my lids, an ever-shifting blaze of reds and oranges mirrored the way my body felt as he caressed it.

"Beautiful Jade." He circled my navel with his tongue. "So sexy, so responsive."

I was all sensation. I lost the ability to think, to speak, and melted into a warm, molten, orange-red mix of alternating arousal and satisfaction. When my body was relaxing from orgasm, Quinn was already laving and nibbling another part of me, perking me again to trembling need.

Finally, he sheathed himself and slipped inside me, and my channel gripped his cock eagerly, his bold hardness such an erotic contrast to all the teasing, seductive drifts of touch he'd been lavishing on me. Yes, this was what I needed now. He'd reduced me to a melting mass of femininity, and I wanted to be filled to the core with his powerful masculinity.

I lifted my hips to meet him as he drove into me. "Oh, yes, Quinn," I panted as he stroked all my most sensitive spots and tension built inside me. "Fill me up. Hard and fast."

"Christ, yeah." His voice rasped and his hips pumped and jerked. "Come for me," he demanded urgently. "Again. Now."

And once more I shattered, my climax blending with his and again going on and on.

When it was finally over, I collapsed bonelessly and Quinn flopped down beside me, breathing hard. I linked my little finger with his. "Poor men," I managed to say. "Only being able to have one orgasm."

He laughed softly. "Doesn't take me long to recover." When I turned my head to look at him, his gaze held a promise and a challenge.

"That's a good thing. Because I'm not finished with you." I was for the moment, though. The wind, the sun, the sex, all the events of the day and the feelings ranging from anxiety to bliss, had worn me out. The gentle rocking of the boat lured me toward sleep, but the occasional sharpening of the breeze and screech of gulls kept me from dozing off.

"We should put on sunscreen," Quinn said.

It wasn't like me to forget. On the other hand . . . "First, I want to lick you all over."

That enticing thought was enough to make me roll on my side and gaze at him. "Had enough recovery time?" I asked seductively.

His dimple flashed. "Why don't you find out?"

And so I did. I was aiming for being as thorough as he had, envisioning licking a leisurely path down his body, but once we'd kissed and he'd started to harden, his cock was too tempting to resist. So I sucked him in, loving the way his body arched, his muscles clenched. Then, my hair cascading across his belly, I deep-throated him until he begged for mercy.

My idea of mercy was to straddle him and, naked breasts filling his hands, ride him until we both cried out as loud as the gulls.

It didn't occur to me until I collapsed back onto the mattress that I hadn't worried for one moment about rolling overboard, or being seen by anyone.

A few minutes later, we went below to dress in shorts and apply sunscreen; then Quinn attached a small barbecue to the boat railing. He'd bought skewers with prawns, green peppers, onion, and tomato, and fresh sourdough bread from Terra Breads, which we slathered with butter.

Turning the skewers on the barbecue, he said, "Help yourself to a glass of wine."

"I thought Aidan said no alcohol." Or didn't Quinn obey that rule?

"None for me, because I'll be sailing us back. But you're just sitting around looking pretty." His admiring gaze told me he meant it, and that he liked having me on his boat.

And, to my surprise, I liked it too. We smiled at each other with a sense of connection that went way beyond sexual attraction. Frightening, when I knew we couldn't have a future. I hurried below to get an Aranciata and a Coke.

Then we lounged on the back deck over dinner. "You never drink when you're sailing?"

"If I'm anchored or docked for the night, I'll have a couple beers or some wine. How about next time we do that? An overnight trip. Now you see it's not so terrifying."

No, sailing wasn't so scary. But the thought of spending the night with Quinn was. And far too appealing, which made it even scarier. I'd sworn not to go on second dates with men who had no Prince Charming potential, and here I was spending more and more time with my faux fiancé. An adrenaline junkie who got his kicks from risking his life.

Or did he? Maybe I'd prejudged him too. "Why do you love sailing?" I nibbled a prawn, watching his face as he reflected.

"That's hard to put into words. A feeling of freedom, I guess. Scenery, wildlife. A different, slower pace of life."

"Slower? So it's relaxing rather than exciting?"

"It's both. Relaxing when it's like this. Or you're anchored for the night in a scenic bay, a burger on the barbecue, a beer in your hand. Watching the sun set." A quiet joy lit his eyes. "Seals swimming around, Canada geese honking, a couple great blue herons fishing for dinner."

"That does sound wonderful," I said softly, imagining the scene he'd described.

"Other times, it's pretty damned exciting. Being out in a stiff wind, pushing the boat to her limits, testing your own skills. Or the times the weather takes an unexpected turn, and you're in rougher water than you'd anticipated."

That dose of harsh reality made me shiver. "Dangerous." Facing the elements and risking death. Not so different than the way my papa had once faced criminals on the street.

Quinn put down his plate and leaned toward me. "You learned how to operate your car, how to watch the traffic, drive defensively. Right?"

"Sure, but a car—"

"Isn't that different than a boat."

"The ocean's different than a road."

"Only because you're not familiar with it. Jade, more people die in car accidents than from any other cause. Something happens—another driver screws up or has a heart attack, a tire blows, there's an oil slick. And sure, your instincts, your skill and experience, come into play, but there's no guarantee you'll come out safe. Those things could happen every time you take your car out, but you still drive."

I'd never thought of it that way. "Okay, I see your point. But, Quinn, tell me the truth. You like speed and excitement, don't you?"

"Sure." He took another piece of bread. "You saying you don't?"

"Um . . ." I didn't like danger. On the other hand . . . "I like the wind in my hair when I drive my Mini, and it was exciting being on the bike. The sailboat, yes, when we were darting across the ocean, that was fun. But we were only going six miles an hour. So maybe it's not speed, but the sensation of speed?"

"Sure. It feels faster because you're out in the world, really experiencing it. Excitement comes from being *there*, in the moment, not having a barrier between you and the world."

Had I been living life behind a barrier? Was that why my friends said I was too cautious? Might it even be the reason I'd never connected in a meaningful way with a man? Except, just possibly, the one in front of me?

Might my faux fiancé actually be my Prince Charming? I'd been fighting my feelings for him, but maybe it was time to open my heart. It would be so easy to do.

11

Companionably, we tidied up the dishes, then put on warmer clothes for the sail back. The sun was low in the sky, and the air held the nip of oncoming night.

I settled back to enjoy the first pink tones of sunset, the snap of the sails, and the sight of Quinn at the wheel. My mind played back my bad first dates and compared him with those men. He was fit, capable, didn't boast or exaggerate, had a great relationship with his only family member, was generous . . . "I forgot to ask. Did you get in touch with the Big Sibs people?"

"Yeah." He glanced at me, then away again to stare at the ocean.

"And?"

He snorted. "They need references."

"Use Aidan. And your superiors in the fire department."

"The department's the problem."

"But . . . you won a commendation."

The sky was a rich, glowing rose now, but his face, partly in shadow, looked grim. So was his voice. "From the City." He paused. "From the department, I get reprimands."

"Reprimands? But I thought . . ." That he was a hero. "Why?"

"We don't agree on how to fight fire. I say, the beast wants to kill. It's our job to stop it."

"What other opinion could there be?"

"That it's about rules. Playing it safe."

"I'm not sure what you mean."

"If it's about rules, risk analysis, talking the shit out of it on radios, innocent people die."

I thought about the rules of the road. "Surely the rules are there for a good reason."

"That's what they say." He wrenched the wheel and the boat took a wave head-on, shuddering, making me grip the railing. "If firefighters had gone into the house when I was a kid," he said bitterly, "they might've got Patrick out. Maybe my parents. But they didn't."

"They didn't go in?" How terrible. "Why?"

"Said the house was fully involved."

"Fully involved?"

"It means the whole place is going up."

"Then," I asked gently, "would your family have still been alive? I hear about people dying from smoke inhalation and—"

"There was a chance. There's always a chance, until you find them. But those guys figured it was too fucking risky." The anger in his voice was a force field between us. "Shit, firefighters sign on for a job that's all about risk."

And that was the big reason I couldn't get involved with Quinn. All the same, I wanted to understand. "But surely they shouldn't go in unless the chances are good they'll survive and be able to rescue people."

"If a guy's gutless, he shouldn't be a firefighter."

What a stupid comment. I bit my tongue to keep from saying so. No man or woman who chose that job was a coward. And they and their families deserved proper safety precautions, or more spouses and kids would go through the hell Mom and

I had. "So, you just rush into any burning building, regardless of how dangerous it is?"

He glanced my way. "No, but I'll go when other guys hold back. Jade, d'you have any idea what it feels like, hearing people crying for help and you're told you can't help? They're going to die, and you're not allowed to try and save them?"

The agony in his voice pierced my heart. "No." It was unimaginable.

"Well, it's crap. So I rescue people who'd have died, and I get a reprimand."

"Don't you worry about dying?" If my husband was a firefighter on active duty, I'd worry every moment.

"Fire's not going to get me. Learned that when I was fifteen. It had its chance, and I walked out. I always walk out. Only difference now is, I save as many people as I can."

I gaped at him. "You sure have a God complex." No wonder he'd been reprimanded. And what about the other firefighters on his team? Did he think they were invincible too?

"No." His voice was more sad than angry. "I'm just a guy doing a job. Waging a war against the beast that took my family."

I could sympathize with his motivation and his survivor's guilt, but in his passion for his mission, he'd lost touch with reality. "We'll have to agree to disagree. You think you're invincible, and I'm danger-averse."

"Didn't say I was invincible," he muttered. "Hell, I wear a helmet when I ride a bike."

We'd never see eye to eye. It seemed as if, on the subject of firefighting, he was stuck back at the age of 15. And any hope for us having a meaningful relationship had just died. A wrenching sense of loss filled me.

I sighed deeply. "I'm sorry we got onto this subject." I wasn't going to apologize for what I'd said, though.

"Me too." He sounded more despondent than mad.

We sailed on in silence. The sun slipped below the horizon, and I was glad for my heavy sweater and the warmth of the life vest. I huddled inside them, cold and depressed. So much for our lovely afternoon.

And what about our faux engagement? Was he still prepared to play the role? Did I want him to? He aroused such a strange mix of feelings in me, perhaps I should say good-bye now.

As we headed toward the Burrard Street Bridge, he lowered the sails and started the engine.

"Quinn, there's another Triple-F event next Friday, but . . ."

"You don't want me to do it. Don't want to be engaged, even if it's just pretend." It was so dark I couldn't read his expression, but there was pain in his voice.

And I knew I did want to see him again. He drove me nuts—my own feelings drove me nuts—but I didn't want things to end tonight. Like this. "I'd like you to come. But I'll understand if you don't want to."

"I made a commitment."

"Thanks." Yes, he was a man who honored commitments.

"And I want to see you again," he said. It sounded like a grudging admission. As if he, too, realized we were better off saying good-bye now yet couldn't bring himself to do it.

"It's a dinner dance. Uh, can you dance? I mean, not that you'd have to, but—"

"I do okay on the dance floor." Now I heard the hint of a smile in his voice. "Especially with the slow dances."

Now I remembered the auction, and how he'd mentioned dancing, and I'd fantasized. Oh, yes, I could imagine being in his arms, moving to seductive music, the dance a kind of foreplay.

No, wait. I shouldn't have sex with him again. I was so damned mixed up, knowing Quinn was utterly wrong for me and yet feeling so drawn to him. Briskly, I said, "I'll fill you in on the details of the event."

And so I did, as he motored to the marina and docked the boat. I left him on deck, tying ropes and tidying things up, and went below to gather my scattered clothing.

When I came up, he touched my shoulder, his face drained of color in the moonlight. "You could stay."

I fought temptation. "I don't think it's a good idea."

The dimple, the sexy teasing, the twinkle in his eyes were all missing. "Maybe you're right. I'll drive you home."

As we rode through the summer evening, I circled his waist with my arms and leaned against him, too drained and confused to be anxious about being on a bike.

When we got to my place, he walked me to the door of the building. He ran his hands through my messy hair, cupping my face. "Guess we're too different, after all."

"I knew that from the beginning, but we have so much chemistry. I figured we could have sex a time or two without . . ."

"Anyone getting hurt." His tone was almost flat, but there was a thread of bitterness, and I knew in my heart that he'd been developing feelings for me too.

"Yes," I said regretfully. "So, now we should keep it to business. Maybe just the dinner dance. The board will be making their decision in a couple weeks."

"I hope you get the promotion. I know how much you want it, and you'll do a great job." His mouth twisted. "And I hope that serial first-date thing works out and you find the right guy."

"Thanks."

"I wish—" He shook his head, then turned away and strode toward his bike.

"Wish what?" I whispered.

I knew what my own wish was. That Quinn was a lawyer or doctor or teacher, even a ditch-digger, so long as his job was a safe one where he wasn't driven to put his life on the line.

12

Amarjeet, in a fuchsia pink top that complemented her dark coloring, sat curled up on the couch. Kimberly, her mass of blond curls in disarray after a day of dealing with grade four kids, sprawled in my reading chair. I sat cross-legged on the floor, closest to the coffee table on which sat sustenance: a bottle of Yellowtail Shiraz and two pizza boxes from Flying Wedge. It was Monday night and we were catching up.

"My mother and I have agreed," Amarjeet said, stretching over for a slice of Szechuan Chicken pizza. "We'll look for an Indo-Canadian man, not someone in India. I'm not moving there, and I don't want a guy marrying me to get Canadian citizenship."

I swallowed a bite of Broken Hearts pizza, with marinated artichoke hearts, onions, mushrooms, tomatoes, and cheese. "I still can't believe you're considering an arranged marriage. Why not try my way first?"

"The one that's working so well for you?" she asked.

"Good point." Kimberly topped off our wineglasses. "Jade, your first date plan is turning up a pondful of frogs."

"An army," I said. "Frogs in a group are an army. A fact I learned in elementary school from Tommy Hornmeister."

"Ooh, that geeky kid who had a crush on you?" Amarjeet asked.

"I'm now thinking of an army of rejected frogs," Kimberly said in a horror movie voice. "Mounting a revenge attack on Jade. A hopping, croaking, very, very green attack."

Amarjeet laughed, but the best I could summon was a smile. After Saturday with Quinn, my heart wasn't in much better shape than the broken artichoke hearts on my pizza. Not that I had let myself love him or anything, but maybe—

"My plan's efficient," Amarjeet said. "The man who's selected will be compatible, and our horoscopes will match. Mom has agreed I can spend time with him and have veto power."

"*You've* sure struck out on compatibility," Kimberly said to me. "Except for Quinn. All those rules you're making? He's the one who meets your criteria."

I hadn't yet told them about Saturday. "Except for the biggie."

"The danger thing?" Kimberly said. "You really have to get over that."

"I agree," Amarjeet said. "Crossing the street involves risk, but one doesn't stay home."

"Maybe I'm figuring that out, thanks to some motorbike riding and sailing."

"Oh my God, you didn't?!" Kimberly's eyes widened.

I filled them in on Saturday's activities. "It was great, until we started talking about his job. He takes crazy risks. And I won't go through what Papa put Mom and me through."

"It was bad," Kimberly said quietly. "I remember."

"It was," Amarjeet said, "but I always envied you your father. Mine has a safe job, he comes home every night, but he's so distant. Rarely did he play with me when I was a child, or hug me or kiss me good night. Never has he said he loves me."

"Amarjeet, I'm sure—" I started.

"Yes, yes, I know he does, in his way. But he doesn't express it as your father does. If I'd had a choice, I might have taken your father—dangerous job and all—over mine." She turned to Kimberly. "I also remember when your grandma died. You and she were so close, and you missed her so much. And *she* died of cancer, not a hazardous job."

I rubbed my forehead. "I see where you're going with this, but—"

"Jade," she said, "we love people and we lose them. Everything that lives will die."

"Thanks for that wisdom, Madam Philosopher," Kimberly teased gently, lightening the mood. "I'm glad you're putting those doctoral courses to good use."

Amarjeet made a face, then said earnestly, "Should that stop us from loving people? From loving fully, making the most of our time with them, not holding back? Look at us three. If I lost either of you, my heart would shatter. But my life is so rich, for loving you."

"Aw, sweetie," I said, and we got up to exchange a misty-eyed group hug.

"There's a difference between us and Quinn," I said. "He goes into danger every day." Like Papa did, before he was injured and went off active duty. But at least he'd obeyed the rules and not believed he was indestructible. "Quinn has a thing about fire. It's like he's fifteen, in a personal war with the beast that killed his family. He takes risks other firefighters don't, and thinks fire will never get him."

"Good God, that's just plain stupid," Kimberly said, and Amarjeet and I both nodded.

"All right, you've convinced me," Amarjeet said. "It would be foolish to care for him."

It would be. Except, I already did. And I had to get over it. "We'll go to the dinner dance; then I'll say good-bye."

From: Jade Rousseau [jade_rousseau@shaw.ca]
To: 'Amarjeet Nagra'; 'Kimberly Brock'
Subject: What happened to basic courtesy?

People who are late suck, right? Like, their time matters more than ours? Know what's worse? You're at the restaurant, you've ordered a drink, you're waiting for late guy, and he texts—TEXTS—that he can't make it. OMG, what a jerk! I have a new record. I can write a guy off without even one date!

Frog detector rule: I demand R-E-S-P-E-C-T—and more than A LITTLE. LOL.

Friday after work, I showered, shaved my legs, then put on a slinky black dress that clung to my curves, had a thigh-high slit up one side, and plunged a bit at both front and back. Appropriate for a work-related function, but sexy enough to—

Damn. No, no, no! Tonight was business and then goodbye. I changed the dress for a tailored evening suit and coiled my hair tidily rather than letting it tumble loose.

The plan was for me to pick up Quinn in the marina parking lot. My stomach churned with nerves as I pulled into the lot, hoping against hope he would for once look anything other than mouth-droppingly appealing.

Well, he didn't, but only because he wasn't there. Five minutes passed, and still no Quinn. Remembering my bad no-date, I checked my cell. No voice mail, no text messages. I called his number and went to voice mail. Sighing impatiently, I got out of the car and went to the locked marina gate to peer in the direction of his boat.

A man in shorts with windblown hair and a red nose walked up the ramp on the other side of the gate. "Can I help you?"

"I was supposed to pick up my date, but he must still be on his boat getting ready."

He held open the gate. "You don't look dangerous."

"Thanks." High-heeled sandals were definitely not the way to traverse a skid-stripped ramp, or the wood-planked docks. I muttered curses under my breath.

The door to the *Padraig O'Malley* was locked, and my knock brought no response. "Damn!" So much for honoring his commitment. He'd blown me off. Clearly, I'd been wrong in thinking Quinn was a decent guy.

Furious and hurt, I went to the dinner dance and spent the evening telling people my fiancé had to work and listening to them rave about what a wonderful man he was.

By the time I got home, I had a splitting headache and was close to tears. There was, of course, no message from Quinn. I took pills for my head, stripped off my suit, put on a robe, and let my hair down. Then I made a cup of tea and turned on the TV for company. But I wasn't really paying attention to the news, I was too busy fuming.

The only good thing to come out of tonight was confirmation that I was right to forget all about Quinn O'Malley.

"... and O'Malley." Had the TV voice just echoed the name I'd been thinking?

Hurriedly, I looked at the screen, where the ruins of a cheap hotel belched smoke. In front, a blond female reporter, mike in hand, said, "The two firefighters are in critical condition."

Foreboding shivered down my spine. "What were those names?" But she was gone, replaced by the weather forecast.

Surely she didn't say O'Malley. Frantically, I dialed Quinn's number, only to get voice mail again. With trembling fingers I leafed through the white pages to find Aidan's number, and again got voice mail. Another shiver chilled me.

I looked up the number for Quinn's fire hall. This time, a

real human being answered. "Is Quinn O'Malley there?" I asked desperately.

"Um, who's calling, please?"

"Jade Rousseau."

"He's not here, Ms. Rousseau. Are you, um, a relative?"

Oh, shit. "I'm his . . . We were supposed to go out tonight."

"Look, I hate to tell you, but—"

"The fire. It was him?" Tears filled my eyes.

"You heard the news? Yeah, I'm sorry, that was Quinn and one of our other guys."

I hugged my knees to my chest with my free arm, holding myself together. "H-how bad?"

"I've heard critical condition. You could phone the hospital for an update. They're at Vancouver General Hospital. I'm really sorry, Ms. Rousseau."

I hung up; then immediately punched the autodial number for Black Top cabs. No way was I in shape to drive. I barely managed to pull on jeans and a shirt, then grabbed my purse and flew down to meet the taxi. Maybe Quinn wasn't the right man for me, but damn it, he was badly hurt, I cared about him, and I couldn't sit at home and wait for news.

When I reached Vancouver General, I asked about him, unashamedly lying and saying I was his girlfriend.

"He's in surgery," a nurse with an understanding smile said. She directed me to a waiting room, where, through a cluster of large, fit men I guessed to be firefighters, I saw Aidan O'Malley. He sat beside one of the men who'd been at the auction with Quinn. The two weren't speaking and Aidan's face was buried in his hands.

I rushed over. "Aidan? How's Quinn?"

He gazed up, face strained. "Jade. I'd have called but I didn't know your last name."

"You're Jade?" the firefighter said. "The girl from the auction? I'm Ben. Quinn said—"

I grabbed his arm, his skin warm against my icy fingers. "How is he?"

"Sit down." He stood, offering his seat.

"How bad is it?" I sank down, knees weak. "What happened?"

"The surgeon hasn't come out yet," Aidan answered. "But I—"

"You a friend of O'Malley's?" another male voice cut in.

I turned to see a burly guy about Quinn's and Ben's age. "Yes. Will he be okay?"

"He was unconscious when the ambulance took him and Rossi away." To my surprise, below the worry in his voice, there was an undertone of censure.

"Walt, this isn't the time to get into it," Ben said. Then, to me, "We got the call, a fire in a cheap residential hotel in the Downtown Eastside. We knew the building. It wasn't up to code. The owner'd been warned to fix it or close it down. Fire had started in an apartment on the third floor, and when we got there it was blazing pretty strong. Most people had evacuated."

I listened impatiently.

"We went in, looking for people. Information was, there were a couple stoners who hadn't made it out." He glanced at the other firefighter. "Walt and me bust in their door, found them passed out from smoke inhalation. And found—"

Walt made a jerky movement. Aidan was slumped back with his eyes closed, and I guessed Ben had already told him the story.

"It was a meth lab," Ben said. "Chemicals and other combustibles. Flames licking the far wall. Place was gonna blow. Walt and I grabbed the stoners, radioed the chief, got the hell out."

"And Quinn?" I demanded. "Where was he?"

"Playing fucking hero again." Walt spat out the words.

"Shut up, Walt," Ben snapped. "The guy's in surgery."

Aidan sat up, staring intently at Walt.

"It's his own damned fault." Walt's voice was lower but no less fierce. "He was a time bomb waiting to explode, and he could've taken any of us with him. Figures it'd be that probie, Rossi. Guy treats O'Malley like he's God."

"*What happened?*" Right now, I didn't care if Quinn had been right or wrong, I only needed to know he'd be okay.

"Chief radioed everyone to pull out," Walt said. "There was gonna be a big explosion any moment. It could take out the rest of the building."

My heart clutched. "Quinn didn't make it out in time?"

"Could've, if—"

Ben overrode him. "We had info there was a little girl in another apartment. He and Joey Rossi'd broken in the door. They were so close, didn't want to quit."

"O'Malley broke protocol," Walt said. "Again. And maybe got Rossi killed."

Aidan's fists clenched. The fact that he didn't defend Quinn spoke volumes.

"Quinn told Joey to exit the building," Ben said. "You heard them on the radio. But Joey ignored him, went into the apartment."

"Probie was just following O'Malley's example. All the times he fucking rushes in without thinking."

"Anyhow," Ben said heavily, "Quinn followed Joey in. The chief radioed again, saying get the fuck out—pardon my French. Said the girl had turned up safe. The guys started to evacuate, but the meth lab blew." He swallowed hard, his stark expression suggesting he was reliving the moment. "We had radio contact. Sounded like Joey got struck by a chunk of ceiling, knocked out. Quinn got hit, too, but got Joey out before he passed out himself."

But they'd both got out. I still didn't have a sense of how serious Quinn's injuries were. "So, Quinn was hurt by a falling ceiling?" I asked Ben, wishing Walt would go away.

"And inhaling chemicals and smoke. Their airpacks got knocked off." Ben rested a hand on my shoulder. "The ambulances were there, the guys got the best care possible. Look, Jade, Quinn's tough. It's not the first time he's been hurt."

I gaped up at him. "He said he always walked out. That fire would never get him."

He huffed annoyance. "Want to look at it that way, he walked out this time too."

And if he survived, would he see it as further proof of his invincibility?

"Rossi didn't walk out," Walt muttered. "Chief shouldn't have teamed him with O'Malley. But then—" he shot Ben a narrow-eyed gaze—"not many guys are willing to go into a fire with O'Malley."

"He's a good firefighter," Ben said.

"Whatever." Walt stalked away.

Aidan glanced at me, then away, and I had a feeling nothing he'd heard was a surprise to him.

Ben shook his head. "Quinn *is* good. Could be the best. But he's a loose cannon. He won't listen to me. He's been screwing up his career, and now Joey's hurt."

"I've tried to talk to him," Aidan said. "He has a blind spot when it comes to fire."

I nodded, having seen it myself.

"You should try, Jade," Ben said.

I had. Well, not really. I'd backed off because I figured I'd never change his mind. If I'd forced the issue, was there any chance he and Joey Rossi wouldn't have been hurt? I bit my lip. "I doubt he'd listen. It's not like I'm his girlfriend."

"No? From the way he talked, I thought . . ." Ben shrugged.

"So did I," Aidan put in.

"Really?" Despite my misgivings and my worry, my heart gave a foolish thump.

"He said, ever since you won him and made him cook dinner for you, you've been a challenge." Ben gave a half smile. "Quinn's not a guy to turn down a challenge."

Like the challenge of waging war with fire. That attitude could get him killed one day.

And that day might even be today.

The fact that he might die hadn't really sunk in before. Now that it did, my eyes flooded. I turned to Aidan. "You're a surgeon. Can't you pull strings and find out what's going on?"

"I have." He took my hand. "Some of it's easy. A dislocated shoulder and a broken arm. Then there's inhalation of chemical vapors. If he's damned lucky, he won't wind up with permanent respiratory problems." He paused, took a breath, let it out. "Then there's the serious stuff. An acute subdural hematoma. In lay terms, a blood clot putting pressure on the brain. They're operating. All we can do is wait."

"Oh my God." A wave of dizziness and nausea hit me, and next thing I knew Aidan was forcing my head between my legs and telling me to breathe.

When I'd begun to recover, I asked, "What about the other man, Joey? How's he doing?"

"He's concussed, but so far there's no swelling or bleeding in the brain. He has a broken shoulder, fractured ribs, and a collapsed lung. He was in surgery until half an hour before you arrived and came through well."

"I hope he'll be okay." I stared pleadingly at Aidan. "Do you think Quinn will?"

He shrugged tiredly. "I hope so. The boy's a fighter."

He'd said "hope," not "think." Which meant Quinn's injuries were very, very serious.

"They're strong guys, both of them," Ben said firmly. "They'll make it."

God, I hoped so. I felt sorry for Joey, but I didn't know him. I did know Quinn. And I knew that, even if he had a God complex when it came to fire, at heart he was a good man. A man who, despite my best intentions, I'd truly come to care for.

And that meant I should walk out now, before I put my heart any more at risk.

I was still there a couple hours later. Quinn was out of surgery and in recovery, and we'd been told that first Aidan, then I, then Quinn's chief were allowed a quick visit.

When Aidan came out, he squeezed my hand. "He's doing well. So far, so good."

The reassuring words didn't prepare me for the sight of Quinn in a hospital bed, hooked up to machines, looking drawn and groggy. Even his body, normally so vital, seemed smaller. A dressing covered part of his head, a reminder that he'd had brain surgery. The smile he gave me was a shadow of his normal vivid, sexy one, but it did brighten his eyes. "Jade."

I sank down in the chair by the bed and clasped his hand gently, trying not to cry. How could I be so relieved and so worried all at the same time?

"Stood you up," he managed slowly, voice croaky. "Sorry."

"It's okay." I blinked back tears. "How do you feel?"

He moved his head slightly and grimaced. "I'll be okay."

"Of course you will." In the waiting room, I'd pried details out of Aidan obsessively. I now knew way more than I'd really wanted to about possible postop complications. Information I wasn't about to share with Quinn.

"Gramps says that—" he paused, swallowed, went on— "Joey's doing okay?"

"Yes. Your chief was in with him and his parents after the surgery. He came out and told the guys that Joey's good." I squeezed his hand. "The chief's waiting to see you too."

Quinn turned his head away. "Too tired."

Or was he feeling guilty, or afraid the chief would ream him out? "He's waited for hours. He wants to make sure you're okay."

"You tell him."

"All right."

The nurse who'd shown me in held up her arm and tapped her watch.

I nodded. "Quinn, I have to go."

Slowly, he turned his head back and gazed at me, through bruised eyes clouded with anesthesia and a pain I thought went beyond physical. "You'll come back? See me again?"

I shouldn't. I'd been going to say good-bye tonight. If I wanted to get married, I had to concentrate on my plan, my serial first dates, not waste time with a man I'd written off.

I bent down and pressed a gentle kiss to his forehead. "I'll see you tomorrow."

13

From: Jade Rousseau [jade_rousseau@shaw.ca]
To: 'Amarjeet Nagra'; 'Kimberly Brock'
Subject: My crazy week

Somehow, Quinn almost getting killed has given me a new perspective. I couldn't keep on lying at Triple-F, so I confessed to the chair, crossing fingers they wouldn't fire me. She was pretty cool. A little stunned—hadn't realized how discriminatory the "image" thing was. I told her I believe firmly in marriage and want to be married, and the good news is, I still have a shot at the promotion.

As for Q . . . I'm so freaking confused!!??!!!

I'm supposed to be dating, right? (And, seriously, I have to find a new coffee shop. I've met so many guys at my old one, the staff are looking at me like I'm a "working girl." <g>) OK, so now Triple-F knows the truth, the pressure's off re the job, but I still do want to get married and start a family, and the dating plan seems like my best bet. (At least before I hand myself over to Amarjeet's mom. LOL!) But I'm just not into it. I postponed a couple dates this week but did have lunch with a colleague of Papa's because he'd set it up. Anyhow, this guy was really nice. Not a single fault. Except, there was no spark. He's cute, fit, smart, considerate, funny, easygoing. I should feel a spark!

I know, I know, Amarjeet, no man is perfect. And yeah, Kimberly, relationships call for compromise. Just not when it comes to CHEMISTRY!!

Frog detector rule: Sparks are mandatory <g>.

Then there's Q. Each night I visit the hospital, I tell myself it's the last time; then I'm back the next night. We can't have sex (people around, and he's battered), but we hold hands, talk, fool around. Irresistible chemistry, but it's more than that. I confess, I'm falling, falling, maybe even fallen. Him, too, I think. His job is a fatal flaw, though. Not something I'll compromise on. Am I crazy for thinking maybe he might???? He's going home tomorrow. It's time to talk.

After I'd sent off the e-mail, I thought about compromise. Was there a chance Quinn would give up firefighting? We'd avoided talking about his job, but two things were clear. First, that he felt crappy about what had happened to Joey Rossi. Second, that he chafed when they said he'd be doing a desk job until he was in shape to return to active duty.

Now I wondered how Papa had decided to give up active police duty and become an instructor. Had it been a realization of his mortality, or had Mom persuaded him?

It wasn't late, so I phoned home and put my question to my mother.

"Oh, Jade, those were horrible days." Even so many years later, her voice was filled with pain. "When that gang kid shot your papa, I went to pieces. So did you, of course. I'm so sorry, honey, I wasn't much use to you. All I could think was, we could lose him."

"I know. Me too." The memory still made me shudder.

"I told him we couldn't go through it again."

"And he said he'd give it up?"

"No, he tried to reason with me. But honestly, what could he say? Every day he was out on the streets with criminals, gangs, druggies. It could happen again." She sighed. "I know it was hard for him. He loved his job."

"I remember."

"Back in the hippie days, we wanted to create a world where people could live in freedom and peace. Most kids just smoked dope and dreamed, but your papa was focused, mature, a man to respect." She paused. "Jade, why are you asking? Is this about one of your dates? That colleague of Papa's? He works at the Justice Institute, not in the line of fire."

"It's not him. There's a special guy, and I . . . could fall for him. But he's a firefighter."

"Oh, honey."

"How did you live with it, before Papa got hurt? When he went out every day carrying a gun, facing dangerous people?"

"Well, he was trained, capable, had good judgment. I never thought he'd get hurt. When he did . . . Maybe that's part of why I fell apart. I'd never expected it."

"Me either." My papa had been a superhero, and superheroes always won. But then he'd almost lost his life. And now so had Quinn. Maybe I could get my lover to listen to reason.

After I hung up, I sat with a cup of tea and thought about what I might say.

When the phone rang a half hour later, I saw my parents' number. "Mom?"

"*Bonsoir, ma pierre précieuse.*"

"Hi, Papa." *Ma pierre précieuse*—literally, my precious stone—was my Québécois father's pet name for me.

"What's this I hear about my Jade getting serious about a firefighter?"

"I know, it's crazy. But he was just injured in a fire, and maybe he'd consider shifting his career the way you did."

"Mmm. You think he'd want to do that?"

"No, but he might listen to reason. You did."

There was a pause. "Does the man love what he's doing?"

"I think so. It's kind of a mission. His parents and younger brother died in a house fire, and Quinn walked away."

"Survivor's guilt?"

"Some. And he's out to save the world."

"The world can use all the help it can get."

Sprawled in my favorite chair, I imagined Papa in his den at home. In his fifties, fit and strong, he was still a superhero to me. "You're helping the world *and* staying safe."

"*Vraiment, mais ce n'est pas la même chose.*" When Papa was tired or emotional, he'd lapse into his first language.

"Why isn't it the same thing?"

"Sometimes a man needs immediacy. Doing things firsthand, not at a distance." There was a heaviness to his voice that I rarely heard. It sounded like . . . regret?

"Papa, do you ever miss being on the street?"

There was a very long pause. "Jade, if I tell you something, you must promise never to tell your mother. It would only hurt her."

A ripple of tension tightened my muscles and I sat up. "Uh . . . okay."

"I miss it every day."

I sucked in a breath. "I had no idea."

"Nor does your mom. And she can't. It was my choice. I did it because she wanted it so badly, and I love the two of you more than life itself. But, yes, I miss being a real cop. It's like a part of me is gone."

A gang member had shot my father twice, one bullet nearly missing his heart. And yet it was my mom, her love and her fear, that had robbed my papa of a part of himself.

"Promise me, Jade, you won't tell her."

"No, of course not. But why did you tell me, after keeping it a secret so long?" I wished he hadn't. Now, whenever I was with them, I'd think of the sacrifice he'd made for her.

"Ah, *ma pierre précieuse*, because now it's about you and your happiness. And because you are like your name. You're Jade. Lovely, decorative, precious, but also a stone. Strong. Stronger than your mother, I think. Perhaps you can live with the man your firefighter really is."

I thought about Quinn, his strengths and his flaws. The loose cannon was not a man I'd ever live with. But what if he were a normal firefighter, one who obeyed the rules? He'd still be in danger, but would it be better to be with him and worry, or not be with him at all?

"Know this." My father's firm voice broke my train of thought. "I have no regrets. If I had it to do over, I'd make the same decision."

"I believe you." He would give up a piece of himself out of love. Yes, when I was with my parents I'd think about his sacrifice, but mostly I'd think about the strength of their love.

If I loved Quinn, what kind of compromise was I willing to make?

The next day, I cancelled another lunch date because I couldn't imagine being with any man other than Quinn. And yet, I couldn't be with Quinn if he didn't change his ways. Not, of course, that he'd asked me, but I saw the expression in his eyes, the one that mirrored my own.

Tonight, Quinn was home. Aidan had said he'd drive him to

the boat and try to make him rest. I'd promised to drop by after work with dinner.

Fed up with hospital food, Quinn had requested Indian, so I drove to Vij's Rangoli on 11th and picked up kalonji chicken curry, garam masala lamb, ginger and coconut curried green beans, rice, and naan. When I reached the marina parking lot, I called his cell.

Peering through the gate, I watched him walk toward me. In shorts and a T-shirt with the sleeves ripped out, his body looked strong and masculine, only the cast and sling on his arm to show he'd been injured. A nurse had buzz-cut his hair so the shaved patch wouldn't be as obvious, and the look suited him, with his nicely shaped head and strong features.

He swung open the gate. "Man, Jade, it's great to see you. Out of the damned hospital."

I held the take-out bags to the side and we gave each other a one-armed hug. He felt so wonderful, hot and strong and sexy, an instant aphrodisiac. Fooling around at the hospital had been frustrating, and now we embraced urgently.

Before things got out of hand, I asked, "Is Aidan still here?"

"No, it's just you and me."

"Good." I tilted my head up and we kissed fiercely, mouths demanding and devouring. My feelings for this man were so damned complicated, but at the moment all I cared about was being together. And getting naked. He'd almost died and I had to make love to him, reassure myself he was all right, feel him fill me and merge with me again. Yes, there was a physical need—sexual longing tightened my nipples and dampened my pussy—but it was emotional too.

"Christ, Jade," he groaned. "I need you now."

"Me too."

Gripping each other's hand, we hurried toward the boat. Inside, the take-out bags fell somewhere, our clothes got tossed somewhere else, then we were on the bed, entwined, kissing and rubbing against each other frantically. His thigh was between my legs and I ground against it, clit swollen and throbbing as each touch fueled my arousal.

It wasn't until he groaned with pain rather than pleasure that I remembered his injuries. I jerked up. "Quinn, I'm so sorry."

He lay back, injured arm cradled across his body, and drew a long, shuddering breath. "Give me a sec."

"Maybe we shouldn't do this."

"Not an option." Head on a pillow, he gave me a sexy, dimpled smile. "Woman, the last week has been hell, being together but not being able to make love. I have to be inside you." His erect cock told the same story. "But you're going to have to do most of the work."

I remembered the times he had pleasured me while I lay back and enjoyed. "I think I can handle that." Leaning over him, I let my hair drift across his chest, then bent to take a nipple between my lips, being careful not to jostle his bad arm.

Using his good hand, he grabbed a handful of my hair and pulled my head away. "Not slow. Not this time. I can't wait." His voice was rough, his expression heated.

His urgency rekindled my own. I found a condom in the drawer by the bed, sheathed him, then straddled his hips. Lowering myself slowly, I took him in, inch by delicious inch, absorbing his hard heat into my slick, sensitive vagina.

He groaned again, and this time it was a sound of pleasure and satisfaction. "Oh yeah, that's good. That feels right."

Yes, it did. Our gazes met and held as I began to ride him, slowly at first, savoring the exquisite sliding press of flesh against flesh.

The gleam in his eyes told me he was enjoying the view.

I straightened my back, thrust out my chest and tossed my hair, cupped my breasts in both hands and played with my nipples.

"That's one beautiful sight."

I smiled down at him. "You don't look so bad yourself." Despite the cast and shaved head. And that thought reminded me that this man, seemingly so strong, was vulnerable. I faltered, broke rhythm.

"Jade?" Using both his good hand and his bad one, he stroked my knees, my thighs, his touch bringing me back into the moment. His hands caressed higher, roughened fingers trailing across the soft flesh of my inner thighs, focusing my attention, my arousal. My anticipation.

"Oh, yes," I sighed as his thumb brushed my sensitized clit. "Touch me there."

I had to move faster. My body craved the driving force of his cock invading my secret places. Marking them, claiming them, bringing them alive in a way no other man had ever done.

We did belong together. My body knew it, and so did my heart. And in the passion of our locked gazes, I thought Quinn knew it too.

His hips rose to meet me, his cock plunged fast and deep; then he caught my clit gently between thumb and index finger and squeezed.

I whimpered with pleasure. And then my orgasm started, coming from hidden female places deep inside, from the erotic pressure of his fingers on my clit, from the intense intimacy of his gaze. Everything came together in an explosive burst of sensation and emotion.

Quinn's dark eyes blazed, and his exultant cry joined mine as we climaxed together.

It took forever to find enough breath and energy to lift myself off him and sprawl beside him. He tucked his good arm around my shoulders and I curled into him, head on his chest.

"So good to be alone together," he said a few minutes later.

"It is. Bet you're glad to be out of the hospital."

"Oh, yeah. And to think of getting back to work. Even if it's on the desk for a while." There was my opening. Before I could take it, he rolled to face me, taking care not to jar his injured arm. "You know I'm crazy about you, Jade."

I started. This was the first time he'd put his feelings into words, and the genuineness of his smile told me he was sincere. "I'm crazy about you, too, Quinn. But—"

"No buts. Let's just enjoy the process."

"Process?"

His lips moved as if he was searching for the right words. Unfamiliar ones. "Falling in love," he said softly. "I've never done it before."

My heart stopped. For a moment I couldn't breathe. Then it lurched back to life and my eyes grew damp. "Me either." But I knew this was what was happening to us. Had been happening from the night we met. Would continue to happen unless I stopped it.

"Quinn, I can't relax and enjoy the process. You scare me. You and your job."

His face tightened. So did his hand on my shoulder. "I'm a firefighter. That's who I am."

"You're a decent, caring man. A grandson, a sailor, a lover. All sorts of things other than a firefighter. You could become an instructor."

He gave a harsh laugh and sat up, pulling his arm away. "With my record, I'm sure as hell not going to get a job as a trainer. Besides, I don't *want* to. Are you really asking me to give up my job? Is that what I have to do, to make you love me? Because, damn!" He shook his head, expression dark, almost tortured. "That's one hell of a high price tag to put on yourself."

All the same, he hadn't said no. "Quinn, it's not your fault Patrick and your parents died. You don't have to spend the rest of your life saving people to make up for not having saved your family."

He frowned, reflected, then shook his head. "It's not about Patrick and my folks. Lives can be saved, and that's what I want to do. It's who I am." The certainty in his eyes blazed bright as any fire.

No, I didn't want to do to Quinn what my mom had done to Papa. "I think I understand. But please try to understand how hard it is for me—a woman who saw first my papa and then you almost lose your lives on the job—to think about you fighting fires every day."

Again, he frowned in thought, then slowly nodded. "I hear the other firefighters talk about how their families worry. I don't want you to go through that, but I can't just let you go. You're . . . I see a future for us."

Tears slipped down my cheeks. "I do too. But I want a man I can have kids with. One who'll do his best to come home safe. Not a . . ." I swallowed. "They call you a loose cannon. A time bomb. They say—"

"I've heard it." He held up a hand, and muscles in his jaw and throat worked.

"When you sail or ride your bike, you're careful. You don't take needless risks. If you brought that same attitude to firefighting . . ."

"Could you handle that?" Gently, he stroked tears from my cheeks with the rough pad of his thumb.

"I'd still worry." But I'd be with Quinn. I knew now that there was no perfect Prince Charming out there. There were only men with flaws. Besides, it's not as if I was flawless myself. Each relationship involved compromise, but better to compromise for a man I loved. If he was willing to meet me halfway.

I took a deep breath. "Yes, it'd be hard, but I think I could handle it. But, Quinn, *can* you change? Follow the rules? Even if you know there's someone who needs to be saved, and your instincts tell you to rush in?"

"It'd be hard," he admitted, echoing my words. His eyes squeezed shut, then opened again. "But the past week has been hell. Joey Rossi . . . It was my fault." I saw the pain on his face.

The probie's injury, and Quinn's admission of guilt, had both cost him.

I touched his arm. "No reprimand was issued. Everyone heard Joey on the radio, insisting on going in after you'd told him to evacuate."

He scrubbed a hand over his face. "Only because he'd seen me do the same thing before."

I nodded. "You were his hero. He wanted to be like you. When you're a role model . . . Look, think about the Big Sibs thing. If you do get approved and get a little brother, and you take him sailing, you're going to make him wear a life vest and teach him to be safe, right?"

His mouth twitched. "Yeah. And, while fire may never get *me*—" When I started to protest, he said, "Okay, maybe I'm wrong about that. But right or wrong, the thing is, other guys are affected by what I do. Probies, friends like Ben, everyone on the team. If we hadn't got out, the chief would've had a tough decision. Whether to risk other guys' lives to come in after us."

He did understand. A huge knot of tension inside me began to release.

"And that's not fair," he went on.

I shook my head. "Even if you're desperate to save a life, it's not fair to put your colleagues in that position."

"They've been trying to hammer that into my head since training, but I was too thick-skulled to get it." He sighed wearily. "I am who I am, and that's a firefighter. But I'll do my best to follow the rules and be a team player, even if sometimes it really pisses me off."

What a very Quinn way of putting it. "That's wonderful."

"So here's the question, Jade. Is it fair of me to ask you to live with that?"

"I—"

"No, wait. Let me say something else first." He took my hand and held it gently. "You're the best thing that's ever happened to me. Maybe it was fate, that night at the auction. I was onstage, saying how I was waiting for the right woman to come along. And there you were."

I remembered what he'd said. About wanting marriage and kids, and not having found the right woman yet. "And I was doing my serial first-dating, but no man ever got a second date because I compared them all to you."

A hopeful smile softened the lines on his face. "So, what's your answer?"

If I was with Quinn, I'd worry about him. If I wasn't with Quinn, it would be like what my father had said. Like a part of me was gone. Papa had said I was strong. And I *had* survived both his near death and Quinn's. Could I be stronger than my mom?

Well, I had to be. Because I wanted this man.

I touched his cheek, the spot where I knew a dimple lurked. "It's taken me a long, long time to find you, Quinn O'Malley. I'm not going to let you get away."

"Thank God." With his good arm, he pulled me close.

We kissed gently, lovingly, to seal our agreement.

When our lips parted, he grinned and that sexy dimple flashed. "Now that we're officially a couple, guess you're taking me to the next Triple-F event?"

"Bet on it."

"Hey, Aidan brought us a present. I think it's the perfect time to open it." He swung out of bed and, naked and gorgeous, walked out of the room. He returned carrying a bottle of champagne. "But you'll have to do the honors, since it takes two hands."

I chuckled. It seemed that Aidan, like my papa, knew me better than I'd known myself.

THE FIREFIGHTER WEARS PRADA

Rachelle Chase

Acknowledgments

To my family, as always, whose love for me continues to unfold in wonderful ways. I love you.

Special thanks to Leigh Michaels, who never says no to my cries for help and never tires of being bombarded with my life's trivia; Calista Fox, for continuing to be my friend, even when we disagree; Ethan Jackson, Myron Scott, and Ken Smith of the SFFD, for letting me peek into the life of real firefighters; Rand Powdrill, for correcting my basketball blunders (any remaining errors are my fault) and of course, most importantly, my readers, who make writing worthwhile.

1

Oh. My. God. There he is.

Delta Ballantyne nearly stumbled in her spiky heels. At the sight of Evan Marshall in the flesh, she felt like a toddler, taking her first step in her Jimmy Choo slingbacks. Tightness clenched her chest, squeezing the breath from her lungs and pushing heat to her abdomen. Dizziness invaded her head, threatening to topple her.

She paused, giving her body time to adjust to the shock—and her eyes a chance to look their fill.

Across the street, Evan stood in front of the fire station, turned slightly away from her, talking to a group of firefighters. Though they all wore station uniforms, to Delta's prejudiced eye, only his fit him perfectly, as if designed by Giorgio Armani himself. The midnight blue shirt was wrinkle free, as was the top of the matching T-shirt, visible underneath the two unbuttoned white buttons. The fabric hugged his perfectly honed chest before disappearing inside impeccably creased pants of the same shade—pants that traced muscular hips and tantalized with hints of well-built thighs.

God. He was even sexier than his photo.

Her breathing quickened, signaling her body's inability to return to equilibrium.

She had to get a grip. She was at San Francisco Fire Station #27 for business, not sex.

Business. Business. Business.

Using the words as her mantra, she took another step. This time, her foot was steady.

Good. That was it. She just had to remember her priorities.

She continued forward, picturing her new line of men's underwear. The image of Evan in the new Playing with Fire undershirt flickered in her mind. But as she stared at Evan, the image vanished. In its place, he stood shirtless and she stood speechless, admiring his powerful chest with her fingertips. She ran her hands over his smooth skin, letting his nipples caress her palms. Her own nipples tightened in sync with his. Her gasps echoed his. As her hands moved down, over his abs, the hard muscle quivered under her touch, begging her to slide lower, to dip her fingers under the waistband of his pants—

Evan turned his head toward her, capturing her gaze.

Delta gasped, startled by the irrational belief that he'd read her mind.

His gaze flitted over her—a guy's natural instinct to check out a woman who enters his line of sight—too quick to be insulting, but long enough for him to form an impression.

The impression must've been favorable, for sexual awareness flared in his charcoal brown eyes, before his expression became inscrutable. His look was intense, the effect deadly. It seemed to pierce her skull and swirl through her mind, stealing all oxygen.

Once again, she felt light-headed and breathless.

Business. Business. Business, Delta chanted as she continued forward; fortunately, without missteps. At her arrival, conversation stopped.

She forced a polite-yet-friendly smile and greeted everyone

before turning to Evan. "Good afternoon, Lieutenant Marshall. I'm Delta Ballantyne."

Delta held out her hand.

Evan's gaze flickered to her hand and his lips twitched, as if something about it amused him. "Good afternoon, Delta Ballantyne."

His hand wrapped around hers. The friction from his palm, slightly work-roughened, against hers shot a ripple of lust up her arm. The visual of her small hand lost in the grasp of his bigger one, coupled with the firmness of his grip, sent a flutter of femininity to her stomach.

"What can I do for you?"

Oh, you can take that hand that's igniting little tremors inside me and draw little circles with your fingertips against my wrist, then slide under the cuff of my silk Marc Jacobs blouse and—

The echo of his words pierced through her fantasy fog as she withdrew her hand. The lack of contact restored a bit of functionality to her brain. And with it, a flicker of confusion.

"I'm here for our three-o'clock meeting."

"Our meeting?"

Had Donnye gotten the day wrong? "My assistant scheduled a three-o'clock meeting with you to discuss the details of my offer."

"Your assistant didn't talk to me. But it would be my *pleasure . . .*"

He dropped his gaze to her breasts.

The air swooshed from her lungs.

He continued downward, his gaze circling her hips.

Heat rushed to her stomach.

As his eyes lingered on her bare legs, it was as if a hundred silken threads brushed against her skin. A flash of dizziness shot through her head.

His gaze reversed direction, repeating its knees-to-rubber-inducing inspection.

He finally looked into her eyes. "To discuss your 'offer.' "

This time, his thoughts were transparent. The dark glint in his eyes said that his "pleasure" would involve his hands caressing every inch of her body that his gaze had touched. The sexy quirk of his lips seduced her into believing that all "discussions" would be tactile, with his lips nibbling hers, before leaving to lick every curve of her body.

And his "offer" was infused with carnal delights.

While her body throbbed from the onslaught of sensuality, the raw sexuality in his gaze sent a zap of excitement through her mind. Now, *that* was the look she wanted to capture in the ad campaign. If the photos caught even an ounce of the heat flaring in his eyes, the underwear would fly off the shelves. No woman would be able to resist buying them for her man.

Delta looked away from Evan, allowing the excitement to ebb from her body and flow to her mind. She looked at the other firefighters. They stood with expressions of curiosity, amusement, or both, soaking up every word.

Calmed by the reminder that they were not alone, Delta returned her attention to Evan. She ignored the seductive pull of *his* offer and forced her mind to focus on hers. "I read that heartwarming story of you saving the family of five—"

"My *team* saved that family."

"Yes, I know." Her professional tone, belying her physical turmoil, restored her control. Delta withdrew a news clipping from her purse, unfolded it, and held it up between them. She tapped a photo of Evan, dressed in full firefighter gear, exiting a burning building. He clutched a round glass bowl containing a small goldfish between his gloved hands.

"But the *San Francisco Chronicle* featured *you* on the front page, detailing how you'd gone back inside for the little boy's pet."

Evan shrugged. "It's what I do, Ms. Ballantyne."

His humility and courage sent a wave of warmth to her heart. Delta smiled. "Please, call me Delta."

"Evan." The dark glint returned to his eyes. His long spiky lashes, framed by dark, thick, naturally arched brows, intensified the sultry look.

Her mind zoomed back to his invitation to pleasure.

Don't go there.

Taking her own advice, she dropped her arm, refolded the article, and returned it to her purse. After clearing her throat, she continued, "Which is why I'm here. Because I think you're the perfect man to model Too Brief's new line of men's firefighter-themed underwear."

The listening men catcalled and whooped.

Evan didn't join in.

With her last eighteen words, the remnants of desire that'd been burning in his eyes was replaced with polite disinterest. And his body, which she had imagined hard with need, was now tense with annoyance. And his hands, which she'd fantasized about gripping her hips, before reaching behind to grasp her ass and—

Well, *those* hands were now clenched at his sides, as if resisting the urge to strangle her.

What had she said wrong?

"I am a firefighter, Ms. Ballantyne. I do not 'model.'" He said "model" in the same tone he'd probably use to say "play Barbie."

A hunky firefighter with creamy, roasted-coffee-bean-colored skin and a dazzling smile stepped forward and positioned himself in front of Evan. "Well, I *do* model, Ms. Ballantyne."

A couple of firefighters groaned.

Another one grinned and gave him a friendly shove. "Since when did being the Pinot Wine King, wearing nothing but a wine barrel and a crown, count as modeling, Carter?"

"Don't be a hater just because you're jealous." Carter said with a grin before turning to Delta. "See, unlike *Senor Machismo* here, I'm comfortable with my manhood and—"

"Carter, aren't you on toilet duty?" asked Evan.

"Nah, I've got kitchen—"

"Would you—or anyone else—*like* to be on toilet duty?"

"Oh." Carter winked at Delta. "Speaking of jealousy, looks like I've gotta go. But remember me. I'm your man."

Delta laughed. "I will keep you in mind."

After the fear of toilets had driven the other firefighters away, Evan turned back to Delta. A wry smile curved his lips. "Don't encourage him."

Despite Evan's tone, the banter, along with his smile, suggested that he and Carter were friends. "Well, if you say yes, I won't have to."

Evan snorted.

About Carter? Or modeling? Delta guessed the latter.

"So, then—what do you have against modeling?"

"Well, contrary to Carter's belief, it's not *machismo*." Evan's smile turned sly. "And my manhood is most definitely intact."

A thrill shot through Delta as definitions of "manhood" zipped through her mind. "Manliness," which Evan's broad shoulders and strong hips easily defined. And "cock" . . .

Her thoughts lingered lovingly there, while visions of his hardness and satiny smoothness—pressing against her inner thigh, before moving upward—teased and taunted her.

She blinked in an attempt to clear her mind.

Evan licked his lips, as if savoring the images flooding her mind.

"*Machismo* and . . ." penis *or* cock *or* ". . . manliness never occurred to me as your objections to modeling. So . . . ?"

"I dislike 'designer labels'—and what they stand for—that models sell."

"I don't understand." His words converted the watts of arousal to kilowatts of irritation. " 'Designer label' stands for fashion. And fashion stands for self-confidence and self-expression. So, you dislike men and women looking and feeling good about themselves?"

"Not at all."

"Evan—"

"Delta." Evan lifted his hands, palms up, in a stopping motion. "Let me give you an example. Let's pretend that a charred wooden beam fell on my head."

A lovely visual. Much stronger than my fist.

"And induced amnesia."

Wonderful. You are now reasonable!

"And filled me with an overwhelming urge to strut around in clothes."

Be still my heart.

"Target would be the first company I'd call."

"What!"

Lord, give me strength.

It was hard to believe that, mere seconds ago, lust had been overheating her circuits, causing a physical meltdown. For now, shock pummeled her insides, overloading her mind.

Surely, he did not just say he preferred Target over Too Brief.

"Because Target sells everyday clothes."

Yep, that's what he'd said.

Delta took a deep breath and ran a perfectly manicured hand along her Dolce & Gabbana skirt, smoothing nonexistent wrinkles, before plucking at invisible lint. The feel of the expensive virgin wool soothed her—in a way that her threadbare cottons had failed to do twenty years ago.

Finally, she looked up. Evan waited, his eyes shining with dribs of victory and drabs of the Deadly Look.

"Target markets celebrity labels," she said.

"Yes, but at affordable prices. Designers slap a 'designer' label on everyday clothes, mark them up two thousand percent, and brainwash weak people into believing that they *need* them."

He stepped closer and fingered the lapel of her suit between his thumb and forefinger. His knuckles accidentally grazed the swell of her breasts.

Delta stifled a gasp.

His eyes flared. The Deadly Look still glimmered in their depths. But something darker—and far more dangerous—sparkled within, changing them from charcoal brown to a smoldering mocha.

"Is this five-hundred-dollar suit really necessary to make you look and feel good about yourself?"

The smooth pitch of his voice dribbled over her skin like warm maple syrup. Though her body responded, her mind bristled at his words.

And suddenly, Delta realized that there were times when fabric was not a cure-all. Like right now. For even if the heavens opened and dropped a bolt of Scabal's $8,000-a-yard vicuna cloth into her lap, fondling it would not give her the superpowers she was going to need to win over Evan Marshall.

She was on her own.

Delta squared her shoulders and decided to take the firefighter by the horns. Because, suddenly, it was no longer about him and modeling.

It was about his attack on her ideals.

Delta stiffened and drew herself to her full height, wishing she could tower over him. "Actually, it's a twenty-four-ninety-five-dollar suit."

This time, his mouth dropped open. "Twenty-five bucks? Seriously?"

Delta smiled sweetly. "No, two thousand four hundred ninety-five dollars. And, yes, I do think it's necessary, Lieutenant Marshall."

2

Evan struggled to keep his expression blank as he gazed into the challenge sparkling in Delta's eyes.

He'd never found challenge especially sexy in a woman, but feeling it arc through the air from her liquid brown eyes seemed to do funny things to his chest. Like make his lungs feel too large and his shirt too small.

This tightness merged with the shock waves that still rippled through his body.

Though he wasn't quite sure what shocked him more: the physical response that had slammed through him at the sight of her—her tight body sheathed in the curve-hugging pink suit, the long, shapely legs made to wrap around a man's hips, and the seductive sway of her hips caused by the ridiculously tall heels; or the fact that they still slammed through him.

Despite the fact that she wore a $2,495 suit.

Because Evan was not usually attracted to fashion divas. His ex-wife, along with a $47,000 "fashion" credit card bill, which he was still paying off, was living proof of that.

A $2,495 suit should have been an erection buster.

But as Evan let his gaze drop to her rosy lips, his cock twitched to life. The fact that her mouth was twisted in annoyance did nothing to stop a sizzling fantasy from streaking through his mind. Of her lips on every part of his body—nibbling his ear lightly, then urgent and demanding as they moved under his, then firm and skilled around his cock.

Down, boy.

"And do you know why?"

He yanked his attention back from the sexual abyss and returned his gaze to her eyes. An unfamiliar bout of confusion swirled through his mind.

Why I'm getting a hard-on for a woman covered head-to-toe in clothing I don't believe in?

"No." *Not a clue.*

"This is finely woven worsted wool, the strands tightly coupled to give it a softness that belies its strength."

Coupled . . . her body, stripped of worsted, woven, whatever, naked under his, trembling and eager, ready and waiting to couple—

"And the cut. The smooth, no-nonsense lines." Her fingertips traced the lapels of her suit. "Give it a hint of masculine power, making me feel like I can butt heads with the best of men."

Masculine power . . . butt . . . his hands gripped her butt. Her ass cheeks filled his palms, firm and tight, as he used every ounce of masculine power *within him to enter her slowly. To ignore the urge to thrust, ram, take, and possess.*

Evan's blood rushed downward, stiffening his cock.

Her eyes flashed. "While the color—the palest blush of rose— gives it a touch of femininity without eroding into girlishness, and lets men know I'm a woman."

The palest blush of rose . . . like, the hot, wet, rosy inside of her pussy, bared by his fingers. A feast for his eyes, tongue, and cock.

His stomach knotted.

She lifted a leg and pointed her toe outward. "And these shoes. The supple leather wraps itself around my skin, hugging and comforting, while thrusting me a few inches higher, giving me the height to look people evenly in the eye."

Leather . . . wrapping . . . hugging . . . thrusting. Ah, fuck.

She lowered her leg.

He lowered his eyes, following the movement of her leg, unable to look away from the smooth skin.

"All of which is a juxtaposition of illusion with reality, giving the illusion of softness, of yielding, while hiding the reality of strength and power. And that makes me feel like I can do anything."

"Softness" and "yielding" were enough to send Evan crashing through the wall of fantasy into reality. He prayed for the strength to do nothing. That is, not to act on the thoughts battering his mind like a Shoring hammer.

"When an outfit from Target makes me feel all this, I will be the first one there."

So, instead, he forced the lewd images fueling his cock from his mind and focused outward. He concentrated on the effect her words had on *her*, not him.

And as he did so—as his eyes scanned her face, seeing the conviction glittering in her eyes, the flush in her cheeks, and her pursed pink lips—another kind of awareness throbbed through him. But, for once, this awareness had nothing to do with sex.

Okay, well, it had a *little* to do with sex.

For it suddenly dawned on him that Delta truly believed the expression that "clothes make the man"—or in her case, woman. While his ex-wife had unemotionally bought clothes because of the price, Delta passionately bought clothes in spite of the price.

And once donned, Delta's clothes turned her into a corporate version of Superwoman.

But once removed, did she turn into a sexual dynamo, wild and uninhibited and insatiable in bed?

The heat that'd flowed through his body before being reined in by his thoughts now zipped to life. Adrenaline surged through his limbs. Awareness coursed through his veins.

And, yes, this time, it had *everything* to do with sex.

Now, the challenge was to prove that he was right. That the (wo)man makes the clothes, not the other way around.

As the beginnings of an idea formed in his mind, Evan smiled.

Delta's eyes widened in surprise.

"Well, then, Delta. Whadda ya say we put all those *feelings* behind that two thousand four hundred ninety-five-dollar suit to the test?"

3

Delta was miffed. But that didn't stop Evan's sexy smile—beautiful teeth, straight and white, that complemented his toasty lips—from causing delicious tendrils of sensation to do salsa steps across her skin. Nor did it stop her blood from dropping to her stomach, where it swirled and boiled, struggling to break free and move lower.

Which further annoyed her.

"What do you mean?" she asked.

"You pass the test; then I'll model."

"Just like that, you've changed your mind about modeling and 'overpriced designer labels'?"

"*If* you pass the test." Mystery laced his smile.

He turned, obviously expecting her to follow.

Delta almost turned as well—in the other direction.

Confusion swirled inside her. First off, she'd never had such a strong instant lust attack for a man she'd just met. Sure, Evan was sexy as hell, but she saw dozens of sexy men at auditions for her ads.

Yeah, but with those men, it's all about business.

And that was the heart of the matter.

For somewhere along the way, Evan had turned a business proposition into a personal one. Starting with the article's portrayal of him as a hunk with a heart. That had sparked romantic fantasies that had nothing to do with business. And then today's encounter, which was definitely personal. Sneering at her ideals, well, that was a personal . . . rejection.

Which brought out the desire to prove her worth, sending her back in time to twenty years ago, when she'd been a penniless tomboy named Delilah Bonnet.

Then, she'd fought the teasing boys.

Today, she felt compelled to beat Evan.

So she turned and followed Evan into the station.

And as she walked down the aisle between the two fire trucks, her resolve solidified. She *would* pass his silly test, whatever it was.

The tap-tap of her heels against the concrete gave her mental strength.

The hard curves of his ass, visible as the wool tautened across each cheek with each step, made her physically weak.

Once again, her mind stripped him of his clothes. This time, she pictured him in Too Brief's new Playing with Fire briefs. The organic Pima cotton clung to the muscular half moons. As her hands cupped his ass, the feel of the fabric's downy softness against his brawny hardness flung her into sensual euphoria.

Delta swallowed hard.

Evan stopped.

Delta stumbled to a halt, a hairbreadth away from the butt she'd been admiring. Not that having her pussy pressed against his ass and her breasts flattened against his back would be a bad thing.

A shiver coursed through her.

"Have you seen the ball?" Evan asked an apron-clad Carter, who stood chopping onions in the kitchen.

Ball?

Carter looked up. Tears filled his eyes. He swiped the back of his hand across his eyes. "Nah."

"I'll be right back," Evan said to her before moving in the direction of the stairs.

While the low hum of lust buzzed through her limbs, curiosity filled her mind. Delta had never been inside a fire station before. She'd never really stopped to imagine what it looked like, beyond picturing a garage housing the trucks, or thought about what went on inside of a station, beyond firefighters waiting to go put out fires.

Her eyes darted from Carter to the firefighters clustered around the wooden tables, then moved to the lanky iPod-toting firefighter mopping the floor.

A voice sounded over a loudspeaker, the cryptic message startling her.

"Don't worry about that. You only need to jump if you hear the tone," said Carter, grinning between his tears.

"Tone?"

"Siren." He waved toward the table with his knife. "Please, have a seat. And I can tell you why you're wasting your time on him."

She smiled and stepped forward. "Thank y—"

Her movement and answer was interrupted by Evan, who bounded into the room. "She doesn't have time."

Her eyes barely had time to take in a flash of blue and the blur of toned flesh, before he breezed past her.

But her body had plenty of time to notice, as his arm brushed against hers. The blood whooshed in her ears, seconds before pooling in her stomach.

"Come on," Evan said over his shoulder, jogging out the door.

"That dude's like a deranged Energizer Bunny, showing up when he's never wanted," said Carter, with an exaggerated sigh. He waved her away. "Go. I'll regale you with my skills later."

With a parting smile and a hasty good-bye to Carter, Delta exited the kitchen. She walked through the patio and around the corner, just in time to catch Evan dribbling a basketball.

She couldn't help but notice that he'd removed his shirt, revealing the Persian indigo SFFD T-shirt that outlined his muscular back with each move. Or the way that the cotton shorts cupped his ass and the muscles corded in his leg with each jog. Not a single body part jiggled as he ran and jumped. He was 100 percent solid muscle.

That damn light-headed breathless feeling was trying to surface.

Delta took a deep breath to combat it.

Evan dunked the ball, then caught it as it dropped through the hoop. Tucking it under his arm, he walked to her. "Do you play basketball, Delta?"

"No." *She* didn't. But Delilah had.

"Good." Evan grinned. "Then, here's the deal. A game of one-on-one, and if you win, I'll be your posterboy for designer duds."

"You don't expect me to win?"

"Nope." His grin widened. "But you can prove me wrong." And with that, he pivoted toward the hoop, jumped a good foot from the pavement, and arced the ball toward the basket. The ball circled around the rim, before falling in. He ran to retrieve it and returned.

What a show-off.

Delta barely stopped herself from rolling her eyes.

"If your Superwoman suit gives you the 'self-confidence' and 'self-esteem' to race tall basketball courts and slam-dunk in a single bound, I will concede defeat and admit the error of my ways." He raised the ball to his chest and passed it to her.

Delta reached out and caught it.

"Well?"

"And if I lose?"

"Then you spend two days—beginning today—using the

superpowers wrapped up in that miracle suit to clean the station."

"Don't you have fires to fight?"

"Nope, not until the tone goes off. Do you have meetings to hold?"

"No, you were my last appointment."

"Well, then. That takes care of any excuses." Hands on his hips, teeth glistening in challenge, Evan was cockiness personified.

Delta eyed the hoop and considered his skill—what little she'd been able to glean from his show-off-manship.

It was enough, though. No doubt about it, he was good.

Yeah, well. So was Delilah. But that had been eons ago.

She eyed the hoop again.

Hmmm.

She turned back to Evan. "Let's discuss terms. So you don't try to weasel out of it, when you lose."

He raised an eyebrow. "When I lose?"

"Yep, so you'll do two ads for the new Playing with Fire line. I'll pay you fifteen thousand dollars. Plus, ten percent of all sales from the line will be donated to your favorite charity. That work for you?"

Surprise flitted across his face before he masked it. "Fifteen percent."

"Twelve point five percent."

He grinned. "All right. But it's a moot point, since you won't win."

Delta smiled. "That remains to be seen." She stepped forward and held out her hand. "You're on."

For the second time that day, he shook her hand. But this time, the jolt that buzzed up her arm and across her chest carried a tingle of excitement at winning, mixed in with the jangle of lust. And this time, identical heat flared in his chocolaty eyes.

Delta blinked, snapping herself out of her mini-trance. As

her attention turned outward, she saw that a small audience of curious firefighters had, once again, gathered. A couple she recognized from earlier, in front of the station, though most were new.

Setting the ball on the ground, she shrugged out of her jacket and purse, and walked to the friendly blonde who'd heckled Carter. "Would you mind holding these for me?"

"No, ma'am."

She thanked him and turned back to Evan, who still seemed dumbfounded. His eyes skimmed over her ruffled blouse before following the movement of her leg, as she lifted it sideways to unbuckle her shoe. His gaze traced her ankle and her calves in an invisible caress.

Tingles cascaded across her skin.

"My 'superpowers' have limits, so I need to take off my shoes." Her voice sounded breathy.

"Be my guest." His voice was a deep rumble, hinting at an invitation for her to remove more than just shoes.

Delta took a calming breath. "If I could borrow a pair of athletic socks . . . ?"

"I'll get 'em," volunteered a voice behind her.

"Please remove your shoes, Evan. I'd hate to have my toes crushed after you stomp on them."

"No problem." And off came his shoes.

"Here you go, ma'am," said the blond firefighter, still clutching her belongings, as if guarding them with his life. "They're clean."

Delta smiled. "Thank you. I appreciate that."

"Yes, ma'am." He stepped back.

As Delta kicked off her heels, Evan stared at her feet. His eyes seemed to be riveted on her Passion Pink Parfait–covered toenails. The intensity of his gaze sparked visions of a deliciously decadent kind of parfait—one that featured her foot covered with whip cream and her toes poking through the frothy confection like pink cherries, right before being licked and suckled by Evan's mouth.

Delta gulped and hurriedly covered her toes.

Evan blinked. "Uh, okay. Here are the rules. We'll play up to seven, win by two, with a nine-point dead end. That means—"

"That the first person to score seven points, with a two-point lead, wins." She smiled, relieved to be back on nonsexual ground. "If there's no two-point lead, the first person to score nine wins."

His eyes narrowed suspiciously. "Right. All baskets count as one point, except shots behind the three-point line—those count as two points. The three-point line—"

"Is nineteen feet nine inches from the hoop."

"That's for women."

"Well? I am a woman."

"I noticed." He dropped his voice to a deep whisper that only she could hear.

His words, coupled with the silky tone, sent a thrill through her.

"We don't have the marking for women," he continued, his voice a bit husky. "So we'll eliminate the three-point line scoring."

"Okay." Her voice had a nervous girlish ring to it. She lowered the pitch. "And I want no 'winners take out.' The person who makes the shot passes the ball to the other. All right?"

"I thought you said you'd never played basketball."

"I never said that."

"When I asked—"

"You asked me if I *play* basketball, which I don't. But I'd like to now. So, are we going to talk or play ball?"

Evan's lips curved into a smug smile. "Pretty cocky for someone who's going to lose."

Delta snorted.

He tossed her the ball. "Ladies first."

The last flickers of lust disappeared from her mind as she dribbled the ball low to the ground with her right hand. She considered her options as Evan came toward her. Raising her left forearm in an attempt to shield the ball from him, she darted to the right.

Evan reached out, immediately stole the ball from her, raced down the court, and did a layup.

He tossed the ball back to her.

She tried to blow past him with a speed dribble.

He stole the ball, and made the shot.

Again. And again.

With each point, his grin grew wider and Delta's frustration grew bigger. Until he won: 7:0.

Carter groaned. A couple other firefighters made polite sounds of sympathy.

Creamed. The most humiliating loss ever. And she couldn't even blame it on the restricted movement allowed by her skirt.

Disgust flowed through her limbs.

Evan came toward her, all smiles. "Gee. Guess your suit's not working. Must be the worst wool."

"Worsted wool," she said, gritting her teeth.

"Hmmm. That doesn't sound right. Maybe you mean the 'worser wool'? Though my advice is to wear your *best* wool next time. Not that I'm the expert here."

If she wasn't so angry at herself, the teasing glint in Evan's eyes and the humor in his smile would cause an answering twitch in her lips. And the look he spared her "worser wool" suit, glimmering with appreciation that had nothing to do with fabric, would send the all-too-familiar rush of heat to her limbs. And the glance caressing her heaving chest would cause her to go all trembly with desire.

But she'd wanted to win too much for more than a smattering of sexual feeling to intrude.

How could she have played so badly? Granted, it had been a

long time since she'd held a basketball, but it should be like riding a bike.

A little rustiness was understandable, but a total lack of skill? For heaven's sake, she hadn't made a single shot.

Maybe it was because she'd tried too hard. Delilah had always *known* she'd win. Delta had *wanted* to win.

For the first time in decades, Delta wanted to be Delilah.

You can't. You've buried her under mounds of Chantilly lace and batik tulis.

"Do you want to change into the clothes that make you *feel* like the janitorial Cinderella?"

She returned her attention back to Evan, ignoring the jibe. "No, I want to play another game. Double or nothing."

"Hmmm" He dribbled the ball, then stopped. "No."

"No?"

"Not double or nothing. You lost the first game. You still have to clean."

Delta frowned.

"*Two* weeks of cleaning."

"One week."

"One and a half."

"Fine."

Evan passed her the ball. And stole it back again to score the first two points.

Come on, Delilah. Help me out here!

With her third miss, after he'd rebounded and scored another point, Delta was fuming.

Evan dribbled the ball over to her, smiling. "Nice try."

Maybe he was being serious. Or maybe he was ribbing her. Delta didn't care. Frustration made her raise her hand and flash him the finger.

"My pleasure," he said with a wink. A flare of heat lit up his eyes. "Later." That husky rasp turned the word into a promise.

An involuntary thrill raced through her.

Focus.

After he passed her the ball Delta paused, summoning long ago feelings. The deep-seated, cellular-level belief that she would win.

The game is mine. The game is mine.

And with that, she feinted to the right. Evan took the bait.

Pivoting, with her back to him to protect the ball, she raced toward the basket and hit a jump shot, milliseconds before Evan reached out to block it.

The ball hovered on the rim.

Go in! Go in!

The ball went in.

"Yes!"

Applause and encouraging shouts greeted her ears.

Grinning, she passed the ball to Evan, serving him a taste of his own medicine. "You want to borrow my Jimmy Choos?"

"Your what?"

"My heels. They might've helped you block that shot."

Oohs sang out from the guys, followed by laughs.

"She's trash-talking you, man," taunted Carter.

"Not for long," muttered Evan.

And with that, Evan did a crossover dribble, bouncing the ball rapidly from one hand to the other. Delta kept her legs spread, her knees bent, her eyes on the ball, trying to guess which direction he was going to fake.

She guessed left.

Evan darted right.

Too late, she ran up to him and jumped, hands raised, attempting in vain to steal the ball.

He easily dodged her attempts, and slammed the ball through the hoop.

"Yes!" he shouted, hands in the air. "Perhaps *you* should go strap on your Jimmy Choos."

"Gimme the ball."

"Sure you can handle it?"

She sidled up next to him and snatched the ball from his grasp. "I can handle anything you have to give me," she purred. Running her tongue slowly across her lips, she trailed a fingertip down the front of his shirt.

Evan's Adam's apple bobbed. He looked down, his gaze seemingly mesmerized by her hand.

Delta yanked her hand away, pivoted around him, jumped high, and released the ball into the air.

"Foul!" he shouted as the ball swooshed through the net.

She turned to him, arms outstretched. "How was that a foul?"

"You distracted me."

"So? There's no rule against that. It's not my fault your brain dropped into your pants."

The firefighters around them hooted with laughter.

The game continued. Delta ran and jumped. Whirled and twirled. Stole and blocked. She felt as if there were springs in her shoes and wings on her back. She was exhilarated. Invincible.

Carter announced the score: 8:9.

Cheers rang out.

"Oh my God. I won! I won!" Delta bounced up in the air, slapped an invisible high five, and came back down to earth on the pads of her feet. She did it again. And again.

Her blouse was stained. Her suit had brown smudges from the ball. Perspiration beaded her forehead and trickled down her back, and her hair felt like a bird's nest. And yet, for the first time in years, she didn't care. She couldn't remember feeling so free, so alive, or having had so much fun.

Maybe because she was chained to her desk, never allowing herself to have fun.

Thanks, Delilah.

Applause and whoops circled the yard.

The loudspeaker came on. The men began to disburse.

All except Evan.

He came toward her, looking ridiculous holding her dainty jacket, purse, and shoes.

"Are you coming over to 'concede defeat and admit the error of your ways'?"

He smiled, but neither his lips nor his eyes seemed to tease. Instead, the Deadly Look seemed to be back.

Delta's pulse spiked.

He held out a handkerchief to her. She thanked him, then swiped it across her brow and down the back of her neck.

His eyes followed the movement, as if he wanted to be the wisp of cotton.

Delta gulped, as another blip of awareness shot through the victory flooding her bloodstream.

"Actually, I was coming over to tell you good game."

The compliment surprised her. She'd expected him to glower or make some crack about beginner's luck. She did not expect to see the dark and dangerous look sparkling in his eye, especially since she couldn't think of anything she'd done to put it there. And it certainly couldn't be the way she looked, since last she'd checked, dirt and grime weren't on the Top Ten Things Men Find Sexy list.

But contrary to all logic and reason, something sexual glimmered in his eyes.

She patted her face with the cloth, this time hot for a different reason.

"And to see if you're ready to clean."

Her heart skittered at the request, the intensity of his gaze making her feel as if he'd just asked her on a date. "Clean?"

"You lost the first game."

"Oh, right."

So wrapped up in the glory of winning, followed by the jab

of lust, Delta had forgotten about the first bet. But even that didn't put a dent in her mood. As she trailed behind Evan's glorious backside, she was still on cloud nine.

She followed Evan toward a four-story structure that was used for training. The "building" had windows on two sides, with fire escapes traversing both sides, and a metal platform in front of each window. The building looked like a rectangle, turned on its short side, and was about as wide as a small bedroom. A couple burnt-out cars were parked on either side.

Evan took a set of keys from his pocket and opened the door. He flicked on the light and stepped inside. "Here we are."

Delta's smile instantly disappeared as her gaze circled the room. Fire hoses resembling piles of cooked spaghetti noodles squiggled across the cement floor. Heaps of rusted car parts and bulging black plastic bags were propped along the walls. Directly in front of them, flush against the far wall, stood a large metal bookcase filled with tools. And in front of the bookcase was a table, covered with mounds of papers and newspapers, many yellow with age.

The look of the room, coupled with the musty smell, convinced Delta that they were the first visitors to enter in months. Or years.

"Wow."

A flicker of remorse went through her, for no D&G garment should be subjected to this. This might tax even the talents of Mighty Lee's Dry Cleaning.

"You don't have to do it," Evan said.

She raised a brow.

"Bet's off."

Delta laughed. "Ooooh, I get it. No way. I'm not letting *you* off the hook. It takes more than a little dirt to scare me away."

But as she turned, her fingertips grazed his and the heat from his body met hers. A jolt to her chest sent her heart racing like a rabbit's. And the sudden flash of what appeared to be a similar burst of lust darkening his eyes made her legs feel as limp as the flat fire hoses.

On second thought, maybe she did scare easy, for the shakiness filling her insides felt like fear.

Fear that she'd forget about cleaning and go for an entirely different activity.

With that thought, Delta pivoted, suddenly consumed with an interest in housekeeping never before experienced. Since walking without tripping presented a problem, she decided to tackle the floor first. She reached for the nearest stack of hose, which proved to be heavier than it looked.

"Let me do that." Evan's voice sounded gruff—or lustful. She couldn't tell. Though given the thrill the gravelly sound sent through her, she hoped for lust.

He bent down and started coiling the hose, as if it were as light as rope. As the loops of hose grew bigger, so did his muscles.

His biceps bulged.

Delta's heart raced as erotic uses of his muscles swam through her mind: his hands, cupping her ass and lifting her off her feet as she wrapped her legs around his waist; his arms, supporting her weight as he pumped his hips, plunging in and out of her.

Delta's mouth felt dry like sheep's wool.

God, what was wrong with her? She had to get a grip on these lustful images. Distance was what she needed. Mental and physical space between them.

She swallowed hard and made herself look away.

Turning, she walked through the small aisle he'd cleared. When she got to the table, she stopped and began stacking the papers. Her hands trembled.

"I didn't think you'd do this," he said.

"Clean?" Relief sighed through her at the normalcy in her tone.

"Yeah."

"Just like you didn't think I'd play ball? And win?"

"I didn't think you'd risk getting your suit dirty. By playing or cleaning."

She embraced the annoyance that flickered through her, grateful for the distraction. "Where do you get your ideas about women?" *Specifically me.*

As she turned to look back at him, her annoyance faded.

Something unreadable passed through his eyes, giving her a glimpse at what looked like vulnerability. And then it was gone, making her think that she'd imagined it.

"You don't fit many of the ideas I have about women—or rather, about you."

Had she said that "specifically me" part out loud?

He set the coiled hose on top of the car hood leaning on its side against the wall, and walked toward her.

"You're into fashion because of passion, not status."

The soft tone of his voice made the compliment erotic.

He stopped beside her and reached for the top shelf of the case.

His closeness set her body abuzz.

"Success has not eclipsed your desire to give back."

His arm brushed her shoulder as he grabbed a box of garbage bags.

A shiver rippled through her.

"You don't back down in the face of impossible odds to get what you want."

He removed a garbage bag.

"While I don't share your interest in fashion, I admire your passion, drive, and apparent ethics." He looked her directly in the eyes.

She struggled to keep her expression calm.

"And that's why I agreed to model."

His matter-of-fact tone clashed with the blaze sparking in his eyes.

Delta's heartbeat tripled. She stood rooted to the spot as the heat pulsating from his body pummeled her in waves. She took a small step back, struggling to find space to think.

She nibbled her lip and searched for something sensible to say. "Despite your opinion of designer labels?"

His gaze dropped to her mouth. "Perhaps all designers are not the same."

His eyes returned to hers, all hot and smoky.

Her body shook.

Evan shook open the bag. "After all, you're the first designer to beat me at basketball." Though his words were light, his tone was heavy, laden with sinful undertones from before.

Delta strove for levity. "The first designer wearing a Superwoman suit."

He grabbed a stack of papers and dropped them into the bag. "Do you really think you won because of the suit?"

Delta chuckled—from a desire to release a little sexual steam, not mirth. "No, you're the one who called it a miracle suit, not me."

She picked up a stack of paper, turning serious. "Clothing can't change a person into someone they're not. It simply brings out the confidence they already have."

She placed her pile in the bag.

"I won the game because I believed I was going to win. In spite of a wholly inappropriate suit."

"Yeah, well, I believed I was going to win too." A disgruntled note entered his husky timbre.

But you didn't need *to win.*

And the fact that it'd taken the return of Delilah to do it . . . Delta was going to have to think about that later. When she could focus. Because right now, with Evan standing close enough for her to sway against, her mind was fighting to string together coherent sentences, let alone thoughts.

She grabbed another stack.

"No offense, but I can't believe a woman beat me." He opened the bag wider for her next load. "I'm good."

"Oh. So a woman can't be good?"

"A woman can be good."

Innuendo replaced disbelief in his tone.

"Spectacular."

His hoarse rasp seduced her mind.

"Sensational."

His glittering eyes seduced her body.

"Mind-blowing."

Delta inhaled sharply. The papers began to slip from her grasp.

Evan caught them with the bag.

"But a woman being all that at basketball is not the first . . ."

He dropped the bag and took her hands, sliding his palms along her hands. Spasms of desire clenched her stomach.

His fingers lingered, lightly caressing. " 'Sport' that comes to my mind."

Basketball was not the athletic activity entering her mind either. Bed sports consumed her thoughts. His broad chest above hers, the sheet draped against his ass. His hips clasped between her hands. His skin slick with sweat, hot from the heat consuming their bodies.

Delta dropped her gaze to his neck, hypnotized by the rhythmic pulsing of the vein near his throat, lured by the need to lick the throbbing vessel.

"Uh . . ." Conversational skills suddenly deserted her. She cleared her throat. "I'm sure, as a firefighter, you meet lots of women interested in 'sports.' " Her voice was a croak.

His hands moved over her wrists, smoothing the fabric and gliding up her arms. Delicious tickles raced over her skin.

"It's the uniform thing. Women seem to go for that."

The dismissive tone drew her eyes to his face. His eyes were half closed as he watched his hands slide up her arms. His lashes cast soft shadows against his cheekbones, making her fingers itch to reach up and trace them.

Instead, she stood frozen, locked into place by the sparks zapping her body from his touch.

"Well, you're wrong." Her voice was uneven. "The uniform is only part of the attraction. It's what your suit symbolizes— you as a caregiver, a rescuer."

His hands stopped. His palms rested atop her shoulders. His gaze met hers, the heat in them searing her thoughts.

She forced her mind to ignore the lust building in her body, impassioned with the need for him to understand.

"You're that romantic knight we fantasized about as girls, rushing to save the damsel in distress. *That* is what women see in the uniform."

His nostrils flared. His thumbs stroked the sides of her neck.

Delta gasped. She drew in a breath and forced herself to continue. "The fact that you look good in it is a bonus." The words were a strangled whisper.

His thumbs moved to her jaw, tracing with feathery strokes. "Are you speaking for all women?"

One thumb moved to her mouth, tracing her bottom lip with deadly intent. "Or is that how you see me?"

His eyes were molten.

Urgent need ripped through her body.

She was done skating around the issue, of pretending that she was standing in the middle of a storeroom of sorts, getting her dusty suit dirty, purely to uphold a bet or get him to model. Because somewhere between the time she'd taken the basketball and now, the focus had shifted, once again. It'd stopped being about her ideals or business and started being about him.

And the need he sent zinging through her body.

It was time to admit the truth.

"Yes, Evan. That's how *I* see you."

His nostrils flared. "Well, then, Delta." His voice was deep and rough. "Let me fulfill my role. Because *you* are a damsel in distress."

Her lungs struggled for air. "I am?"

His gaze dropped to her chest. "You seem to have trouble breathing."

"Oh . . . yes."

He tilted her head up and lowered his head to hers. "So it's my duty to resuscitate you."

"Yes." She barely got it out before his lips touched hers.

The light pressure teased.

Delta teased right back, reveling in the softness of his lips, thrilling to the sureness, marveling at the fit—and the fact that her movements seemed to naturally follow his.

And when his hand slipped behind her head, bringing her closer to him and her lips harder against his, a jolt electrified her. For his lips no longer teased. Instead, they sought and craved. And with each thrusting quest, Delta's spine weakened.

Her body melded to his.

A groan rumbled in his chest.

Her hands went around his neck.

His hand slid down her neck, to the small of her back, caressing lightly and restlessly.

She pressed herself tighter against him, wanting to get closer.

His groan was muffled against her lips.

Her gasp was caught in his mouth.

The kiss seemed to go on and on. Heat cascaded through her body in waves, spiraling through her chest and swirling through her stomach, before making the familiar downward rush. Though, perhaps not so familiar, for it'd been months. Which gave it an edgy sensation. And a stroke of uniqueness, as if it were the first time.

Perhaps that explained why a single kiss was leaving her with more nerve endings tingling in her body and more heat raging through her limbs than she could ever remember. Maybe that was why she didn't want it to ever end. And why she wanted him to keep moving those deliciously firm lips over hers, to keep slipping his tongue inside her mouth, swirling inside in its riotous thrusts until every inch had been explored and memorized. Until—

He pulled away, removing the lips Delta suddenly craved, until they no longer touched.

She resisted the urge to cling to him. Her eyes snapped open.

"I think you've been resuscitated."

"Resuscitated?" She blinked, trying to connect the dots between his words and her brain.

"Perhaps not." A slight smile quirked his lips before his head, once again, lowered toward her.

Delta's eyes involuntarily slipped closed.

The siren suddenly blared.

Delta jerked.

Evan cursed.

He took her hand and pulled her out of the room at a run.

4

Delta stood in her bedroom with her BlackBerry cradled against her ear. For the fourth time, she listened to an important message from a new fabric supplier. And like the other three times, the voice faded away into nothingness as she stared at her bed.

The new paper-white sheets were starched so stiff that a wrinkle wouldn't have the nerve to appear. The new pillows were plumped so perfectly, a person's head wouldn't dare to dent them.

Lights were aimed at the bed like mini-beacons, turning the whiteness into near blindness.

What had possessed her to let Donnye convince her to use her bedroom for the shoot? God, if she was this rattled replaying a simple kiss over and over again in her mind, what memories was she going to put on continuous rewind after seeing Evan in her bed?

We'll finish this later.

Evan's last words after the siren had gone off and he'd rushed her out of the station. And for the last week, the words had been jammed in her mind. X-rated actions involving their naked bodies and lascivious sensations had been etched in her brain, leaving her craving.

With a sigh of disgust, Delta clicked the key to disconnect the voice-mail message. At that moment, Donnye came into the room, with Evan behind him.

"I cannot work with the firefighter," he announced in a huff.

Delta heaved another sigh. This time, in anticipation of the drama ahead. She'd kept her fingers crossed that, for once, a photo session could progress with a happy Donnye. Once again, the fashion-shoot gods had let her down.

She tossed her BlackBerry onto the modern overstuffed chair. "What's wrong?"

"*He* doesn't like the T-shirt."

Delta turned her eyes from Donnye's expression of outrage to Evan. Amused calm merged with a smoldering look of desire identical to the one that'd consumed her thoughts. As if on queue, her nipples tightened.

Business, Delta.

She dropped her eyes to the white T-shirt. The fire hose wove around the goldfish swimming across his muscular chest, before curving downward. The nozzle was like an arrow, drawing one's gaze down, over the muscular abs, to the waistline of the Prada air-washed jeans.

And lower.

Delta attempted to be objective—to ignore the vision of delectable manliness in front of her and push aside her body's urge to satisfy its desires.

"What's wrong with the T-shirt?" Her voice was husky.

"He said the cartoon design will appeal only to five-year-old boys!"

"He asked my opinion." Evan's voice was rusty.

Donnye stiffened. "It's whimsical, showing the playful side of masculinity. The man who wears this is making a bold statement, telling the world that he's not afraid to embrace his inner youth." Donnye's tone bristled. "I already explained this to him and he said—"

"I said, it's cute, but no firefighter would be caught dead in it."

Donnye was flabbergasted for the second time. "It is the merging of manliness and fun. Just as these—"

With a flourish, Donnye whisked the box from under his arm, opened it, and withdrew a pair of white briefs. He dangled them from a perfectly manicured finger.

"Combine the flush of innocence with the flash of sexiness."

Evan's calm deserted him. "I am not wearing those."

"Unlike the vibrantly bold images on the T-shirt, the goldfish is understated, while the hose emphasizes—"

"I see exactly what the hose emphasizes."

As did Delta, imagining the series of loops nestled up against Evan's cock.

Heat swirled through her chest.

Donnye smiled with faux politeness. "Never fear, Mr. Marshall. Should you find yourself lacking in the required fit, wardrobe can supply the proverbial sock."

"I do not need a sock."

Delta struggled to keep her eyes away from his crotch, and her lips from twitching at Evan's affronted glower.

"Donnye, Evan is not objecting to wearing the shirt so, regardless of the differing of opinions, there is no problem."

"But—"

"Donnye. No buts."

"Well." Donnye's smile was strained. "Since there is 'no problem,' I will go check on the photographer. If you will excuse me . . ." And with that, he pivoted. Back held straight, chin pointed skyward, he flounced out, slamming the door behind him.

With his departure, the room was pin-drop silent. The air suddenly felt thick, as if every lustful thought had broken free from Delta's head and wafted through the air on gossamer threads, clogging her lungs and cloaking her body.

She couldn't breathe.

Her body throbbed at Evan's nearness.

Taking a slow, deep breath, she forced a calmness she wasn't feeling. "I apologize for Donnye. He's great at his job but can be a bit diva-ish."

Masking her desire, she forced her eyes to meet Evan's.

His desire was unmasked.

She stifled a gasp. "So, what's your objection to wearing the briefs?"

"They're Too Brief, pun intended."

She ignored his syrupy drawl and gave him a smug smile—or so she hoped. "Shy, Evan?"

Evan's smile was sly. "Private, Delta. I prefer to show my . . . 'socks' to a woman, alone."

Delta's smile slipped, as her mind zoomed back to the vision of the organic cotton caressing Evan's cock. "Well . . . that is the point. The woman looking at the ad wants to imagine that you are wearing them for her, alone."

His response was interrupted by a knock at the door. At Delta's invitation, Donnye poked his head in the door. "Wardrobe's done with the girl and the photographer's ready to take exposure readings on *him*."

"Give us another minute, please."

With a terse nod, Donnye left.

Delta turned back to Evan. And gasped.

His hungry gaze was on her lips. "Well, then, Delta. Since you're speaking for *all* women, once again, it would be a pleasure to fuel *all* women's imaginations."

Delta's blood trilled at the sultry threat, while her stomach tightened with dread.

Good Lord.

How on earth was she going to keep her professionalism intact and her lust at bay for the next few hours?

5

Evan watched Delta scribble notes and check off items on her clipboard. As she directed the crew and made requests, her voice rang with confidence. Today, she was the picture of poise and professionalism.

But last week, she'd been a wanton temptress, paralyzing him with a simple kiss.

Okay, it hadn't been quite that simple. Her tongue had mated with his, matching his, swirl for swirl and thrust for thrust. Her lips had ignited flames in his body that had sent him crashing down into lust. As she'd pressed her tight little body against his, he'd almost forgotten he was at the station. Thank God for the tone, because he'd been seconds away from hiking that skirt up over her ass—an ass that had tormented him on the basketball court and stolen his ability to focus on the game, as he'd watched it switch with each jog and clench with each jump.

Evan's groin tightened.

Now is not the time.

With a curse, Evan cleared his mind. Keeping his expression blank, he let his eyes wander over her. Though she was dressed casually in jeans and a blouse, she managed to look elegantly sexy. The jeans hugged her hips perfectly, snug but not skintight. A thick belt with a round silver buckle circled her hips. The top of a light blue T-shirt was visible underneath a curve-hugging off-white jacket the identical shade of her belt. The shoes also matched.

With a smile, Evan wondered if they were Jimmy Choos.

But more importantly, he wondered about her bra and panties. He was a black lace kind of guy, but he'd be willing to bet she could convert him to whatever she was wearing, including bloomers and gunnysacks.

"Okay, let's get started."

Delta's announcement interrupted his musings.

"Evan, this first shoot is to capture the . . ." Her lips twitched, as if she was holding back a smile. "Whimsical mood of the T-shirt. So, act happy, think about something fun, and move around. Pretend we're not even here. We're ready when you are."

Evan smiled, amused by the professional look and tone, reminiscent of when she'd first shown up at the fire station. But a far cry from the woman who'd been pressed against him, her mouth hot and wet and hungry under his.

Something fun and whimsical, huh?

Evan hooked his thumbs in the pockets of his jeans. He imagined Delta with the basketball.

"Want to borrow my Jimmy Choos?"

He stared at the laughter twinkling in her eyes, spilling over into her lips, and making them curve upward in a smile made all the more sexy by her genuine happiness.

He wanted to laugh with her, only he couldn't take his eyes off her lips, or rid himself of the desire to taste them.

He laughed, like he hadn't been able to do then.

The camera shutter whirred.

The mumur of voices surrounded him.

Evan turned sideways, leaning against the doorjamb, and tilted his head back against the frame. Though his head was turned toward the camera, he looked away.

"Gimme the ball," Delta demanded, her lips now in a firm line but no less kissable. Now, he wanted to move his mouth over them, nibbling the full upper lip, licking the tense lower lip, until they relaxed against his.

His smile faded.

"You sure you can handle it?"

She ran her tongue slowly across her lips.

Evan licked his lower lip, returning his gaze to the camera lens. He bent his knee and planted the sole of his shoe against the door frame.

Delta trailed her fingertip down the front of his shirt. He watched her finger, his eyes glued to the pink tip. He wished she'd grab the T-shirt and pull it from his pants. He wanted her to slide her hands underneath the cotton. He craved the feel of her palms smoothing over his abs—

"Good, good, love the sexy look," came a voice to his left.

The camera whirred nonstop.

"Now, smile," came the same voice.

Evan looked at Delta, grinning at him.

He smiled.

Dirt stains darkened the collar of her blouse and a large brown smudge covered her stomach, with smaller smudges dotting her pink skirt. Her hair was tangled, like she'd just rolled out of bed. Which, of course, made him think of his bed—and her writhing in it, her body arching up to his, her head thrown back, and her mouth open in a breathless moue of ecstasy as she—

"Smile, Evan."

Unaware that he'd stopped smiling, Evan curved his lips upward.

His mind unwillingly kicked Delta out of his bed and back onto the court.

"I won! I won!"

He laughed.

He pushed himself away from the doorway and turned his body to fully face the camera.

Delta bounced up and down, peals of laughter spilling from her throat.

Putting his hands on his hips, he laughed again.

His gaze drifted from the curve of her neck to her tits. His eyes were riveted to her breasts as they bounced in time to her jumps.

Evan's laughter faded to a grin.

Another jump. Another bounce. As she landed on her feet, her breasts strained against the silky material, as if they wanted to be free.

Evan's smile faded to a slight quirk of the lips. His eyes narrowed slightly.

"Great," said the woman to his right.

"Cut," said Donnye.

Evan blinked, turning his focus outward. He gazed at Donnye, huddled in front of a laptop, which appeared to be hooked up to the photographer's camera.

He moved on to Delta. Her gaze was businesslike, as she looked at the computer screens. Evan wondered what she was really thinking under the composed mask. Better yet, he wanted to influence her thoughts. To fill her mind with *his* thoughts—thoughts of the two of them naked on her lily white bed, her body open to him like a succulent feast, quivering as he laved and licked and—

"Yes, I think you got some good shots we can use. Great, guys."

She looked up at Evan and smiled. The polite professional smile, which was beginning to irritate him. "Thanks, Lieutenant. You were great."

"No, thank *you*, Delta." His tone was innocent.

Her eyes narrowed slightly.

"Because of your tip, I imagined fun things. Like . . . sports."

Her smile didn't change, but the flush spreading over her cheeks let him know that she got it—the reference to their conversation at the station.

He sent her a you-were-great-too smile. Only his smile complimented her imagined "sports" greatness.

"Uh, glad that helped." Her face flushed darker.

Evan grinned. Satisfaction hummed through him—he'd rattled her. Nice to know he wasn't the only one getting hot and bothered.

She turned to Donnye. "We're ready for Vanessa."

This time, when she looked at Evan, a trace of smugness laced her smile. "It's time for the underwear shot, so if you could change, that'd be great. You can remove everything, except the underwear. There's a bathroom right behind you."

"That's okay." Evan grabbed the bottom of his T-shirt and pulled it up over his head. Next, he unzipped the jeans, pulled them down over his hips, and stepped out of them.

Delta's eyes flicked downward, then darted away. But not before Evan caught the bolt of heat that flashed in her eyes.

His stomach tensed.

Her face flushed brighter.

Anticipation built in his chest.

Donnye swooped in and took his discarded clothes, then pulled the sheet back from one side of the bed. He plucked and smoothed the material with his fingertips, making the just-got-out-of-bed wrinkles perfect. Or so Evan guessed.

"Please lay on the bed, firefighter Marshall." Donnye's voice proved that politeness could sound rude.

Evan lay on the bed with his shoulders propped on the headboard, supporting his weight with his elbows. Donnye leaned in and fiddled with the sheets again, draping the end of one against Evan's leg.

The photographer moved left, then right, taking shots from different angles.

And all this time, Delta looked everywhere but at him. She surveyed the bed, the sheet, and the light coming in through the window. The closest she came to looking at him was when her glance grazed his leg, before bouncing away.

Evan grinned, once again pleased.

Maybe Donnye was wrong. Judging by Delta's reaction, perhaps the skimpy undies were heavy on sexy and light on innocence. Feeling cocky, Evan put his hands behind his head and raised his uncovered leg, bending his knee.

The photographer took a few more shots.

"No, I don't like it," said Delta. "It's looking too much like Beckham's Armani shot."

How did she know? She still hadn't looked at him.

Donnye snorted. "Hardly."

Obviously, Evan's earlier sins would never be forgiven.

"Bring in Vanessa."

At that moment, a gorgeous brunette dressed in a satiny white bra and panty set entered the room. Her C-cups fit her tits snugly. The lacy edging of the cups rested flush against her flesh, giving her cleavage a natural, unforced look. Matching lace stretched across her abdomen to her round hips, before forming a frilly triangle that covered her pubes.

The woman was gorgeous, her voluptuous body proving that curves were in, white lace could be sexier than black, and panties could be more arousing than thongs.

Maybe some things were worth spending a day's salary on. Or, rather, maybe some things were better when not purchased from Target.

"Let's have you both stand," ordered Delta. "Evan, you in front. Vanessa, stand behind him and wrap your hands around his neck. Then try running your hands along his shoulders, then wrapping them around his waist. You might try kissing his neck—not really, just pretend to. The point is, look like you want him—like you can't wait to get him in that bed and have sex with him."

"That shouldn't be hard," Vanessa said with a chuckle.

Those in the room chuckled or smiled.

Delta's faint smile looked forced.

Oh, yeah. This was going to be fun.

"Evan, reach behind and put your hands on her hips."

Evan did as he was told. Her hips felt smooth and firm, as if she worked out daily at the gym. A woman after his own heart. Only, unfortunately, she didn't move him. It seemed that only Superwoman of the expensive suit got his blood burning and his cock primed.

Not that he'd admit it out loud; he could imagine the ribbing he'd get at the station. Especially from Carter.

"Good. Now, Evan, just look sexy. You know that you're going to end up in bed. You want to have sex with Vanessa, but you're confident, in control. It'll happen when you want it to and only when you're ready."

"That shouldn't be too hard."

Real amusement laced Delta's smile. "Ready?"

"Yes," he and Vanessa said at the same time.

Look sexy. Think about sex.

Now, that was a piece of cake.

Evan felt Vanessa's arms around his neck.

He imagined it was Delta's arms around his neck. He imagined it was Delta standing behind him—the heat from her body caressing his naked back, causing nerve endings to strain to the surface of his skin, craning for the spark of her touch.

Evan looked into the camera.

The shutter whirred nonstop, becoming white noise, no longer noticeable.

Vanessa's fingertips skipped along his shoulders.

Delta's breath tickled his shoulders, seconds before her mouth nibbled and licked.

Prickles stormed his skin, sending flames of lust to his groin.

"You're that romantic knight in shining armor," Delta whispered in his ear. "Rushing to aid the damsel in distress."

Vanessa's breath touched his neck.

Delta's breath replaced her lips, caressing the skin made sensitive by the hot wetness of her tongue.

A tremor ran through Evan.

He stared at the camera. His gaze seemed to see beyond the lens, deep into the black nothingness within. It hypnotized him with its blackness, until he wasn't aware of what he was looking at. His mind turned inward, focused on the images flashing through his brain and sensations stroking his body.

Vanessa's hands drifted over his arms. Her chin touched his shoulder. Her hair brushed against his cheek.

Evan slid his hand to Delta's neck. He slipped his hand under her hair. The soft strands parted under his fingers and covered his hand in silky softness. He guided her closer, lowered his head, and pressed his lips against hers. Lightly, he explored. Firmly, he possessed. His tongue met hers, spearing and probing.

Vanessa's hands threaded between his arms and circled his waist, before resting lightly on his stomach.

Delta's hands moved down his arms to his waist. She slipped them under his shirt and over his abs. Her fingernails grazed his flesh, leaving a trail of quivering skin in their wake.

Heat swirled toward his cock.

Evan closed his eyes.

Delta's mouth pressed harder against his, her tongue ruthlessly plunging. Her hands moved restlessly over his chest, up, then down, grazing the waistband of his pants, where they paused. The first button came undone. The second one popped free.

His cock strained toward freedom.

"Oh, yeah," Evan encouraged, *his whisper ragged. He—*

"Cut," said Donnye.

Vanessa's hands slid from his waist.

Evan's eyes snapped open.

Once again, Donnye's forced smile was the epitome of politeness. "It appears that someone is getting into his role a bit *too* much." He waved a hand in the general direction of Evan's groin.

The room was suddenly still, with everyone looking everywhere but at Evan. Delta's cheeks were dark red, her attention seemingly riveted on the clipboard in her hand.

Evan's face felt on fire. He grinned. "Just making sure you didn't need that sock, Donnye."

Relieved chuckles broke the tension.

Vanessa giggled.

"Let's take a five-minute break," said Delta in a strangled voice.

That's not going to save you, Delta.

6

Delta shut the door after the photographer left. With a sigh, she leaned against it and closed her eyes, letting the relief that the shoot was over unknot her limbs.

For hours, she'd been struggling to keep her lust under wraps, to pretend that Evan's hard muscles, glistening under the bright lights, had no effect on her. And for hours, her body had quaked with the desire to feel his hardness against her.

Today, that raw sexuality she'd seen in his gaze the day she met him outside the station was a hundred times stronger, giving her photos sexier than she'd hoped for. The longer she'd watched, the harder it'd been to resist the urge to press her legs together, in a futile attempt to relieve the hot tendrils of erotic pain that'd pooled in her pussy.

Which left her feeling horny—and stupid. For who, but a fool, would believe that the sexuality glistening in Evan's eyes and cloaking his body was for her?

The who and the fool were one and the same.

Because Delta *had* believed that the look in his eyes was for her. Excited and embarrassed, she'd felt exposed, as if their awareness shimmered in the air like a hologram, visible to all.

Instead, it'd been for Vanessa.

But Delta didn't blame Evan.

It was Delta's fault. She was good at her job, picking the right talent for the right ad. Delta had wanted men to go agog over Vanessa—Evan had proved that she'd succeeded. Delta had wanted women to take one look into Evan's eyes and drown in the conviction that Evan was seeing her. Well, Delta, herself, had definitely proved that.

Vanessa and Evan had created a chemistry on camera that would, indeed, help her lingerie fly out the door. Her ad campaign would be successful. And wasn't that the whole point? So, she'd put her stupidity aside, focus on business, and forget that silly little kiss.

Except it hadn't been a "silly little kiss."

It'd been one *huge* kiss that'd sent her heart beating so fast that she'd felt faint. It'd been one body-trembling kiss that'd fueled endless cravings for more. More kisses. More touching. The feel of Evan's hands on her body—her back, her hips, her ass, before moving to the front, up her stomach and over her breasts—

She pinched the bridge of her nose. Best to push those thoughts from her mind, now and forever.

As she pushed herself away from the door, a knock startled her. Turning, she looked into the peephole. There stood the man responsible for her physical distress.

Unlocking the door, she swung it open, and pasted on a smile she wasn't feeling. "Hi."

"Hi. I think I left my wallet in your bedroom."

Delta ignored the ridiculous flutter of disappointment in her stomach. "Come in," she said, turning and walking to her bedroom.

"I forgot to thank you," Evan said from behind her.

"Thank me?" Delta asked without turning. It was all she could do to continue forward, as if having him trail behind her was no big deal. She imagined his eyes on her ass, then moving down to her thighs, and wished he'd be filled with the urge to stop and pull her against him.

"For the gig. I didn't expect to have fun."

Fun? Yeah, well, she remembered exactly how much "fun" it'd been. From the seductive curl of his lips, to the dazed look of arousal in his eyes, to the bulge that'd become noticeable at his groin. All because of a Beyoncé-clone in Too Brief's best-selling line.

Yeah, right. It'd been a barrel of fun.

"Kinda makes a man want to change his mind about modeling."

With a sigh of relief, Delta entered her bedroom. Her eyes circled the room, skimming each nightstand in search of his wallet.

"Yes, you seemed to have fun. I'm glad."

Evan laughed. "Are you?"

Delta frowned. "Of course. Your ability to enjoy yourself proves that you're not as rigid as you originally appeared to be about modeling."

"Hmmm."

"You don't believe me?"

"I believe that my 'rigidity' has affected you. But not in the way I want it to."

Her gaze snapped to his.

The humor faded from his eyes, replaced by the sizzling heat that'd simmered consistently in them during the shoot. "I'm done teasing you."

He took a step toward her.

Delta held her breath.

"I didn't come back to get my wallet. Do you know why I got a hard-on during the shoot?"

God, as if seeing him get hard over another woman wasn't bad enough, she now had to hear why?

"Really, Evan. I don't need to know—"

"I got hard because I was thinking about you. As Virginia—"

"Vanessa," Delta corrected automatically, her heart beating happily at his use of the wrong name.

"Virginia, Vanessa, whatever. The point is, when she wrapped her arms around my waist, I imagined I was picking up where we left off."

"Oh."

He took another step closer. His hand reached out and stroked her bottom lip. "I'd just gotten to the good part, where your hands were unbuttoning my jeans, when Donnye interrupted."

"Oh."

"That's why I wanted to show my socks to *you*. Alone."

"Oh."

That simple word seemed to be the sum total of her vocabulary. For his declaration scattered all logical thought. His words rocked her mind and threw her body off-kilter.

He pointed to the front of his T-shirt and rubbed the palm of his hand across the image. "And then I started wondering: Does this look 'whimsical,' showing my playful side?"

The smile on his face looked downright deadly. In a most torrid kind of way.

Before Delta could answer, he grabbed the bottom of the shirt with both hands and pulled it over his head, giving her the first glimpse of his chest. The chest she had pushed against on the court, brushed against while cleaning, and clung to while kissing.

Only this time, it was gloriously naked.

Her gaze dropped to his hands.

He unsnapped one button at a time, then slid his Levi's over his hips.

Her mouth went dry.

He was still wearing the Playing with Fire underwear. The same ones that she'd fought not to look at.

But she wasn't going to look away this time. Nor was she going to fight her body's response. Her chest felt tight. Her nipples felt hard. And she loved it.

Evan moved his hand to his briefs. His *bulging* briefs.

Heat speared her abdomen.

"Is the goldfish understated?"

He traced the orange goldfish with his forefinger.

Delta's breathing faltered.

His bulge grew bigger.

He smoothed the tips of his fingers over the curves of the fire hose, moving downward, stopping at the "V" of his thighs.

"Does the hose emphasize my cock?"

As if being summoned, his cock lengthened.

"This is what I wanted to show *you* in private."

As if being summoned, Delta stepped forward. Reticence was a feeling of the past. Because all reason to hesitate, to hold back, was gone. It'd disappeared the moment Evan had let her know she was the source of his need.

She ran her palms along the chest she'd been craving to touch. "I think Donnye made a few mistakes in his descriptions." The satiny smoothness of his flesh caressed her skin. "Nothing could look whimsical on this."

She trailed her hands lower, moving to the waistband of his briefs, inching her way toward the graphic.

"The goldfish is understated, but you, most definitely, are not."

She lightly traced the curvy design with her fingertips.

His cock strained to meet her, proving her words to be right. His breath rasped in the back of his throat.

She dropped her hand even lower and pressed her palm against his groin. His cock twitched against her fingers.

Delta leaned forward and placed her mouth against his neck.

She licked his neck in one long swoop, as if his skin were an ice-cream cone, before stopping at his earlobe. "But, this . . ." she whispered in his ear while cupping her hand around his cock and curling her fingertips around his balls.

She squeezed lightly.

Evan's groan brushed her cheek.

"Is the definite 'merging of manliness and fun.' "

Evan's breath was harsh against her ear. His hand closed over hers, dragging it away.

"I'd love to give you a bout of manly fun," he rasped.

Delta shivered.

He released her hand and moved his hands to her waist.

"But first, there's something I need to know."

He stepped away from her and looked at his hands, as they moved up her body and slipped under her jacket. He pulled it off her shoulders and tossed it onto the bed.

"I've been trying to guess the color of bra. And whether you're into thongs."

He grabbed the bottom of her T-shirt.

"I'm guessing something pink with a ton of lace, with a barely there patch in the front of your thong."

Delta wanted to smile. But her mouth seemed frozen. She could barely do more than breathe, and even that felt like a struggle, for the look in Evan's eyes made her feel like a Creamsicle that he couldn't wait to devour.

He lifted the shirt over her head, blocking out all sight, but not sound.

His gasp was audible.

Her sight was restored as he tossed the shirt the way of the jacket.

This time, she gasped at the raw hunger in Evan's eyes. His gaze roved her breasts, leaving no centimeter unseen.

"You got the barely there part right," she said. Her attempt at a joke was ruined by the crack in her voice, making it sound like a jagged whisper.

As he continued to stare, her nipples pebbled against the sheer silk, completely visible to his gaze.

"I should have known it'd match the blue T-shirt."

"Aqua."

"Huh?"

"The color. It's aqua."

"Let's see if your panties are the same shade of aqua."

Her throat went dry.

His hands moved to her belt buckle. He unfastened it, then unzipped her jeans and slid them down over her hips. When she was completely revealed, his hands froze.

"Damn, Delta."

Funny how Evan made the exclamation a compliment. Reverence underscored his words. The heat from his eyes and his touch seared her, as his hands followed her curves.

"Is there anything else you need to know?"

"No, this makes everything abundantly clear."

"Good, because I'm getting a bit impatient for the 'manly fun' part."

Evan's laugh was husky. "Are you always this demanding?"

"Only when there's something that I want."

Evan bent forward and lowered his head to her breast. He wrapped his lips around her nipple. The hot wetness of his mouth seeped into the silky meshlike material. He swirled his tongue, teasing her nipple.

Delta gasped and pressed forward, coaxing him to take more of her into his mouth.

Evan obliged, opening his mouth wider, letting more of her flesh into his hot, moist cave. He lifted his hands from her hips, moving them to her chest. One hand kneaded the breast he was suckling, while the other played with her nipple through her bra.

Delta moaned and braced her hands against his shoulders.

He nibbled and sucked.

She wriggled and moaned.

Heat flooded her limbs and invaded her muscles. His mouth moved to her other breast. With each lap of his tongue, her craving grew stronger. She craved the hot moistness of his mouth, slick wetness of his flesh slapping hers, and the sleek hardness of his cock inside her.

She grabbed his head, moving him away from her.

Leaning forward, she rubbed her breasts against his chest and pressed her pussy against his hard cock, as she strained to reach his mouth.

His body tensed as her body met his. His hands gripped her hips.

She drew his head to hers, crushing his lips against hers. There was no teasing this time. There was no exploring. The time for leisurely action was past. Delta moved her mouth over his, forcing her way inside. She ground her hips against his in a circular motion.

Evan followed her lead, matching his moves to hers. His hands dug into her ass as he gripped. His cock throbbed against her pussy as he humped. The head of his cock grazed her pussy between their underwear.

Delta moaned.

Evan groaned.

Hooking his hands in the elastic of her panties, he pulled them over her hips. He broke contact with her mouth as he pulled them down over her thighs. His mouth nibbled her hips and her thighs, soft nips mixed with wet licks.

Delta shivered.

Her panties fell to her ankles.

She stepped out of them.

Evan straightened and tossed them onto the bed.

Her bra quickly followed the path of her panties, and Evan pushed her gently onto the bed. She sprawled onto her back, watching hungrily, as Evan stripped off his briefs.

The breath froze in her chest as she stared at Evan. He was gorgeous, masculinely beautiful, muscularly perfect, and magnificently . . . hard.

Delta gasped.

Evan sank down onto the bed, straddling her with his knees on either side of her thighs. But he didn't lower himself. Instead, he stared down at her, his eyes probing ebony embers as they traveled the length of her body.

"Beautiful," he breathed.

Delta let her eyes rove his body. From the chest she'd stroked, to the hips she'd gripped, to the cock she'd been dying to see, feel, taste, and touch.

"Damn, Evan," she breathed, mimicking his earlier exclamation.

Evan chuckled.

He changed his position, moving his knees between her legs.

Delta wrapped her legs around his thighs and dug her heels into his ass, urging him forward. Reaching up, she wrapped her hand around his cock, thrilling to the satiny feel of his skin against her hand. She stroked him.

Evan's laugh ended abruptly on a ragged moan.

"Greedy little thing, aren't you?" He closed his hand over hers and moved it away. "I wondered if your confidence would desert you without your miracle suit."

Delta reared up and wrapped her hands around his neck. "Never underestimate the power of the birthday suit." And with that, she pulled him down on top of her.

She gasped as his chest pressed against her breasts.

She moaned as his cock jerked against her pussy.

She stopped breathing as his mouth crushed hers.

And, with that, all conscious thought went out the window. Her body took control, arching up against his. Her hands ran restlessly over his back, over his ass, and to his thighs, then back.

His mouth plundered hers, his tongue thrusting inside. His hips moved against hers, slowly, methodically.

His mouth tantalized.

His cock teased. It brushed her upper thigh, rubbed against her, and then moved away.

Delta pressed closer.

Evan moved back. He lowered his head to her breast, kissing the fleshy skin before circling the dusky circle around her nipple.

Delta moaned.

She arched her back, flung her hand to the side, and groped for the nightstand drawer. After seconds of fumbling, she found it. Her fingers closed around a small square packet.

Reaching for Evan's hand, she gave him the condom. "Come on, Evan."

"This is called foreplay, Delta." He closed his mouth over her nipple. He sucked. He bit. He nibbled.

Delta writhed beneath him. "I don't want foreplay, Evan."

He moved to her other breast, repeating the action.

His tongue lapped.

His cock throbbed.

Her grip tightened on his ass. "Evan. Please."

He gave an exaggerated sigh against her breast. "What about my needs, Delta?"

She jerked her hips upward. "*This* is what you need, Evan."

Evan groaned and jerked away.

Delta heard the soft sound of paper tearing, seconds before his sheathed cock entered her.

Delta cried out, the shock of his entry sending waves of pleasure crashing through her body.

Evan groaned. "God. I think you're right, Delta."

And with that his hips pumped.

And Delta luxuriated in the feel of him, in his body thrusting against her, entering her, filling her, fulfilling her. Sensation overwhelmed her body, sparking every nerve and caressing her flesh. Emotion overloaded her mind, warm feelings floating through the gray matter, ingnited by the endorphins coursing through her blood.

Delta met Evan's thrusts, her hips rising and falling, her hands clenching and relaxing. Frantic need swam through her body, generating heat that circled her stomach and curled her toes. Her pussy clenched, clinging to Evan, craving release.

Which Evan's deep thrusts and hard cock delivered.

Delta froze. Her chest tightened. Her nipples hardened. The blood roared like a wildfire through her ears. Building in strength, exploding with heat, her muscles gave in to a wave of spasms.

Her quaking body sent Evan into a frenzy. His hips pumped harder, driving him deeper, desperate to answer his body's silent plea.

Which didn't take long. The shakiness had barely begun to subside before Evan tensed and jerked inside her.

7

As Evan's ragged breaths began to slow, Delta smiled. She was glad to know she wasn't the only one who'd gotten a workout. And what a workout it'd been. She still felt breathless and her body still tingled from the force of her orgasm. "Well, that certainly was a manly bout of fun."

"Yeah." Evan chuckled. He slid off of her and rolled onto his side, leaving their legs entwined. "But just don't ask me to do it again right this second."

It was her turn to chuckle. As they lay there in silence, Delta thought about how odd it felt to have a man in her bed. How long had it been? Six months? A year? To make matters worse, that one incident had been a break in a serious dry spell. And it wasn't even a memorable break in the dry spell.

Maybe that's why she'd nearly attacked Evan, desperate to skip the preliminaries. Why she'd felt so turned on that she hadn't even *needed* the preliminaries. What woman in her right mind resisted a man's insistence on foreplay?

She should feel embarrassed, but she didn't. Evan's cocky self-confidence brought out her competitive instinct. It challenged her to go for what she wanted, to stand up for what she believed in.

But in a good way.

Whereas Delilah had had to fight to be accepted, Delta fought to be heard. And it was fun to "fight" with Evan. Because, despite the cocky exterior, he listened.

Like he'd listened to her love of fashion, despite the fact he didn't get it—or agree. Being able to tolerate different viewpoints was a key ingredient to a successful relationship.

Relationship?

Delta laughed. A giddy, happy laugh.

One week, two face-to-face meetings, one instance of spectacular sex, and the word *relationship* had flickered through her mind?

"What's so funny?"

"I was thinking that I gave new meaning to the phrase 'jump your bones.' " Which wasn't a lie, since that was what she'd been thinking about before the R-word. Kind of.

Evan laughed. His fingertips swirled along her stomach. "Yeah, but I like a woman who's not afraid to go after what she wants."

Like I just said.

Delta smiled.

His fingers began tracing the underside of her breasts, then suddenly moved to a spot above her head. He returned with her sheer underwear.

How the hell had those gotten up there? Her mind traveled back to when Evan had stripped the panties from her hips, nibbling and kissing and licking his way down her body, before flinging them aside.

Oh, yeah.

A flush of warmth zoomed to her stomach.

He fingered the mesh fibers. "So, why is designer fashion so important to you?"

Her mind focused on his question. "I already told you."

"You told me how it makes you feel. Not why."

Delta played with a strand of Evan's hair, focusing all her attention on curling it around her finger and postponing the answer to his question. It wasn't exactly that she was ashamed of her background. She just didn't feel the need to discuss it, if it wasn't necessary.

Well, if your mind's letting the word relationship *slip out in reference to a man you just met, perhaps it* is *necessary. Plus, you don't have to tell him everything.*

That was true.

Delta's lips quirked up into a faint smile. She let go of the lock of Evan's hair and smoothed her fingertips against his temple instead.

She still didn't look into his eyes.

"I wore secondhand clothes to school coming up. And was always fighting the boys who called me Little Miss Castoff." She shrugged in an attempt to lessen the importance. "So I promised myself that, when I grew up, I'd buy new clothes and no one would ever tease me again. Only, I didn't plan on liking *expensive* clothes."

She stopped fiddling with Evan's hair. Finally, she looked him in the eye. "But, I do love them. They're a big part of my life."

Placing her panties on the tip of his forefinger, he twirled them in the air. As he watched them go round and round, his lips curved into a wry smile. "Until today, I never thought I'd be thankful for expensive clothes. Specifically, panties."

Delta smiled and relaxed beneath him, previously unaware that she'd been tense. "Why are you so against fashion?"

Evan's smile faded. "Tasha, my ex-wife, got into fashion. She bought them solely for the label and the instant status she felt they gave her." This time, he shrugged. "And then, suddenly, my Target duds failed to pass muster."

And so did I.

Delta wondered if that was the rest of the reason. If so, their experiences—of not being accepted—were similar. Empathy for him swirled through her heart.

"So let's just say it left a bad taste in my mouth when it comes to fashion."

Before she could respond, he smiled. His finger stopped twirling and her panties floated down around his hand. He pointed them at her. "But this doesn't look like Target."

He rubbed the fabric between his thumb and forefinger. "It doesn't feel like Target."

He raised them to his face, placing the crotch under his nose. "It definitely doesn't smell like anything from Target."

Delta laughed and snatched them from his hand. So he wanted to make fun of her and Target, did he? "Well, speaking of Target, what did you think of your jeans?"

"The fit was different from my Levi's, but I liked them."

Delta smirked.

"What?"

"They were designer jeans by Prada."

"Prada?" Evan groaned and rolled over onto his back. "Fire-fighters do not wear Prada."

"You did. A three-hundred-forty-dollar pair of designer jeans."

"No!"

"Yes."

She sat on top of him, with her ass resting against his groin and his balls flattened against her pussy lips. She wrapped her hand around his cock. "Which you filled out quite nicely."

Evan tensed.

She moved her hand down to the base of his cock, then back up, feeling him grow in her hand.

Evan shoved his hips upward, driving his cock forward and pushing her hand flush against his groin.

She stroked.

He pumped while staring at her fingers.

"Why, I bet you'd like to buy a pair of those jeans, wouldn't you?"

His palm flattened against her ass, pressing her hard against his thigh as he fucked her hand.

"To wear to the station."

"Uh-huh." His tone was distracted. He raised his head for a better view.

She changed the motion of her hand, adding a corkscrew swirling motion to the upward stroke.

Evan grunted. He bit his lower lip.

"And another pair for the weekends."

"Yeah." He pulled his hips back, then thrust them forward.

"And another pair for around the house." She squeezed the base of his cock.

He groaned.

"Right?"

"Yes, yes, yes." His tone was impatient.

"Yes, yes, yes, what?"

"To whatever you just said."

She removed her hand from his cock and placed them on either side of him, then moved her hips back, pressing them against his. His cock felt hard and hot against her.

Delta shivered.

She leaned over him, her breasts dangling tantalizingly close to his head, and moved against him, using her hips and thighs to position him right where she wanted.

Her pussy lips kissed his cock.

Evan groaned and thrust his hips upward.

Delta moved her hips slightly backward. "Tell me what I said."

He gripped her hips, pulling downward. "You said, 'Do you want me to fuck you, Evan?' "

He raised up and craned his neck, taking one of her nipples

in his mouth. He swirled his tongue around her nipple, before suckling.

Jolts of need shot to her pussy. Delta gasped.

"And I said . . ." His voiced was muffled against her breast. He removed his hands from her hips and placed them on her breast, squeezing, forcing more flesh into his mouth and the nipple to spear his tongue.

Delta groaned in ecstasy.

"Yes, Delta . . ."

His mouth went to her other breast, licking and sucking. He moved his mouth back and forth, from one to the other. He nipped. He bit. He sucked.

Delta arched her back, pressing her chest forward, greedy for more.

His mouth left her breasts, and he dropped back down onto the bed and raised his hips. His cock parted her lips.

"Fuck me," he finished.

His cocked throbbed between her lips, urging her hips to slide down and take every hungry inch inside of her.

Delta gritted her teeth, wanting the sweet torture to last a minute longer.

"While I do want to fuck you, Evan . . ."

She moved her hips down, letting his cock inside an inch.

"Oh, yeah," he said.

She moved her hips down another inch.

"That wasn't the question."

Evan's jaw was clenched. His eyes were black embers, burning with a heat that promised to stoke the fire in her core. His hands grasped her hips, gripping and urging.

Power surged through her. The power to seduce.

Need and frustration flickered through the smoldering orbs. "You're a bully, Delta."

You're a bully, Delilah.

The words from the past zapped her power. Unease tumbled through her.

Evan jerked her hips down, ripping the unease from her and shocking her body with pleasure.

Delta gasped.

"That's it," breathed Evan. His hands tightened on her hips, pulling her away from him, then forward again.

She began moving her hips. Up, withdrawing his cock from her moistness, then down, burying him back inside her.

Evan cursed.

On the next downward movement, he thrust his hips up to meet hers.

His hands slid to her waist, supporting her weight as he lifted her on the upstroke, then pulling her down on the downstroke.

The power in his hands, permeating her body from his grip, mingled with the power radiating from her pussy, leaving Delta with a never before equaled high. She couldn't remember the last time she'd taken control during sex. Perhaps she never had, never felt the need before. With what little ability she had to think, she wondered faintly why not—until Evan's grip tightened, his hands urging her faster, the glazed look in his eyes begging her to give him the release she felt, once again, building within her. The sweat glistening on his forehead, beading on his upper lip, and slicking his body, telling her she was making him hot. With lust. With need.

The experience was heady.

Delta gave up control, giving him what he wanted. She fucked him, her pumping hips driving all thought from her mind and need through her body. Beads of sweat rolled along her cheek, dropping onto Evan's chest, merging with his. Her orgasm was unexpected. One second, her hips were humping, the rhythm hypnotic, focusing her mind on nothing but the movement and the heat consuming her body, and the next second her muscles were quaking and weakness had invaded her body, forcing her to accept Evan's support.

His hands supported, keeping the pace going, until he joined her seconds later. His grip on her tightened, his fingers digging into her flesh in a grip that bordered on painful. His groan was guttural, overpowering her ragged breaths in its intensity, until it faded.

His grasp on her began to relax.

Delta let herself fall against him, her body, slick with sweat, rubbed against his. Her chest heaved with his. Her grip on his cock began to relax as he slowly softened inside her.

They panted together in silence, limp against one another until even that stopped.

Delta remained against him.

He moved his hands to her back, lightly caressing.

He chuckled softly.

It was her turn to ask what was funny.

"I honestly can't remember your question."

"What question?"

"Exactly my point."

Delta smiled into his chest. What had she been trying to get him to say, right before he'd asked her to fuck him, driving every other thought but the desire to do just that right out of her mind? Obviously, it wasn't important. It'd just been part of the game. The teasing that'd made her feel omnipotent.

"Well, you're still a bully."

Unfortunately, she remembered that, and the unease that'd flowed through her.

Evan rolled her off of him and onto her side. His cock came out of her with a sloppy kiss. He curled against her, his groin against her ass.

"No one likes a bully," he said against her neck before giving her a soft kiss.

Yeah, that's what she was afraid of. She thought she heard him say, "except me." Not that it made a difference. The damage had been done.

But she knew the perfect solution. That was her last thought before she drifted off to sleep.

8

Evan stepped out of the fire truck and closed the door. As he walked into the station, he whistled the tune to Usher's "U Got It Bad," which seemed quite appropriate, given that he couldn't seem to get Delta out of his mind.

Though it was a bit too soon for 98 percent of the lyrics, the part about feeling it was pretty right on, as was the title.

He couldn't remember the last time a woman had made him feel like smiling, let alone whistling.

He gave an absent greeting to a few guys and continued on to the kitchen.

Carter, once again clad in a white apron, raised a brow. "Whistling? What's up with that?"

"That's what I was wondering," Evan said with a grin and went back to whistling.

Carter snorted. "You're stultified."

"Stultified? Where'd you learn that word?"

"You think that just because I'm black I can't use big words?"

"I didn't think you'd use *archaic* words."

Carter harrumphed. "I know what that one means too. I graduated from—"

"Stanford. Summa cum laude. *Everyone* knows."

"Speaking of cumming . . ." He motioned to the paper on the table. "Guess that's why you're whistling."

Evan swiveled the edge of the *San Francisco Chronicle* toward him. His gaze flickered to the photo of him, shirtless, with Vanessa—or was it Virginia?—circling his neck. Thankfully, the photo was cropped at the waist.

His gaze zoomed in on the image of Delta leaning against a doorjamb, arms crossed. Her lips were curved into a half smile, and her eyes sparkled with mysterious secrets.

He'd seen that look, right after she'd said she gave new meaning to the phrase "jump your bones."

And then she'd gone on to do the opposite—tease the hell out of him. He'd also liked that. He'd had her pegged all wrong, from the reason why she was into clothes to the belief that, being so girly-girly, she wouldn't get dirty.

Or sweaty.

He'd seen her sweaty two times and neither time had she batted an eye, or made a mad dash to the shower to instantly wash off.

Another thing he liked about her.

So far, other than an interest in clothes, she was the exact opposite of his ex-wife.

How could he have made the mistake of thinking that she was anything like Tasha?

Maybe it was time to tell her. A serious declaration about the "error of his ways," since the whole fashion thing that started their interaction was a big deal to her.

Maybe he would. He looked at his watch. He had about fifteen minutes before she was due to arrive. He'd make the rounds, the first one being to make sure the public bathroom had been cleaned.

"Why didn't you think about me?" groused Carter.

"What?"

"She's more my type than yours."

"What are you talking about?"

Carter's mouth dropped open. His gaze returned to the paper. "Was it that unmemorable?"

Seeing that Carter was looking at his photo shoot image, Evan finally got it. "I didn't sleep with her."

Carter's frown instantly cleared. "Really?" He picked up the paper. "Cool. Then you can introduce me."

Carter turned back to Evan. He narrowed his eyes. "Then who did you sleep with?"

"Carter, since when do I owe you an explanation of my sex life?"

A slow smile spread across his face. "Oh. So it's like that, huh?"

Evan kept his face expressionless and his tone nonchalant. "Delta's coming by to drop off a poster of the shoot."

Carter's grin said he wasn't fooled. "How nice."

"And I believe she is coming with her." He motioned to the newspaper in case Carter didn't get it.

Carter's smile evaporated. "When?"

"In about ten minutes. She wanted to come by for a mini-celebration."

"Shit, man. Why didn't you tell me?"

"I'm telling you now."

Carter snorted with disgust and started untying his apron hurriedly. "I'd better get ready."

Evan laughed. "Get ready?"

"Yeah, this kind of woman doesn't go for the country bumpkin look."

"No, but women love a man who can cook."

Carter paused in the process of bunching the apron in his fist. "You think so? Even hot models?"

"Especially models. I'm sure they're used to being catered to."

"Hmmm." He looked down at the apron in his hand. "Then I'd better go iron it."

Evan laughed.

Carter shot him the finger.

Whistling, Evan turned back to the newspaper.

"Oh, what's her name?"

"Who?" His lips quirked higher as he read Donnye's "whimsical" description of the designs.

Carter rattled the paper. "Her!"

"Virginia."

"Virginia . . . I like that." He turned and left the room.

Evan's smile softened as he read Delta's passion-filled description of the fabric. "Supple," "limber," and "pliant" leapt off the page at him, sending a wave of heat to his cock as if he were reading porn.

Damn, but she had a way with words. Maybe he'd ask her to describe him the next time they were in bed.

Evan grinned.

Hopefully, "next time" meant "tonight."

But his smile began to fade as he read about Delta's new suit, the one she'd been photographed in for the article—an $8,948 Versace something or other.

Okay. A $2,495 suit was barely understandable. But he'd been willing to chalk it up to a difference of opinion, to her feelings about expensive clothes.

But an $8,948 suit? How could he reconcile that one and shrug it off as no big deal? If she had one, then she probably had a dozen or more. And he'd be willing to bet there'd be others, even more expensive, to come.

Why would a woman need a suit that cost more than a Chevy Aveo? Or closetful that rivaled a car lot?

Why don't you ask Tasha?

His thoughts were interrupted by the sound of voices at the front of the station, followed by the clatter of heels.

Spiky heels.

Evan pushed the paper back to the center of the table. As he headed to the public bathroom, he no longer felt like whistling.

9

Stupidity was becoming a common feeling when it came to being around Evan. Once again, her thoughts weren't on business. Though, this time she wasn't exactly trying to stop herself from thinking about him.

Well, a little bit.

Just enough to wipe off the dopey grin that screamed "I just had mind-blowing sex" to everyone.

Delta walked slowly to the entrance of the fire station, once again concentrating on her steps. Nervousness wasn't the cause of her carefulness this time. Instead, she was being practical: Her hands were full with a plastic bag, a gift-wrapped poster, and the Miette Patisserie & Confiserie's Tomboy Cake—three layers of decadent chocolate cake with a rich vanilla butter-cream filling. She hoped the firefighters of SFFD Station #27 liked chocolate.

Delta grinned. Now, there was a dumb thought, for who didn't like chocolate?

Reaching the open roll-up metal doors, she replaced the goofy grin with a professional one.

"Hello?" she shouted. "It's Delta Ballantyne. May I come in?"

"Sure," said Carter, coming toward her with a welcoming smile. "Here, let me help you with that." He took the poster and cake from her hands. His smile faded. He peeked over her shoulder and looked around. "Are you alone?"

He sounded disappointed.

"Yes, but one of the models is on her way."

"Ahh. Good, good." He perked up. "Well, come with me."

As she entered the kitchen, she said hi to the smattering of firefighters sitting at the table.

"Nice article, Ms. Ballantyne," said the blonde who had held her jacket during the basketball game.

"Thank you. And please, call me Delta. That goes for everyone."

"Well, I commend you, Delta. You performed a miracle," said Carter.

"How's that?"

He tapped the paper. "You did an excellent job of finding a model that makes Evan look good. Why, my eyes pass right over him. He's like a human tree trunk, supporting the real fruit."

Several firefighters chuckled. Until the clickety-clack of heels announced the appearance of Vanessa. "I'm sorry I'm late but—"

Delta hid a smile at the men's reaction. The room went suddenly quiet; then all the men jumped to their feet at once to offer her a seat.

At that moment, Evan entered the room. While everyone gawked at Vanessa, Delta's eyes immediately zoomed in on Evan. He wore the same station uniform he'd worn the first day. Only now Delta had proof of all that she'd fantasized about. The feel of his hard body rubbing against hers. The salty taste of his skin as he made love. The smell of sex wafting through the air after they both came.

Heat rushed to her face. Her professional mask froze.

How does one greet a relative stranger at their workplace on the day after passion? Should she be polite, yet friendly? Businesslike and confident? Warm and familiar?

She needn't have worried, for Evan answered her question when his eyes swung to hers. His expression was masked. His lips curved into a polite smile. "Hi, Delta."

Disappointment zinged through her. "Hi, Evan." She turned, busying herself with the paper plates and plastic silverware.

"Virginia, please take the seat of honor," said Carter, drawing Delta's attention from Evan. Carter cupped his hand on her elbow and led her away from the men at the table. "You don't mind if I call you Virginia, do you?"

She gave him a tight smile. "I wouldn't if that was my name. But it's Vanessa."

A few firefighters snickered.

Carter glared at Evan, before turning back to Vanessa with smiles. "Forgive me. Some imbecile gave me the wrong name. Have you ever seen a fire station?"

She motioned back at the table. "Actually, I—"

"It's actually quite fascinating . . ." he began, and steered her away.

Once Carter left, other than the sporadic conversation amongst the seated firefighters, the room remained quiet. Delta busied herself with cutting cake. Evan chatted with a female firefighter. And Delta's disappointment gave way to anger.

If he'd changed his mind and didn't want her around, he could've called and spared her the trip. She could've sent the damn poster.

What the heck was his problem anyway?

When he'd left her bed, all had been good—great even, for they'd shared a quick breakfast. Which was another first for Delta, for usually she didn't eat breakfast and rarely with a date.

Not that Evan was a date.

He was in that unlabelled zone that made actions—and expectations—fuzzy.

Well, that's what she got for leaping before looking. She didn't know him, didn't know what he wanted. For all she knew, it could've been a one-night stand. She could've been an easy lay.

Delta flinched.

The one time she decided to go with her urges . . .

Carter and Vanessa returned to the room. Carter's smile seemed strained and Vanessa seemed tense.

Trouble in paradise before the plane even got off the ground?

Delta could relate.

Summoning a pleasant smile, she passed out cake to the fire-fighters and handed the poster to Evan. "It's time for your unveiling."

10

Delta picked up the stray piece of wrapping paper from the floor and tossed it into the garbage. Though the firefighters had repeatedly told her that she didn't need to clean up, she'd done so anyway. After all, she'd been the one to suggest the little celebration. Which, judging by all the laughing and teasing—which had made it feel like a roast for Evan—she thought went well.

Next, she picked up the "gift" Carter had given to her—an autographed copy of his Pinot Wine King poster. He'd assured her that it was a limited edition collector's item that would be worth millions on eBay one day. Despite the silliness of the photo, Carter was photogenic and his sexiness blazed in the photo. To his genuine surprise, she really did want to use him in a future ad campaign.

That'd made his night, seeming to perk him up a bit after whatever had happened between him and Vanessa.

She wished that all men were that easy to please. Why couldn't she have fallen for him instead of Evan?

With a sigh, Delta grabbed her purse and said good-bye to

the lounging firefighters. As she headed to the door, Evan came toward her.

"Thanks for the cake and the poster. I'll walk you to your car."

"O-kay." A ripple of unease shot through her at his polite tone, confirming that something was wrong. She could shrug off his politeness in front of others, but not now that they were alone.

Delta preceded him outside. The night was uncharacteristically warm for late fall in San Francisco. Usually, she relished the warmth and took a moment to appreciate it. And perhaps, if she'd still been in a giddy-goofy state of mind, she would have.

But happiness was a far cry from what she was feeling.

As they walked in silence, dread burrowed into her stomach. With each step, she felt that much closer to hearing the "breakup speech." Which was ridiculous because they weren't even dating, so there was nothing to break up.

Then why did she feel like crying?

Because, dumbass that she was, she *liked* him. She liked his competitiveness, his intelligence, his teasing, and most of all, his acceptance. He was fun, he made her laugh, and yeah, he gave great sex. And she'd been looking forward to getting to know him.

She'd thought the feeling was mutual. How could she have been so wrong?

Delta took the last few steps to her car and pressed the remote. The electronic beep, followed by a mechanical click, signaled that the doors were unlocked.

Evan leaned down to open the door for her.

She stared at the door, unmoving. "Look, I'm not sure how to ask this since we don't know each other very well, despite . . ." *hours of sex and two orgasms.*

Oh, damn.

"I read your article in the paper," he said.

Delta turned toward him and waited.

He remained silent, as if that said everything.

"And?" she prompted.

"And I saw your suit."

She waited for him to continue.

Once again, he remained silent.

"Evan, I have no idea what you're getting at."

"Eight thousand nine hundred forty-eight dollars for a suit?"

"What?"

"You spent that much on one suit?"

"God, what is it with you and this—"

She looked away in frustration, her eyes roving the street and passing cars in search of the right word. "This . . . obsession with the cost of my clothes?"

"I just don't get it."

"Yeah, well, I don't get it either."

"You're beautiful, intelligent, successful. I don't understand what you have to prove—and to whom—by buying clothes that cost a small fortune."

"I don't have anything to prove."

"Oh, come on, Delta. No one buys a nine-thousand-dollar suit just because they like the way the fabric feels. Let's be honest here."

Delta's mouth dropped open. The blood roared through her veins at a speed that left her light-headed.

Stupidity was definitely a disease that she'd contracted when she'd first met Evan, because it had just struck her again. She'd actually thought they'd moved beyond this. That, though he didn't share her passion for fashion, he'd accepted it.

But she'd been wrong. He seemed incapable of acceptance.

He's incapable of accepting you. Isn't that what you were afraid of?

No!

Then what are you trying to prove?

Nothing!

How dare he!

"Evan, how about if *you* try being honest. Your refusal to accept my appreciation for—"

" 'Appreciation?' Appreciation is buying a little scarf or—"

"Like the silk Hermès Passiflores scarf for three hundred ninety-nine dollars?"

"That's not my point and you know it."

"Okay. Then let me get back to the point. As I was *trying* to say, your refusal to accept my appreciation for fashion has nothing to do with me. This is about your ex-wife, isn't it?"

His lips tightened.

"You think that any woman who likes clothes is like Tasha."

"I think that any woman who spends hundreds of dollars on every article of clothing that touches her body is buying them for some other reason than because she 'likes clothes.' "

She narrowed her eyes and snorted in disgust.

"Tell me, Delta, do you own a single piece of clothing, including underwear, that's less than several hundred bucks?"

"What dif—"

"Or a single suit that's less than several grand?"

She clenched her jaw, refusing to answer. He wasn't going to listen, anyway. His mind was made up.

"I didn't think so."

"What's it to you? It's not coming out of your pocket!"

Suddenly, the anger faded from his eyes. "I've been there, done that."

You're a bully, Delilah.

"Yeah, well, so have I." She got into the car and slammed the door. She revved the engine and drove away without looking back.

11

Delta smoothed her hands over the hips of her sage Muriel Valdoni contour pants. She straightened the collar of the cotton floral shirt. Turning to the side, she eyed herself critically in the floor-to-ceiling mirror in her closet.

"How do I look, Donnye?"

"Hideous," he said with a shudder.

She turned, viewing herself from the opposite side.

"Really, Donnye. I'm serious."

"So was I."

"Donnye!"

He heaved a huge sigh. "Delta, your entire ensemble costs less than my tie."

"That's the point." She swiveled around, checking out the back. "Do these pants make my ass look wide?"

"Yes."

She sighed in irritation. "Oh, forget it, Donnye."

Turning out the light, she exited the closet. She closed the door and walked down the hall to the kitchen.

Donnye trailed behind her. "I don't understand why you're doing this."

"Because Evan was right. Partly." Her gaze scanned the table. The honey gold plates sparkled under the muted light. The ebony napkins were perfectly folded. The Baccarat crystal glasses glistened.

"I can't believe *that* man could ever be right."

Everything looked perfect.

"Donnye, don't you think there's something wrong if *every* item in your closet is expensive?"

"Most definitely not!"

She closed her eyes and inhaled deeply. The faint spicy scent of citrus and cloves soothed her nerves. "And that perhaps you're setting out to prove something?"

"Of course. That you have impeccable taste."

Delta snapped her eyes open and looked at the clock.

"Oh, never mind. It's getting late." And she still needed to warm the seafood lasagna. Delta spun around to Donnye. Ignoring his look of disgust, she grabbed his arm and led him to the door. After they exchanged air kisses and good-byes, she ushered him outside. "Thanks for stopping by to look at the final proofs."

He waved his hand dismissively.

She turned to go back inside.

As she closed the door behind her, nervousness once again hit her. Evan had called last night, stating that they needed to talk.

That had to be a good sign. Surely, he wouldn't ask to come over if he wanted to discuss business.

The doorbell rang, startling her.

Patting her hair, she opened the door. Evan stood holding a bouquet of gardenias and a gift-wrapped package.

But that wasn't what caused a thrill to race through her heart.

It was the soft look in his eyes and the warm smile on his lips and the Playing with Fire T-shirt and the—

Her eyes roved his muscular legs. Her mouth dropped open.

Was he wearing Prada air-washed jeans?

Delta laughed and slipped between his full arms. She stood on tiptoe, leaned forward, and pressed her lips against his. She kissed him with gladness. She kissed him with passion. She kissed him with fear. Every emotion that had stormed inside her was let loose in her kiss.

He kissed her back with a matching intensity. His lips crushed hers. His tongue chased hers, swirling over her teeth and then sweeping the roof of her mouth.

Breathless, Delta pulled back. "Hi."

"I think you already said that."

She smiled. "Well, then, come in."

She took the flowers from him and lifted them to her nose, inhaling their sweet, pungent scent. "Thank you," she said. "And what's this?"

"I think it's obvious that it's a gift. But first, I'd like to talk." The smile faded from his eyes. "I owe you an apology."

"No, I—"

He interrupted her with a soft kiss.

"Let me finish."

Dazed by his lips, she simply nodded.

"You were right the other night. Though I don't understand your"—his lips curved into a faint smile—"appreciation for fashion, it wasn't about you."

He placed the gift on the table and sighed. "The last four years of my marriage were rocky. But I thought it was just a rough spell. And then Tasha became interested in clothes." He stopped and looked into space for a moment, then ran a hand through his hair. "She was happy—for a minute. But the more she bought, the unhappier she became. Then she started faulting what I wore, the way I cut my hair."

His gaze returned to the present and he looked at Delta. "And I got mad. I told her I'd buy her things, but I wasn't going to change. And that was that."

Delta frowned. "That was what?"

"She said she didn't love me anymore and moved to New York City the next week, leaving me with a hefty credit card debt."

"Oh." Delta remained silent, waiting for him to continue. She reached out and touched his hand, letting him know by action what she didn't say in words, for the tension in his jaw and the twist of his lips let her know he wouldn't appreciate words.

"I was totally floored. It felt like she'd turned into someone else. It didn't make sense. So when I met you, and discovered your love of clothes—clothes that seemed to be more expensive with each discovery I made, I freaked. I didn't believe you could be different. And then when you started trying to get me to wear these jeans."

"I never did that!"

"In bed."

"But I was playing."

"I know. I didn't even know it'd registered then. It wasn't until I thought about why I blew up, that I put everything together." He lifted her hand to his lips and kissed it. "Now, you can interrupt."

"All I can say is, I understand. Because that night in bed, you also said something that served as a trigger."

"I did?"

"Yeah, when you called me a bully."

"But I was playing."

"Yeah, I know. What I didn't share when I told you my story was the one boy that I really liked. He'd never called me names and we'd never fought. But after a pretty nasty fight, during which I broke a boy's nose, he looked at me with disgust and said, 'You're a bully.'

"All this time, I'd been fighting to be accepted. But I realized that boys—nice boys—didn't like girls who fought, who were bullies. So from that day forward, I stopped fighting. I stopped being Delilah, which is my real name, and I became Delta.

"When I met you, I let out Delilah. It was exhilarating and exciting—the basketball game, the verbal sparring. You challenged me. But it was scary, since you were a 'nice boy—'"

"I'm not a nice boy!"

"Figuratively speaking."

He snorted.

Delta smiled. "Anyway, that caused a fear of rejection. And when you called me a bully, that triggered my fear that maybe, over time, you wouldn't accept me. So I went out and bought the most expensive outfit I could find.

"So you were right. First off, I don't need a nine-thousand-dollar outfit. And, second, yeah, I do love fabrics and the way they make me feel, but when I get scared, I also use clothes to prove that I'm a desirable woman and that I'm worthy. In this instance, to hide Delilah."

"You are desirable and worthy, and I like both Delilah and Delta. And I don't care if you wear expensive clothes like this." He fingered the fabric of her blouse.

Delta bit back a smile. "Even if it's twenty-four ninety-nine?"

"Nope, not even if it's two thousand four hundred ninety-nine dollars."

"No, I meant twenty-four dollars and ninety-nine cents."

"No!"

"Yes." Delta stepped away from Evan and strutted like a fashion model on a runway. "Delta Ballantyne is wearing an original Muriel Valdoni cotton, shirred-shoulder blouse and cotton pants from Target. Notice the fine stitching along—"

"Thank you," Evan whispered before pulling her against him.

"Thank you," she said, her hands slipping into the back pockets of his jeans.

His mouth covered hers. His tongue branded. His lips possessed. And when he was finished, Delta was dizzy. "Now, open your gift." He unhooked her arms and pulled away from her, then reached down and scooped the box off the table.

Delta took it from him. She unwrapped the box, opened the lid, and laughed. "A basketball?"

Evan smiled. "Yeah, all of us at the station autographed it. Carter said it'll remind you to come by and beat me periodically." His smiled faded and his eyes became serious. "And I say it'll remind you to keep playing with me."

Happiness flowed through Delta's body. "Well, I think you're both right. But I have another game I want to show you."

"Oh, yeah? What's that."

"Sheet wrestling." With a smile, she took Evan's hand and led him to the bedroom. "The loser has to finish making dinner tonight."

"That's a moot point. Because I'm going to win."

The game is mine. The game is mine. . . . Thank you, Delilah.

PLAYING WITH FIRE

Jodi Lynn Copeland

1

The acrid smell of smoke rolled through the cracked, second-floor bedroom window of Lincoln Gabriel's townhouse. Instinct had his mind screaming to alertness from a dream straight out of his wettest fantasies. Reality had him denying the urge to jump from bed, yank on his clothes, and hustle to the source of the smell.

For the better part of a decade, waking from a dead sleep and taking on blazes that ranged from minor to hellacious minutes later had been Linc's job as much as his life. As of three months ago, fighting fires played no part in either.

No matter how clear he'd made his decision to put to rest his work as a fireman, some people weren't ready to accept it. Some people like Erica Donelson.

Guessing his neighbor to be in listening range—probably standing in the bed of fast-fading flowers she'd planted beneath his window back in the spring—he kept his eyes closed and grumbled into his pillow, "Go away, Erica."

No answer. No surprise.

As long as she pretended not to be responsible for the pungent scent, there was a chance he would succumb to ingrained temptation and respond. There was a lot better chance of blocking out the smell and returning to his dream lover. Make that set of lovers. Identical blondes with the most talented and benevolent mouths he'd ever had the fortune of coming across. Or, more accurately, coming inside.

"Help me." A broken sob shook the words. "My cat . . . s-she ran up a burning tree and now she's trapped!"

Ah, hell. The smell he could block out. Erica's begging, never.

With a groan, Linc flopped onto his back. The covers shifted to expose his naked torso to the crisp October air, and his irritation kindled higher. "If I come down there, the safety of your cat's going to be the least of your concerns."

"Please, Linc." Her voice took on a breathy note. "I need you."

Damn, so much for his irritation.

She'd always known just what buttons to push. Only this time, he didn't believe Erica knew what an erotic invitation her pleading sounded. Didn't think for a second she realized what a perv he was when it came to thoughts of her, him, and need. Didn't believe for a heartbeat she'd buy he would rather have her lips on his body for an instant than a pair of brick-house blondes satisfying him all night long.

So much for the chilling effect of the morning air seeping through his window too. Thoughts of Erica's mouth, or any other part of her short but curvaceous body, delivering him to ecstasy had Linc's internal temperature skyrocketing.

Remembering his annoyance, he tossed back the covers and climbed from bed. Thirty seconds later, he'd pulled on black sweatpants and journeyed downstairs to the front door. Yanking open the door revealed Erica a dozen feet away, sneakers planted amidst the dying remains of his flowerbed and her face tipped to his bedroom window.

A light breeze toyed with the ends of her short, curly, auburn ponytail. That same breeze lifted the smoldering leftovers of what was either the world's smallest tree or several dozen leaves from a large orange ceramic pot near her feet.

"If there was a cat in that tree, it was a damned small one," he accused.

Erica's attention flew from the window to his face. Guilt widened eyes as blue as sapphires before they returned to their usual slightly slanted, slightly sleepy shape.

A month ago, when Linc had regained his vision following exposure to severe flash burn while on an emergency call, the sight of her had been one for sore eyes literally. Today, he was determined to remember that being awoken before eight on a Saturday morning, by her pointless attempt at getting him to return to the Ladder 13 fire crew, had long worn thin.

Crossing his arms, both to ward off the brisk air and to show her that he wasn't amused, he demanded, "What is it going to take?"

Her eyes slanted farther, from sexily sleepy to stubbornly shrewd. "You tell me. The Ladder is your life. You can't give it up over a minor incident that hardly—"

"Erica . . ." On a frustrated breath, he cut off additional words. Reasoning with her had failed time and again. Antagonizing had to prevail.

There was one thing almost guaranteed to get her off his case: making the sexual move Linc told himself he would never make. Not only had she been his neighbor for nearly six years, but up until a little over a year ago, she'd been married to his closest friend and crewmate.

Following his own injury on the job, Nathan had quit the crew. Shortly thereafter, he'd morphed from the guy ever ready to share in laughter or grief, as the situation merited, to the guy who had no time for anyone but himself and a newfound savage temper. No time for anyone including Erica.

Nathan had let her down. Linc had no intention of doing the same.

He'd long ago vowed to see to Erica's welfare—God knew she was rotten at seeing to her own needs. After the way she'd stayed by his side during his recovery months, taking care of him when he'd been a complete pain in the ass bent on a self-pity trip, he'd realized how much he valued her friendship. She was so much more than the one-time wife of a buddy. She was the lone person to remain a constant in his life, as close to a best friend as he had these days, and he was determined to remain a constant in hers by sticking with his vow. That would be an impossible feat from the other side of the grave.

He wasn't going back to the Ladder. The sooner Erica either got that straight in her mind or gave up on trying to change his, the better off they would both be.

In the meantime, if a little friction erupted for acting like he was after her for sex . . . A little friction they could work past in short order. He would let his come-on fester long enough to serve its purpose, then pass it off as the sort of casual teasing he was notorious for.

Leaving his arms to fall at his sides, Linc stepped barefoot onto the cold cement of the covered front porch. "I'll tell you what it's going to take."

Interest flared in Erica's eyes. Moving off the porch and past the stretch of browning grass dotted with dead maple leaves, he joined her in the flowerbed. The bed was four-feet wide at most; the smoldering pot took up nearly half that space, which meant he was inches away from her. Inches away from the lush, pink lips he'd spent his recovery time envisioning and fantasizing over. Inches away from the reality anything he said or did in the next few seconds wouldn't be further from an act.

"A kiss." The words rolled out fierce with longing. His body tightened in anticipation as he leaned toward her. His heartbeat ratcheted up like it hadn't done over a kiss alone in years.

Hell, he *hoped* they could move past his come-on.

Shoving aside doubt, Linc captured her sweatshirt-covered upper arms in a staying grip. He lifted his gaze from the sweet curve of her mouth to those sexy baby blues. The idea was to frighten her with the nearly combustible hunger he knew darkened his own eyes. Instead, he met with the unmasked ravenous want to consume him whole.

Oh, sweet Jesus.

"That's it, one little kiss?" Erica's eyes gleamed with sensuality and secret desires. "Why didn't you say so weeks ago?" Rising on tiptoe, she pressed her breasts to his chest and rocked his world by sealing her mouth against his own.

Even softer than he'd guessed them to be, her lips moved against his. A caress. A nibble. A cock-rousing, heart-slamming stroke. Warm breath, flavored with the taste of succulent female and a hint of hazelnut coffee, rushed in as he dazedly opened his mouth against the velvety pressure of her tongue and let it slip inside.

Holy hell, this wasn't going as planned. This was going a way Linc never saw coming. A way he ought to know better than to journey. He did know it too. But giving in, feeling the carnal flush of body-to-body desire he hadn't experienced in months, felt so damned good he unhanded Erica's arms and let his fingers do some walking.

He glided his fingers down the length of her arms, across the pulse kicking madly at her wrists, around her hips to palm her ass through her jeans. A sexy little moan slipped from her mouth into his as her hands moved around his bare sides. Her fingers splayed across his back. The contrast of her warm touch against his cool skin sent shivers racing through him. The exuberance of her tongue as it explored his mouth, licking at his gums, tangling with his own tongue heated his blood while coursing it in on a reckless path of longing straight to his groin.

His hips shoved forward on instinct. Clothed only in a thin

pair of sweatpants, his cock rose up to press at the vee of her thighs.

So far he hadn't gone completely stupid with lust. He'd seen that things went no further than a red-hot kiss she controlled and some relatively mild groping. Erica changed that. Spreading her thighs, she sandwiched the tip of his solid shaft between them.

Seductive heat laced through Linc with the bold move he would never have guessed in her repertoire. The stroke of her tongue stilled in time with the pulsing of his erection. On a needy whimper, she nipped her short nails into the muscles of his back, tightened her thighs, and shocked him again by grinding her sex against his.

The pistoning of her hips was feverish, primal, like she ached for him to strip her naked and take her right there in the flower-bed. Right across the street from her former sister-in-law's kitchen window.

Shelby's morning routine all but guaranteed she was partaking in her second cup of coffee and a voyeur's view befitting an X-rating.

Linc grunted with the ice-cold slap of reality. He'd set out to scare Erica off, and instead, they'd nearly both gotten off.

While his rock-solid body screamed at him to keep going, he freed his hands of her butt and his tongue of her mouth. The warmth of her hands lifted away. Drawing in mouthfuls of crisp morning air, he took a step back, outside of the flowerbed and onto the prickly grass. The moisture-deprived blades felt like a thousand tiny needles against the bare soles of his feet. It was the distraction he needed. Anything to keep his thoughts off the mad slamming of his heart and the parallel tattoo throbbing the blood through his cock.

If only the poke of the blades was enough to keep his attention from returning to Erica's face. Question filled her murky eyes. Or more likely, surprise over her lascivious actions, as well as his own.

"Now will you go back to the Ladder?" she asked in a sedate voice.

Or maybe it was question, after all, just not the kind Linc expected. Not even close.

She didn't look unruffled with her cheeks and lips flushed scarlet, and her ponytail riding askew. Even so, how the hell could she *sound* so calm and still be thinking about his returning to the fire crew after that four-alarm kiss?

He wasn't calm by a long shot.

Linc played it cool regardless, by reverting to the idea of scaring her off from additional attempts at getting him to go back to the crew. He eyed first the swell of her breasts, then the curve of her mound. Like the hot, bothered, and sex-starved bastard it was, his cock jerked hard against his sweatpants.

Christ, it was just too easy to envision her naked. His face buried against the short, matted hairs of her sex, tongue and lips devouring every inch of her gorgeous, glistening cunt.

Letting the feral, sexual beast that had overtaken his mind curve his lips, he cast a pointed look at his bedroom window. "Nice try, but the kiss was to warm me to the idea. It's going to take a lot more than blowing smoke and a minor lip-lock to make me agree. A lot more action and a lot *less* clothes."

"I wanted his kiss," Erica confessed to her ex-sister-in-law over the rim of her coffee mug. When Erica dropped by shortly after eleven, Shelby had sent her husband and boys outside to rake leaves while she broke out the emergency Danish and Joe stash.

Erica set her mug on the breakfast-nook-style table. She eyed the black steaming contents a few seconds before meeting Shelby's intent brown eyes. They'd been friends before Erica had hooked up with and eventually married Nathan, and she was eternally grateful they'd remained close following the divorce.

Close enough to discuss her getting back on the sex wagon.

Nerves danced in Erica's belly. How had her life changed so drastically in such a short amount of time? As little as eighteen months ago, she'd been dreaming of sharing in the blessing of parenthood with Nathan. She'd been praying for kids as adorable and generally well behaved as Shelby's two-and-a-half-year-old and five-year-old.

Now, Nathan was gone, and children were a far-off dream. Never one to lust after a man or want for sex, she'd thought physical gratification was a distant thing as well. It seemed her hormones had other ideas. That they suddenly wanted for sex in a big, unavoidable, wet-between-the-thighs-just-thinking-about-it way.

Imagining the dark, decadent grin and sizzling hazel eyes of the hard-bodied man ready to cater to those wants didn't help the situation. "I never realized I was attracted to Linc from a sexual standpoint until this morning, but it's all I've been able to think of since. What kind of woman does that make me?"

"A healthy one," Shelby offered from her seat on the other side of the table. "Your divorce was final more than a year ago. Considering what an ass my brother was for the five-plus months before that, I can guess you haven't had sex in far longer. It's time to accept that Nathan is never coming back and move on."

"I know he's not coming back. I don't want him to," Erica asserted for what had to be the gazillionth time. "At least, not for my sake."

Shelby's skeptical look called her a liar, but Erica wasn't lying. There was a time when she'd wanted Nathan back with a vengeance that made falling asleep at night a teary-eyed chore. A time, for many long months, when she'd placed the blame for his leaving on her shoulders. She'd since accepted his inner demons were at fault. Ones she'd held no power to slay.

"This is Linc we're talking about," she reminded unnecessarily as Shelby popped a bite of cherry Danish into her mouth. "Nothing could ever be simple between the two of us. Nathan might not be returning, but his memory would always be there, like a hole in your sock waiting to gobble up your big toe. Then there's the fact that Linc is a fireman. Yeah, he's pretending like he's not, but we both know it's in his blood. Just like we both know I swore to never get involved with another firefighter."

Shelby swallowed the bite of Danish. Sitting back in her chair, she pulled her dishwater blond hair into a makeshift ponytail, the way she had a habit of doing while in thought. "Did you ever consider he isn't pretending? He's always seemed to have a passion for the job, but that doesn't mean he wouldn't have an even greater love for something else. The almost two months he was on disability leave could have—no pun intended—opened his eyes."

"I don't think so. Firefighting was Nathan's calling. The second he got injured on the job and quit the crew to try something else—"

"Linc isn't Nathan."

"No, but at the firehouse, with the crew of Ladder 13, *is* where Linc belongs. If it takes forgetting my vow and sleeping with him to get him to go back, it'll be worth it." Conviction backed Erica's words that she suddenly felt deep down inside.

She'd been there during Linc's recovery time, had grown closer to him as they'd revealed their weaknesses and strengths over a bottle of well-aged whiskey. She didn't remember everything from that night, but she couldn't forget his biggest fear: not regaining his vision and returning to firefighting. He'd regained his vision but was still at risk for succumbing to the second half of that fear. Erica refused to let that happen.

Shelby released her hair. Eyebrows knit, she sat forward. "You think he was serious about wanting you? He talks a big game and even kisses a lot of women, but most of those kisses are nothing more than playful teasing."

Erica's thoughts turned from three months ago to three hours ago. Her cheeks heated as the dampness between her thighs again made itself known. "Trust me, he wasn't in a playful mood."

Never had she known such a dizzying rush from a first kiss. Never had she yearned for the feel of a man's sweaty body beneath her palms, his erection sliding along her mound. Never had her sex grown so quickly soft and slick, her body trembled with such fierce desire she'd forgotten all time and place.

God, in the space of a heartbeat he'd made her willing and wanton like she hadn't thought possible. He'd made her forget everything but her want to feel him buried inside her, putting out her needful blaze with the fervent stroke of his own.

She had no idea why or when Linc had started wanting her, but his kiss was no joke. "He also wasn't teasing."

Shelby smiled knowingly. "From what I could tell out the kitchen window, it didn't look that way to me either." Her smile fell away. "The thing is if he does want you and you can get past the whole 'no sleeping with another firefighter' vow, are you honestly up for casual sex? It took my brother more than ten months of dating to get in your pants."

The warmth died from Erica's face. She didn't want Nathan back, but memories of the good times were hard to swallow. Only were the good times so good, at least from a sexual standpoint, that she'd felt more turned on by Linc in a few minute's time than she ever recalled feeling with Nathan?

It had to be an age factor. Her sexuality peaking as she edged toward thirty. "I was nineteen and a virgin, and I never should have told you that."

Shelby bit out a laugh. "Like it wasn't obvious he'd gotten laid by his grin. I swear the thing took up half his face and lasted for most of the next week."

Erica hid her displeasure for the turn in conversation behind her coffee mug.

Shelby seemed to get that the topic wasn't working for her. The amusement died from her eyes and she waved the observation away. "All that matters is your happiness. If you want to sleep with Linc, short term or otherwise, I say go for it. Just don't jump into his bed merely to cheer him up. And for Pete's sake, don't do it because you want to succeed with Linc where you feel you failed with Nathan. You already played that angle enough when Linc was on disability."

"The two are completely unrelated," Erica affirmed. "I accepted Nathan's withdrawal wasn't my fault and moved on months ago."

"Okay, they're separate. You helped Linc deal with his temporary blindness simply because he's your friend. Nathan isn't just your friend, and I know better than to think you're so far removed from his life. If my brother shows up tomorrow asking for your help to get his life on track, you'll do whatever it takes to make that happen." The hint of a smile played at Shelby's lips. "God love you, and you know that I do, too, but you're a mother hen, Erica, set on seeing to the welfare of everyone around you. That can be a good thing, just not when it means letting your own happiness get twisted and turned around and stomped in the mud, again and again."

There was a time when Shelby would have been right about Erica being a mother hen. It was a facet of her personality stemmed from forgoing the usual teenage antics and obsessions to see to her younger sister Holly's welfare while their parents spent their free time arguing. It was also a facet of her personality that had left shortly after Nathan did the same.

She'd helped Linc in his time of need solely because he was a friend, one who'd done the same for her by not leaving her alone with her sorrows following Nathan's departure. One she craved with a hunger that wasn't the slightest bit motherly.

For the sake of her own happiness, Erica was going to his house expressly for sex. Sure, he was going to spend the time getting happy too. And maybe she would somehow even influence him into giving the fire crew another chance in the midst of dirtying up his sheets. But what kind of friend would she be if that outcome didn't please her?

Of course, she had a feeling they wouldn't be dirtying up his sheets.

He did talk a big game when it came to sex, teased and flirted relentlessly, but she also had it on good authority that he wasn't all talk or taunting.

To put it bluntly, he liked to fuck.

Up against the wall. Over the arm of his couch. Standing in the flowerbed in clear view of their neighbors. Probably anywhere *but* in a bed.

She could handle him. The heady warmth chasing through her pussy said so. As did her boldness in donning a white lace teddy and matching thigh highs. She didn't have shoes to go with the erotic attire, but then Linc's attention wouldn't be anywhere near her feet. Not when the teddy featured cutaway nipple holes and a sheer crotch.

Fingering the curly ends of her free-flowing, shoulder-length hair, Erica studied her reflection in the dresser mirror. Were the smoky makeup, fire-engine red lipstick, and peek-a-boo-style of the teddy enough for a man with Linc's sexual appetite? Should she throw in her newly purchased fuzzy pink handcuffs and matching flogger for good measure?

Better to save them in the hopes of a repeat session . . . given she ever made it across the street for an initial session.

Despite all the signs telling her that she was ready to make this move, anxiety twisted at her belly. Thinking to bolster her nerves, she growled at the mirror à la she-cat on the prowl. Tacking on "Go get 'em, tiger," came naturally.

Too damned naturally. They were words Nathan had used to boost her confidence numerous times.

Before thoughts of her ex surfaced in force, Erica stuffed her feet into her sneakers and made for the door. She stopped to pull her knee-length jacket from the front closet, shrug into it and zip it, and then stepped out into the chilly, nearly black night. Her heart thudded against her ribs, and her breathing grew labored as she crossed the stretch of browning grass that separated her home from Linc's.

Countless times she'd made this trip. Never before had it felt like she was merging into the fast lane without first checking the rearview mirrors.

The thing was, she had checked the rear view and there was nothing good in it but memories that made for cold bedfellows. A long-term future wasn't liable to wait behind Linc's door. A short-term one could. A few-week fling to ease her way onto the sex wagon and, dare she hope, his way back to Ladder 13?

Praying this visit—booty call, if she was being legit—would somehow be enough to accomplish both, Erica stepped onto his front porch and knocked on the door.

Light flowed through a trio of small windows carved into the door, and his truck was parked in the driveway. Even so, he didn't answer her knocking. She waited another few seconds and tried again, louder. Still, no response. A twist of the doorknob revealed it locked.

Obviously, this was going to require the big guns.

She cast a hasty look around. They lived in a sleepy suburban neighborhood in the heart of lower, central Michigan. The kind of place that housed families with young kids, with a handful of singles and retirees mixed in. Lights were on inside many of the homes, but no one appeared to be outside save for herself.

God forgive her if there *was* someone nearby and they happened to be a kid.

Forgoing another round of knocking, Erica unzipped her jacket. Leaving her sparsely clothed body to the ravages of the frosty night air, she opened her stance to provide the best view, then shouted, "Linc, open up! My pussy's on fire and you're the only one who can put it out."

2

Linc groaned into his beer bottle. So they were back to him saving her cat. A cat he knew Erica didn't have.

He should turn up the volume on the TV and continue to ignore her. Or pretend like he'd gone out for the night and left on the living room lights to make it easier to find his way home. The only problem with option two was that she knew he would never tempt fate of the electrical malfunction kind by leaving his lights on while away. Then there was the fact that her cat had suddenly become her pussy.

What if she'd taken his morning's goading to heart?

Curiosity and the fear she wouldn't stop shouting until either he or one of their neighbors responded had him setting the beer bottle on the end table and rising from the couch. A lone wall separated the living room from the front door. Beyond that wall the only things blocking his view of Erica was a door or a vertical window on either side of it. The windows were hidden behind tan mini-blinds. The door had windows of its own. These ones small, uncovered, and revealing a short, built, and nearly naked woman.

Shit. She *had* taken his goading to heart.

Linc's pulse went thready at the sight of her exposed nipples, fully erect and inches away from stabbing against the glass. This morning her lips had been inches away from his, and look how quickly things had gotten out of hand. Opening the door would be a step away from unzipping his fly and showing her that she wasn't the only one with stiff parts.

He dragged his attention upward. Maybe by some miracle Erica hadn't spotted him. But, of course, she had. Of course, she wore a vibrant red smile and the sizzling heat of his greatest temptation in her eyes.

"Can I come in?" she shouted.

He should say no and walk away, flip off the light, go to bed. Feel like an asshole for not being man enough to turn her down when there wasn't a door between them.

Putting on a bored look, he unlocked and opened the door. The strength of 600 million sperm primed at the ready urged him to look down, below her neck. Self-preservation kept his gaze focused on her face. "Sure, if you don't mind feeling like a third wheel."

Her smile diminished. "You have a woman over?"

"No." Damn, why'd he go and ruin what could have been the perfect excuse? Improvising, he added, "But one said she'd probably drop by around eight."

Her smile gained an animalistic edge. "It's almost nine. Doesn't look like she's coming."

Linc's cock thrummed with the way she drew out the word *coming*, like it was a sexual act. He stepped back to let Erica in only for the sake of the neighbors. All right, and because past the sensual heat stifling the air between them, she had to be freezing.

"Thanks." She moved inside and past him.

He registered the soft sound of material sliding against skin but didn't recognize that it was her jacket falling down her arms until he turned around. He didn't mean to look lower than her neck. Movement near the floor had his gaze going south out of habit. The inappropriateness of the sneakers she toed off next to her scanty outfit brought an instant smile. That smile froze on his lips as his attention coasted back up . . . along her thigh-high–covered legs to the tuft of auburn curls peeking through the sheer white lace at her mound to the cold-stung red nipples sitting hard and bare atop heavy breasts barely contained by the teddy's low-cut bodice.

A whistling breath cruised between his teeth. His dick jumped hard against his zipper. What the hell had he done right to have his wet dream become a wet reality?

Only, Linc knew exactly what he'd done. He knew her coming here and offering herself up went well beyond wanting him. That was just one of several reasons he wasn't about to play with the smoking hot fire before him. "If you're here because of this morning, I wasn't serious. I don't want you to sleep with me"—*Liar*—"and doing so isn't going to make me change my mind about quitting the crew."

Amusement flashed in Erica's eyes with her shrug. "You were packing some pretty hard evidence to the contrary."

He sighed inwardly. A shrug should be innocent. When it jostled her beautiful breasts like that it wasn't close to it.

Taking the pansy way out, Linc headed for the living room. "I was trying to scare you away so you'd get off my case about going back to the Ladder."

He was settled on the couch with a much-needed drink of beer chasing its way down his suddenly over-dry throat when Erica rounded the partition wall. A predatory smile clung to her lips as she crossed to stand in front of him. "You can conjure up an erection for the sake of convenience? Now, that's what I call impressive. In fact, I think you've found your new calling. I'd be happy to help spread the word. Of course, I'd need an in-depth performance first, to be certain I wasn't selling a faulty product."

Hell, she had to quit talking. Moving. Breathing, for the way each inhale pressed her breasts snugger against the teddy's top.

Unless she wasn't here to swap sex for his agreement to return to the fire crew. Unless the secret desires he'd sworn he'd seen in her eyes this morning had surfaced along with his hunger for her those long weeks he'd been sightless, he just hadn't had the vision to recognize it then, and she'd masked it since. The impromptu kiss and grope in his flowerbed could have been interpreted as a green light to unveil her want.

Even if that were the case, relenting would be a bad idea. As would letting his gaze travel south again. Given their positions, his face had to be about two feet from her crotch. Twenty-four inches from taking a power dive into rapture. He resisted the urge to inhale in the hopes of catching the scent of her arousal.

Erica brought temptation closer.

Her legs rubbed against the front of his jeans as she lifted the beer bottle from his fingertips. Linc expected her to take a drink. Instead, she set the beer on the end table and herself on his lap. He sucked in a breath as she shimmied upward. Her thighs pressed intimately around his, her barely concealed sex tight to his own. And then there were those soft, full lips. Siren red now but still mere inches away, asking him to open up and agree to fuck her.

Talk about goddamned temptation.

Threading her fingers through the back of his hair, she leaned her breasts into his chest and rocked their pelvises together. Through his T-shirt, his small nipples hardened with the press of her big, bare ones. His cock clamored for release as exquisite sensation arrowed from his chest to his groin and stoked every inch in between.

Erica released a throaty laugh. "Your talent's back. What do you say, Linc, want to use it to try to scare me away?" Eyes slanted in the sleepily sexy fashion that drove him wild, she ground her hips back and forth.

While he was generally closer to a sinner than a saint when it came to indulging in sex with whatever woman turned his head, he hadn't been with a single one since losing his vision. That celibacy played hell on him now. The nearly uncontrollable want to flip her back on the couch and bury himself balls deep in the welcoming warmth of her pussy blistered through him.

He sighed out a warning, "Erica . . ."

"Mmm-hmm." The response murmured across his lips a hot whisper as her mouth connected with his.

This morning she'd kissed him gently, at least in the beginning. Tonight, she kissed him with intent, tightening her grip on his hair as she pressed her lips firm to his and demanded immediate entry with the force of her tongue.

Linc opened out of stupidity, or maybe it was desperation. Either way, from the first fierce flick, he was a goner. Lost to months of unfulfilled desire. Lost to the untamable need to possess. Lost to this woman he'd always considered the girl-next-door type but was suddenly acting like a shameless seductress with a license to thrill.

One second Erica was straddling his lap, commandeering him in a wet, hot kiss with the power to scald his every brain cell. The next he had her on her back on the couch beneath him.

Her eyes widened as he dragged her arms over her head by the wrists and trapped her thighs beneath the muscled vee of his own. Gasping breaths puffed from between her lips. A tangle of excitement and a modicum of fear danced across the soft planes of her face.

She wasn't nearly so composed as she'd been following this morning's kiss. Good. He liked to keep his lovers guessing.

If she was to be his lover . . .

Freeing a wrist, Linc filled his hand with the lush bounty of a breast past its thin covering. Excitement quashed every trace of Erica's fear. A slow, sultry smile formed as she wriggled her hips and pressed her bare nipple against his palm. His cock spasmed, feeling abused in its snug confines.

Damn, had she been this hot for Nathan?

Hating the thought, he lifted his hand and pinched her nipple. Hard. She squeaked out a cry, but then strained her nipple upward, seeking out another helping of the same.

He growled low in his throat. She truly was playing with fire now, egging on the dominant in him. Or he was, by letting her.

"Tell me this isn't about this morning," he demanded.

"It's not about this morning."

Not completely.

She didn't have to say the words. Linc could sense them hovering on the tip of her tongue. The same wickedly willful tongue that flicked out to meet and moisten a fingertip from the hand he'd earlier released.

Erica brought the glistening digit down her body, under his arm, to the small triangle of space that separated her mound from his thighs. With a barely audible swish, it slipped beneath the crotch of the teddy. Before, the material had been sheer. Now, her juices lined it, and he could see her finger drive between her nether lips as clearly as if she wore nothing at all.

She sucked in a sharp breath with the impaling. Another as she thrust the finger deeper. Her breasts rose up, high, firm, and heavy. Her eyes narrowed and then closed completely. "Please, Linc," she breathed. "I need you."

Ah, God, that sexy pleading. That soft voice that had served as his window to the seeing world for nearly two months. That scent . . . so familiar and yet now spiked with something even more potent.

The rich, sensual scent of her arousal clung to the air and took his senses on a joyride of ecstasy. Sweat beaded on his forehead. "Your pussy's still on fire?"

"Only you can put it out."

Probably, he shouldn't. But then, if he stuck with using his mouth to bring her to climax, it wouldn't have to be a big deal. After all, he'd already had his tongue buried in her own mouth twice today. One end wasn't much different than the other, right?

That Linc knew it was, that he'd kissed a lot more women than he'd ever tongue fucked registered and then blissfully faded away as Erica pulled aside the wet crotch of the teddy. Using two fingers, she spread her shimmering labia and exposed the hot button of her pleasure.

Swollen and blood red, her clit begged for his touch, his tongue. She rubbed a finger across the tight bundle of nerves. "I need you here."

And he had to be there. Before his raging cock combusted from too much action on her part and not nearly enough on his.

Releasing her other wrist, he went up on his knees and scooped her butt into his hands. He bent his head to her sex. Two of her fingers still held her pussy open. Up close, the sensual sight was even more intoxicating, and it took all his self-control not to shove his tongue inside and lick until she bathed him in her cream.

He sampled her instead.

Slowly, sinuously, Linc ran his tongue around her opening, through her silken folds, along the succulent pre-cum lining her fingers. She encouraged with little pants and sighs, and the upward roll and glide of her hips. Greedily, he took another slow tour around her opening, through her folds, along her fingers. All the while he pleasured as her pants became ragged, her sex wetter. A trickle of juice leaked down her thigh, and he lazily licked it clean again.

"Please, Linc," Erica begged, her voice a throaty whisper, a desperate plea. "I need you inside."

When he didn't immediately respond, she used one of her own fingers. Piercing her sex, she stroked deep, hard, touching where he hadn't. Where he'd purposefully avoided ... until now.

Squeezing her ass cheek in playful reprimand, he caught the finger in his mouth and guided her hand aside. Then he gave her what she begged for, what he'd fantasized—hell, masturbated— over for months, by sinking his tongue between her engorged pussy lips and tasting her deep within.

Simply, sinfully delicious.

Erica's pants turned to breathy moans that echoed through him like a guttural stroke. Her hips surged restlessly. "Oh, yes!" She drove her fingers into his hair. "Put the fire out, baby. Put it out the way only you can."

While his tongue licked, feasted, savored, Linc's mind jerked alert. Honed in on that word. That one-word ticket to his own personal hell.

Not Linc. Not lover. But *baby*?

It was the endearment Erica had used for Nathan, and it brought Linc's reason for not pursuing his fantasies of her screeching to the front and center.

She'd spent more than a few nights sleeping on his couch during the early weeks of his blindness. He'd woken several of those nights to hear her crying. It didn't take a genius to know who she'd shed those tears for. Not when, over a shared bottle of whiskey, she'd confessed her fear of never loving another man the way she did Nathan. If Nathan entered the room this instant, it was probable that she would forget about Linc to shower her ex with her every understanding and forgiveness, be- cause she still loved him without limits. Linc would be damned— not to mention a damned bad friend—if he pretended otherwise simply for sex.

To err was human. To wrap this moment up in a convenient box and shove it in the recesses of his mind was going to bite big-time.

Taking the first steps in one fluid move, Linc pulled his tongue from her pussy, slid his hands from beneath her butt, and came to his feet beside the couch. Every inch of her stunningly aroused body, from her barely contained, rapidly rising and falling breasts to her shimmering sex, called out to his. Before he became a dick-ruled bastard by answering that call, he trained his gaze on her face.

Erica pinched her eyes tighter after a few seconds of no contact, then opened them. His mind and body frustration had to show on his face. A frown claimed her lips, and she pushed up on her elbows and shook her head. "You're not done."

"We can't do this, Erica. Nathan will always be there to stop us."

Incredulousness followed by anger flitted through her gaze. "I don't want him back," she gritted out. "He hasn't even been in the picture for over a year."

She sounded sincere. If she were any other woman, he might believe her. This was Erica, and he didn't buy her words for a heartbeat. "Fine, then, Nathan's not an issue. Your vow to never get involved with another firefighter is."

Hope replaced her fury, bringing with it the most captivating of smiles. She opened her arms to him. "You're not one, so come back down here and do me right."

God, yeah, if she were only any other woman . . .

"Not tonight and not tomorrow I'm not, but one day I might be again. I'm not about to make you face that day by my side."

3

Erica turned her black coupe into the auto service center where Linc had accepted an assistant manager position earlier in the month. The shop was in one of the worst parts of the downtown area, and although she tried not to judge people by their surroundings, she couldn't help flicking on her locks as she pulled around back of the time-aged brick building. A double set of glass garage doors revealed both of the service bays occupied by other customers.

They also revealed Linc.

She could see only portions of him, those mostly cloaked in plain, navy coveralls. Regardless, her heart beat faster with the reality of how attracted to him she'd become in less than a week's time.

Or had she always been? Had her love for Nathan and then, more recently, her concern for Linc masked her true feelings before this?

The answers didn't matter. Linc had made it clear that, despite their scorching chemistry, he wouldn't take their relationship beyond friendship. Much as it goaded her that he believed she wasn't over her ex, Erica had accepted his rejection of her advances. Accepted it, and still the breath snagged in her throat like an infatuated schoolgirl's when one of the bay doors lifted a couple minutes later and she caught sight of the back of his head.

She'd always liked his hair. It was a shade darker than his hazel eyes, thick, and as she'd learned on Saturday, silky soft. His naturally golden-toned skin made his year-round coloring a thing to envy. His butt, as he bent to grab something from the garage's concrete floor, the sort of thigh-melting masculine perfection even the mostly shapeless coveralls couldn't mask.

Erica's sex throbbed its awareness. Guilt quickly followed. She'd come here to play on his admission he could one day return to firefighting. The last thing she needed was for him to spot her ogling his ass and presume her presence another attempt to get into his pants.

Focusing on the early 20s, lanky blond guy signaling her to enter the service bay, she pulled into the building. The guy was almost to her window when he stopped and looked the other way. She didn't need to follow the blonde's gaze to know that Linc had spotted her. Within seconds, his scowling face filled her window.

Bet I could think of a few ways to turn that frown upside down.

Yeah, and she'd bet each one of them was naughty in nature. Not to mention would make it even harder to forget the wondrously salacious feel of his work-roughened hands shackling her wrists and rubbing against her nipples.

Keeping her attention off his hands, she slid down her window. The shop's warmth rolled inside the car as she offered a friendly smile. "Fancy meeting you here."

Wariness narrowed his eyes. "What are you doing here, Erica?"

"I need a lube job."

His scowl deepened. "Cute."

She recognized the unintentional double entendre and sobered her expression. "I'm serious. I need my oil changed."

Linc continued to eye her suspiciously another few seconds before walking to a low counter ten feet away. He lifted a clipboard from the counter, then returned to the car and handed it to her through the window. "Turn off the engine and pop the hood."

Erica frowned as he disappeared behind her raised hood. She'd expected a potential discomfort between them for a while, but why was he acting so aloof? He fooled around with women and remained friends all the time. Yet in the three days since he'd turned her down, he hadn't even spared her a passing hello.

Hating that distance between them, she pulled a pen free of the clipboard lip and went to work on the customer form attached to the board. She was concentrating on filling out her mileage and car make information when she felt someone watching her. A glance to her left revealed Linc back at her window. For the space of a heartbeat, his scowl was gone, some other emotion weighing in his eyes and over the strong, sexy lines of his face.

His gaze met hers, and the cool look returned. "You could use a new air filter."

"Go ahead and give me one. I trust your judgment." He didn't look thrilled by the response. Well, tough patooties. He could play Mr. Grimface all he wanted. She was going to get out her purpose in using up her lunch hour to make the fifteen-minute trip to this garage.

Erica handed the clipboard back through the window. When he grabbed the top edge, she held tight to the opposite end. "The annual benefit dinner and dance for the families of fallen firefighters is Thursday night."

An "I should have known" smirk curved the corners of his mouth. Dryly, he asked, "Is it?"

"Yes, outside of last year, I haven't missed it in nearly a decade."

"So go."

"I don't have anyone to go with." Seed planted, she released the clipboard. "The last thing I want is to show up solo and have everyone in the place doling out their sympathy."

Linc grabbed the pen from where she'd replaced it beneath the lip of the clipboard. He looked down to jot notes on the customer form. "You're more liable to have Callahan and Foster coming to fists over which one gets to try to take you home."

"I was hoping you'd take me."

"Erica . . ." he warned without looking up.

She hadn't meant to imply she wanted him to take her home. That he took it that way had her mind racing with memories of Saturday night. Of his masterful tongue on her sex, teasing, taunting, and then coming so close to licking her straight to ecstasy while she brazenly moaned and pleaded for more of the same.

Flushing away those memories and the accompanying wet ache between her thighs, she let out a light laugh. "You're developing a habit of doing that."

"You're developing a habit of pushing my buttons."

"It's a good cause." When he continued to fill out the form without responding, Erica tossed out, "Forget I said anything. I'll just send a donation check in the mail. It's not like I don't stay home every other night of the week, anyway. Besides, most of the crew has probably forgotten that I exist by now."

Linc shot her an irritated glance while he stuck the pen back under the clipboard lip. "Trust me, you're not that easy to forget."

Tossing the clipboard onto the counter, he returned to the front of the car. The cacophony of workers shouting over the drone of pumps and other unseen equipment arose. Erica lifted a paperback from the passenger's seat and tried to lose herself in the pages.

Between the background noise and her wonder over the annoyance that clung to Linc's parting comment, she never made it past page two before he returned to stand beside her window several minutes later. He held out her oil dipstick, and she nodded her approval.

"You're going to want to get your radiator flushed before long." He started to turn away, then stopped and looked at something across the garage. "I'll take you."

Or maybe he wasn't looking across the garage, just not at her.

Triumph sailed through Erica. Enduring his irritation, whatever the source, was worth getting him back in contact with his former crewmates. Enduring a night spent ogling his delectable body decked out in a suit and tie didn't sound half bad either.

Playing innocent, she asked, "To get my radiator flushed?"

"You know what I mean." The note of warning returned to his voice. "Be ready by six, and wear at least twice as much as you had on Saturday night."

After returning to the tax accounting office, Erica bypassed her cubicle to head down the hallway to Shelby's office. Along with holding a senior position in the company, Shelby had several years on her in age and a multitude more experience where men were concerned. Erica *could* endure Linc's irritation. She would much prefer to understand it and, therefore, help him work past it and the distance between them.

Erica closed her friend's office door and took a seat across the desk. Shelby looked up from her PC's widescreen monitor. An amused smile slid into place. "So did you get good and lubricated?"

"My car did. I got confused." Erica recounted Linc's behavior and his ornery observation about her not being easy to forget. "I'm thrilled he agreed to go to the benefit, but I don't get why he's acting so out of it in the first place. We didn't even have sex."

"From what I'm hearing, that's precisely the problem. He turned you down out of obligation. That doesn't mean he wanted to do it, or that he hasn't spent every second since wishing he'd kept his mouth shut."

"Why would he feel obligated?"

"He told you why. Nathan will always be between you," Shelby said pointedly. "As I recall, you said much the same thing yourself. 'Like a hole in your sock waiting to gobble up your big toe' to be exact."

"You might also recall that not two minutes after saying that I realized I was mistaken," Erica snapped back. She hated acting bitchy toward Shelby when her friend was trying to help, but she was seriously sick of people telling her where her feelings rest.

"I told Linc that Nathan wasn't an issue," she added more calmly. "I meant it."

"All right, so my brother's not the problem. Per your accounting, Linc also said he wouldn't let you get involved with another firefighter. He might not be one at the moment, but as of Saturday, you both seem to think in time that will change."

"When I made that vow I was talking long term. I don't expect—or for that matter want—anything lasting from him. I just want to get him naked long enough to share a few orgasms between friends." Okay, so she hadn't necessarily made the vow regarding the long term only. Judging by the fervor of her declaration, she was ready to view it that way now. What Erica wasn't any longer prepared to do was accept Linc's rejection of her advances.

Shelby's smile returned. "Then I suggest you drive that point home, because that's clearly what *Erica* wants when she stops thinking about what sounds good intentioned and starts thinking about what promises to feel great."

* * *

Linc's anxiety had been building since agreeing to accompany Erica to the benefit dinner and dance two days ago.

He'd pointedly ignored the bulk of Ladder 13 the last month. The two months prior, he'd chased off those who'd stopped by the house with his self-pity–fueled anger. Seeing them again, experiencing the sense of brotherhood he'd never known as a single child, held the possibility of making his comment about one day returning to the crew more than another attempt at scaring Erica away, this time from wanting the physical.

At least that comment seemed to have done the job, Linc mused as he knocked on her front door. She hadn't done anything to tempt his libido since Saturday night.

Erica opened the door less than a minute later, and he nearly swallowed his tongue along with his thoughts. The strips of iridescent gold, which began at her waist and tied behind her neck, were four-inches wide at best. They covered just enough of her otherwise bare breasts and torso to look enticing instead of trashy.

Damned enticing.

As were the light floral scent of her perfume and the curly, auburn wisps of hair caressing the shells of her ears while the rest of her hair was pulled up and back. Her lips were painted the same shade of siren red as they'd been last Saturday. And like last Saturday, her mouth was far too close and inviting.

His body tightened, muscles bunching in a way that was becoming commonplace. While she might not have taunted his libido in days, his thoughts of her had been taunting the hell right out of it. For all the women he'd slept with and remained friends, he couldn't return to thinking of Erica in friendly terms.

Because they hadn't actually slept together? Because he'd never known this supremely sensual side of her existed and his mind refused to let its surprise go?

Unable to let his sudden frustration go either, Linc met her eyes to snarl, "That's not twice as much."

Frowning, she lifted her right hand to reveal a gold twist earring. She slipped it into place against her earlobe. "It's at least three times as much."

"I meant over your breasts."

At least her nipples were covered, along with her lower half from her waist to a few inches above her knees. Her feet were covered, too, if one counted spiked, gold four-inch heels as covering.

Personally, he called them fuck-me shoes.

Personally, thoughts of her wearing the sinfully sexy shoes and nothing else, while she did fuck him, weren't helping his fight to keep his body in check.

"Plunging halter necklines are the current rage." Erica produced the other earring from her left hand. After slipping the gold twist into place, she went to the closet near the door. She took out her knee-length black jacket and swept it around her shoulders. "If you dislike my dress that much, we don't have to go."

The ease with which she would call tonight off to placate him was precisely the reason they did have to go. Part of her was probably gambling on time with his former crewmates making him anxious to return to work. But he also knew she loved this benefit, and the odds were favorable that she really wouldn't attend alone.

"The dress is fine." He glanced through the open doorway to his truck running in the drive. "Let's go before all the good seats are taken."

Five minutes later, Linc acknowledged that he already had the best seat available, right there in his truck. Erica had neither pushed her arms into the sleeves of her jacket nor zipped it, merely left it in place around her shoulders. While the dress's slim sides somehow managed to stay put, her cleavage swelled to undiscountable proportions beneath the press of the seat belt.

A week ago, he would have joked about the dress's daring

fit. If their friendship stood a chance of getting back on track, he had to do the same now.

Focusing out the windshield, where the first traces of night pressed in on a heavy, gray sky, he asked, "So are your boobs taped in?"

"God, no." She sounded mortified. "Tape and skin equal pain when it comes time to remove the dress. I used Juicy Fruit."

His gaze darted back to her breasts. "You *what*?"

"Used Juicy Fruit. You know, the gum? It washes off easily once it's served its purpose. Until then, a gently chewed piece has the perfect composition to stick to an areola. Anyone who's ever put gum in the washer by mistake knows how well it sticks to clothing."

But to use it on her boobs? He wasn't sure if it was the most entrepreneurial or the most insane thing he'd ever heard of a woman doing at the cost of looking good.

Recalling his purpose, Linc tried at a teasing tone. "Just so long as you don't plan on stealing the spotlight from the benefit by flashing everyone over dinner."

"Not a chance." Erica took her breasts in hand to give each a testing squeeze and jiggle. She flashed a self-assured smile when the dress's sides didn't budge. "The Juicy Fruit's working like a charm."

His cock was working as well, at hardening for her intimate handling.

4
_____

Andy "Trick" Warren approached as Linc and Erica cleared the fire hall entryway. Relief to see Linc shone in the eyes of the mid-40s, stocky fireman who Linc had been close with since Trick had been assigned his mentor nine years, four kids, and close to a thousand practical jokes ago.

After exchanging hellos and handshakes with Linc, Trick looked to Erica. His gaze slid to the swell of cleavage exposed past the risqué sides of her dress, and his dark blond eyebrows rose appreciatively. "Holy mama, that's some outfit."

"It's the current rage," Linc informed him while taking stock of the room dimly lit by the glow of hundreds of white holiday lights.

Between the couple dozen guest tables set up on one side of the place, and the hors d'oeuvre station and makeshift bar and dance floor set up on the other, there had to be sixty-plus women in attendance. Not one of them wore the so-called current rage.

"Whatever it is," Trick said, "I approve."

Erica gifted the man with a wide smile and a kiss on the

cheek. "I always knew you had good taste." She stepped back to give him the once-over followed by a low whistle. "Speaking of good taste, you look great in that suit, Andy. How've you been?"

"Can't complain. At least, I won't bother to." Trick inclined his balding head toward the rear of the room. "Anna and I are sitting at a table in the corner if you guys want to join us." He gave the plunging neckline of Erica's dress another look. "I should probably add that Callahan and Foster came stag and are sharing our table."

Her smile broadened. "This big girl can handle them."

"No doubt that's what they're hoping," Linc murmured.

Ignoring her questioning look, he moved behind her and slipped the jacket from around her shoulders. With the heels on, the top of her head reached his nose. The natural scent he'd come to know like an old friend mingled with the light floral scent of her perfume, rising up in tandem to toy with his senses. Against his better judgment, he peered over her shoulder and got a first-rate view of her barely contained breasts. The generous mounds alone were enough to earn her that "big girl" title.

Dismissing thoughts of Erica's breasts and the warm, soft feel of her skin against his fingertips, he suggested, "Go ahead and have a seat while I check your coat."

"As long as you guys promise not to talk about me the second I'm gone."

"Not a chance."

Linc didn't want to talk about her. He didn't even want to think about her and precisely how much he loved the way she filled out that dress. The extreme sweep of the dress's open back, all the way to the rise of her ass, made that impossible. She couldn't be wearing underwear. He already knew she wasn't wearing a bra.

She pretty much deserved whatever advances Callahan and Foster made for putting herself on display. Or so he was telling himself when she reached the corner table. Trick's attractive brunette wife was away from the table at the moment. The duo of horn dogs were present, both standing to greet Erica with hugs.

Probably to cop a feel was more like it. Linc wasn't betting the Juicy Fruit stayed in place for their eager handling, either.

His gut twisted when she returned their embraces, then sent a look at her chest that concluded with all three of them laughing. She was probably just happy they remembered her. Either that, or she was about to bait them with the same testing squeeze and jiggle of her breasts that she'd baited him with on the drive over.

Had she been baiting him, both with her intimate handling and by suggesting she wouldn't come to the benefit without him?

Hell, he wasn't any longer sure of her motivation. He wasn't even sure he really knew the woman he'd come to consider his closest friend.

Weeks had passed since their shared night of whiskey and weaknesses. Maybe Erica *had* moved past her love for Nathan in that time. Now that she felt she'd seen to Linc's welfare, by getting him here, she was finally ready to focus on her own happiness, by finding a guy to share in the sex Linc had refused. If so, she would be wise to look beyond her current companions.

"Didn't expect to see you here," Trick commented from Linc's left.

"I had no intention of coming."

"The dress twisted your arm."

The dress was doing something to him, all right. The kind of something that heated his blood even as it knotted his gut.

Linc looked at the older man to clarify, "Erica and I came as *friends*."

Amused skepticism gleamed in Trick's eyes. "Never seen you

look pissed over someone checking out a 'friend' of yours."
The levity left his voice. "How are things going at the garage?"

"The job's fine," Linc replied, glad for the distraction from
his thoughts. The truth was, if Erica was looking for a guy for
sex of the no-strings variety, she couldn't find a better bet than
one of her current companions. Callahan and Foster *were* a set
of horn dogs, but their lovers seemed plenty satisfied for the
way they kept coming around the firehouse, trolling for seconds.

Grudgingly leaving her to her own devices, Linc focused on
Trick. "It's routine work, but at least I don't have to worry if
I'll make it home at night."

"Hell, in that part of town, you're more liable to get clipped
walking out to your truck than you are to lose your life fighting
fires." Hopefulness entered his eyes. "Captain hasn't filled your
position. I think he's hoping, just like the rest of us, that you'll
pull your head out of your ass and come back to work."

"I'm not returning to the Ladder, Andy."

Trick looked toward the rear of the room, then back at Linc.
"I could maybe see why if you were involved with Erica. Since
you aren't—or at least you aren't owning up to it—what's stopping you?"

"Self-preservation. I'd prefer to die old and keep my sight
intact for as long as possible in the meantime."

Trick looked unconvinced but gave in with a shrug. "Suit
yourself. Personally, I prefer to live however many years I have
ahead of me to the fullest. Much as it might help Anna to sleep
easier, I could never do that apart from the crew and be completely happy."

Molding his body against Erica's in any manner was missing
from Linc's nightly agenda. Knowing how much she loved to
dance, he might feel badly about that decision. He didn't feel

badly, though. Not when she had a near-constant supply of dance offers from other men, nearly all of which she'd accepted with an eager smile.

Callahan moved her around the floor now. The guy's arms didn't budge from her waist as the slow, sensual melody of one love song segued into that of another. His fingers did move, down the slope of her bare back to centimeters from her ass.

"Friends don't let friends get manhandled," Trick commented a seat away.

Feeling like he'd been caught playing voyeur, Linc pulled his attention from the dance floor. He took a drink of his 7&7 before effecting a careless tone. "Like she said, she's a big girl. Besides, something tells me Erica's right where she wants to be."

"Would that be the 'help me' look she gives you every time he turns her this way?" Anna asked from beside her husband. "Smiles can be forced. Pleas for mercy, even silent ones, tend to be the real deal."

Linc looked back to the dance floor. Erica's face came into view and, as Anna noted, her gaze moved directly to his. There was definite brittleness to her smile. Pleading in her eyes.

"Guess I don't have a choice but to help her." He'd meant the words for his ears alone. Anna obviously overheard them. She gave him the lethal look typically reserved for those times when Trick took one of his practical jokes too far.

Before the brunette could add verbal venom to the mix, Linc pushed back his chair and moved onto the dance floor. Erica's face appeared past Callahan's shoulder when Linc was a couple feet away. Her smile warmed, and she mouthed, "You're awesome."

Aware Callahan wouldn't agree, Linc stepped up behind him and tapped on his shoulder. "Time's up," he said loud enough to be heard over the music.

Most men would have gauged Linc's additional four inches

and twenty-some pounds, and given in to avoid a confrontation. Callahan was just young enough and cocky enough where women were concerned to tighten his hold on Erica while giving Linc a "fuck off" look. "Sorry, dude, but she's mine till the song's over."

Linc clasped the younger guy's shoulder through his dress shirt. "Sorry, *dude,* but she's not. This is the last slow dance this set and I promised to spend it with Erica."

Callahan looked to Erica. She uncoiled her arms from around his neck with a coy smile. "You don't mind, right? Linc and I always share at least one dance at this event, and I'd hate to break from tradition."

"All right." With a slow nod, Callahan lifted his arms from her waist. "But if you get bored, you know where to find me."

"Promise," Erica vowed as he stepped away. In the next instant, she had her arms around Linc's neck and the rest of her molded against his body.

Linc groaned. This was the reason he hadn't wanted to help her get rid of Callahan. Now that that other guy was gone, they were in the precise position he'd sworn wasn't on tonight's agenda. And, damn, she felt too good. Each little move had her groin rubbing sinuously against his, the weight of her breasts caressing his chest past the open sides of his suit jacket.

Like a stupid shit bent on self-torture, he inhaled her scent. It was nearly all natural Erica now with the perfume worn away. That inviting, seducing scent that had his heart rate kicking up while his dick threatened to come along for the rise.

Reminding his libido that her actions spoke of gratitude alone, Linc sent her a teasing smile. "Not such a big girl, after all?"

"I'm plenty big, just not experienced with turning men down. Callahan's a good guy, but—"

"You're not in the market for a fuck-and-run man." He

winced as the words left his mouth. Worse than their crudeness was his all-out relief to think she wouldn't be spending the night with her legs wrapped around some other guy. "Sorry. Being around the crew tends to bring out my inner sailor."

"Like I said, I'm a big girl. I can handle a dirty word or two." Gleaming deep blue beneath the holiday lights, Erica's eyes took on a naughty slant. A healthy dose of sexual honey slid into her voice as she added, "In or out of bed."

Or maybe her actions weren't solely about gratitude.

Fuck, he couldn't handle her advances tonight. Too much already weighed on his mind.

Initially, he'd ignored Trick's observation that he could never be completely happy away from the crew. The last couple hours, chatting with his former coworkers, sharing in the generally good-natured camaraderie he couldn't come close to matching at the service garage made the words impossible to forget.

"Are you happy?" he asked Erica.

Her naughty look turned to one of surprise. A soft smile formed as she looked around the decorated fire hall. "Yeah, I always have a good time at this benefit. Thanks for bringing me."

"You're welcome, but I was talking about in general. Are you happy with life, everything that's happened the last year or so?" Christ, he was on a roll. The way he'd ended the question, she was bound to think he was talking about her divorce.

Her smile stayed put, her body moving in time with his lead. "I'm not depressed by or living in regret of anything. Could I think of ways to be happier, who couldn't?"

Did the lack of reaction mean she really was over Nathan, and did those happier ways she spoke of include using Linc's body to indulge her every wicked desire?

"What about your job?" he asked, returning to safer ground.

"I never would have believed you a tax accountant when we met. I still find it hard to buy that you find it fulfilling."

"It's fulfilling most of the time. Stimulating, not so much."

Right. A fulfilling job kept you entertained while it paid the bills. A stimulating one made you eager to get up for work each morning, or whenever the fire alarm sounded.

Shit, so much for safer ground. Somehow he had to disconnect the fire alarm from that thought. But what if he was no different than Trick, and couldn't make that disconnection and still be happy?

"You used to sculpt," he recalled, preferring to discuss Erica's career choices over his own. "Busts, right?"

"Yes, I'm surprised you remember."

"Work that good's hard to forget. Why'd you stop?"

Her smile went vacant. "It wasn't real work, just a hobby. Then when Shelby got me in at the accounting office . . . I guess I recognized there were better things to do with my time than play with clay."

"What if you gave up on your calling?"

Erica looked away. "I seriously doubt it."

And Linc seriously doubted to the contrary that she felt the need to turn away. He shouldn't push the issue since it was liable to make her push him for information in return, but he suddenly had to know her reasoning.

Catching her chin in his hand, he brought her gaze back to his. As they had that morning in his flowerbed, secret desires filled her eyes. These ones carried a far different kind of passion, and even so, her arduous expression riled his blood and hardened his body.

Even so, he fought the burning want to take her mouth with his. "You'll never know if you don't try again, will you?"

Her lips parted a fraction. Instead of words, a solo puff of breath escaped followed by the tip of her tongue dampening her lower lip. The move could have been about nerves. His cock opted to believe it was about showing him how anxious she, too, was to bypass talk and move right on to the hot and heavy stuff.

Putting on a saucy smile, Erica looked down at the river of cleavage flowing between her raised arms. "Did I mention I have Juicy Fruit stuck to my nipples?"

5

"You should come in," Erica said when Linc pulled his truck into her drive.

She didn't bother to mask the sensual invitation in her words. Since they'd left the dance floor over an hour ago, tension of the "I want you" variety had been mounting. Coupled with the covetous glances she'd caught Linc sending her dance partners, it seemed Shelby had been accurate in her assessment of his irritation. Now it was up to Erica to convince him that she wasn't after more than casual sex, so he need not worry about Nathan or her no-firefighter vow.

Linc climbed out of the truck and came around to the passenger's side. He opened her door looking like tall, dark, and sexy personified. The moonlight gleamed off the white collar of his dress shirt past his suit coat while his rich caramel hair tousled in the breeze, making her fingers tingle to run through its thickness.

His closed-off expression stopped her from doing so.

"Thanks," he said flatly, "but I need to get home."

Sighing, she climbed from the truck. "Like I told you before, Nathan's not an issue. My want for you also has nothing to do with convincing you to return to the crew. This is about you, me, and my burning pussy alone."

"Erica . . ." The now familiar warning sounded in his voice.

Back on the dance floor she'd taken their surroundings into consideration and forewent kissing him. She should make up for that now by dissolving his warning with the warmth and wetness of her mouth. At the very least, lay out the planned offer of casual sex. But Linc had been a true friend, taking her to the benefit against his want to do so. Again, when he'd saved her from having to come up with a polite way to reject Callahan's unspoken advances.

Tonight, she would repay his kindness by ignoring her sex's growing ache to be filled by his. Give him time to go home and consider the evening behind them, how much he'd missed his crewmates. How much he ached for her in return.

Tomorrow, she was going after what Erica wanted, full speed ahead.

This is about you, me, and my burning pussy alone.

The words resounded in Linc's head like a sexual freight train as he locked his front door. Hell, he would need a dozen cold showers if Erica kept talking that way. Mind on a lone, warm shower meant to get her delectable scent off his body, he started up the stairs. Halfway up, with his suit coat off and his shirt sleeves unbuttoned, the phone rang. Calls this time of night generally amounted to one thing: the need for emergency backup.

Pulse accelerating, he dropped his coat on the stairs and hustled down to the living room. He was jerking the cordless off the end table when he remembered the firehouse wouldn't be on the other end of the line. Worse than the ingrained assumption was the smile he felt creeping across his lips over the thought of donning his gear and rushing onto a fire scene alongside the rest of the Ladder 13 crew.

Damn, he should never have gone to the benefit tonight.

Smile gone, Linc punched the Talk button. "Hello."

"Linc?" Erica's questioning voice came from the other end.

Make that a double damn. With her offer still so fresh, the sound of her voice was all it took to have his cock stiffening. "Did you expect someone else?"

"No, it's just . . . you know how I told you I used gum to keep my dress in place?"

As if he could forget. "Yeah, Juicy Fruit."

"I was kidding. I used two-way tape." She made a whimpering noise followed by a whooshing one, both of which sounded pained. "I wasn't kidding about tape and skin not working well together. What I didn't realize was how damned bad it hurts peeling it off. I need help."

Go over there in his current state of confusion and help her bare her breasts? Not a chance. "I'm sure Shelby knows about that woman stuff."

"Probably, but all their lights are out. I don't want to wake the boys with a phone call. Can you please come over?" She sucked in a sharp breath and expelled a far from gentle curse. "I'm afraid if I keep going at it like I have been, I'm either going to pass out from the pain or end up minus a couple nipples."

Ah, hell, she sounded desperate.

Even so, planting his deprived cock in close quarters with her burning pussy and soon-to-be-naked breasts would be asinine. On the other hand, leaving her to suffer would be incredibly cruel and about as unfriendly as a guy could get.

Fine, he would go. But he wasn't going to be happy about it.

Feeling like an imbecile, Erica wrapped a bath towel around her stinging breasts and awaited Linc's arrival. After he'd gone, she'd recognized giving him time to rehash the night really was for the best. Considering how he'd brought up her sculpting and suggested that she may have given up her calling, his mind had to be turning with the wonder if he hadn't done the same. He had to be close to the point where, if she pushed just a little more, he would give firefighting another chance.

The automatic porch light came on moments later. She opened the door and flashed a thankful smile. "Have I mentioned lately that you're awesome?"

Grim-faced, he moved inside and shut the door. "About an hour and a half ago, when I rescued you from Callahan."

"In that case, I owe you double time." Facing the inevitable, Erica unwrapped the towel. She looked to the strips of white tape hanging from her sore, splotchy breasts. "Anything in particular you'd like in repayment?"

"I'm here to help," he clipped. "That's it."

She looked back up. "I didn't mean to imply you wanted my breasts. *I* don't even want them right now."

Linc looked like he wanted to laugh over the remark. Holding on to his glower, he shrugged out of his suit coat and hung it on the front doorknob. "Let's get this over with." He gave the right strip of tape a testing tug. "Do you still have your busts?"

Erica tried not to wince but, damn, maybe she should have gone to the ER instead. And maybe if he wanted her to quit thinking about sex, he should stop talking about her busts when his hands were all but on them.

Needing a safer focal point, she studied a wall photo of herself and her sister taken at Holly's college graduation a couple years before. "I've always heard seeing is believing."

The tugging came to a merciful end. Then he got merciless, cupping her breast in the heat of his palm and massaging the heavy globe. "I meant the ones you made before you gave up sculpting."

"Oh, I'm sure there's a few left in the attic." *Oh, God,* was more like it. As in, *Oh, God, how could he be so evil?*

Each knead of his work-roughened hand shot jolts of carnal longing from her tape-concealed nipple to her crotch. Needful ache fanned through her sex. She wanted to whimper. Wanted to grab his other hand and rub it against her pussy. Wanted to ask if he could smell her arousal thickening on the air. The daring cut of the dress's backside hadn't allowed for panties, and she hadn't taken the time to put any on while awaiting his arrival. The sweatpants she had pulled on felt nearly saturated in the thighs.

Erica closed her eyes and concentrated on the forthcoming pain. After all, he was here solely to help.

But if he'd come over only to help remove the tape, why had he brought up her sculpting again?

She hadn't changed the subject earlier to avoid talking about it because it was a bad subject per se. It was that her reason for giving up the hobby she'd always loved revolved around Nathan. Knowing how much Linc loathed the man her ex had become, the last thing she wanted was to add more fuel to the fire. Not because she felt the need to mother Nathan or still held feelings for him either. Rather because . . . just because.

The sensual torment of Linc's hand stilled. His palm left her breast. "You should get them out. See if they don't inspire you to do more."

"Why do you care—" Her question fell flat as his hand returned, this time to settle over her other breast. Any remaining soreness evaporated beneath his deft touch. Any chance she had of forgetting her arousal went along with it.

Erica pinched her eyes more tightly closed. So long as she didn't see him handling her breast, she could make it through. Somehow.

His free hand came over her unoccupied breast, treating it to the same glorious fondling. Or rather soothing, as was no doubt his intent. She let herself fall under its lulling spell. Let his reason for being here fall away completely.

Remembering the conversation, she tried at her question again, "Why do you care if I'm inspi—"

Lightning bolt pain seared through her breasts, cutting her off short. Gasping in horror, she slammed her eyes open.

Linc stood a foot away, sympathy in place of his earlier severity. A tattered strip of two-way tape dangled from either of his hands. "I just want to see you living life to the fullest."

No, he just wanted to see her bawling like a baby for that ruthless move.

Erica hugged her arms around her screaming chest. At least her nipples were still intact, as it appeared were the rest of her boobs. "On second thought, *you* owe *me* double time. That hurt like a son of a bitch."

"I wasn't the one who put the tape on, backward from the looks of things."

He might not have put it on, but she'd put it on for *his* sake. She'd worn the glaringly blatant dress and bedroom heels for the benefit of *his* testosterone. Was it really too much to ask for him to get over his reservations and do her already?

Obviously, it was, since he didn't give her breasts so much as a passing look.

Linc balled the tape in his hand and took a step toward the door. She expected him to grab his coat and make his getaway. Five minutes ago, she'd mostly wanted him to do that very thing. Now, Erica wanted to forget about letting him off the hook for the night by reminding him in vivid detail how hot he got her.

She kept the words inside when he took a second step that led him not closer to the door but in the direction of her open kitchen. Moving through the living room, he went into the kitchen and pulled a bag of peas from the freezer.

"What do you say we make a deal?" He returned to hand

the bag to her. "You give sculpting another try, and I'll give my all to returning to the Ladder, at least on a part-time basis."

What did she say? That she was either delirious from tape expulsion and hearing things as a side effect, or he'd just presented one hell of a win-win situation.

Option one, delirium, was out. Now that the pain was subsiding, Erica was keenly aware of the situation at hand. There was a whole lot of power to be had in the alliance of her bare breasts and one small bag of peas. There was also a whole lot of feeling good to be had if only he allowed it.

Palming the bag, she brought it to her breast and tauntingly circled the areola. "All right." She *oohed* as the frosty bag made contact with her nipple. The still-red tip beaded, and a flood of liquid happiness further dampened the crotch of her sweatpants. "I'll agree. On one condition."

Linc's throat worked visibly. His eyes no longer averted contact, but locked on her breasts, his irises that dark, decadent hazel and heated with desire. "Do I want to know?"

"It's not a big thing." The words came out throaty, her breathing shallow, as she worked the bag between her cleavage.

For someone who'd never much lusted over a man or hungered for sex, the idea it could be his cock pumping between her breasts came far too easily. Erica was feeling brazen enough to see it happen too. Right after she saw every inch of his deliciously hard body displayed for her eternal rendering.

"It's just that as much as I enjoy doing busts, I've always dreamed of sculpting a nude, and I can't think of a better model."

6

"Where do you want me?" Linc eyed Erica for direction, wary of the hesitation in his voice.

Never had he felt nervous about undressing for an audience. With most women, he would have had them both naked by now, their bodies moving feverishly against the wall, or the couch, or the rug. Or, hell, anywhere so long as they were feeling good. He'd established long ago that Erica wasn't just any woman. Just as he'd established he shouldn't be alone with her when one or both of them was lacking for clothes.

At least he would be the naked one this time.

Agreeing to her modeling request had brought an end to her erotic show with the bag of peas. Over the course of gathering her art pad and pencils, she'd pulled her hair into the ponytail he'd long been accustomed to and covered her breasts in a loose-fitting navy sweatshirt that almost hid the fact she was braless. She sat on the couch now, art pad on her lap, legs extended onto the footstool, and her fingers flexing in preparation.

Anticipation rolled off her in waves.

Linc had known on the dance floor that giving up sculpting hadn't been something she'd done lightly. Getting her back to it was the reason he was still here against his better judgment. In the event he couldn't be completely happy without returning to the fire crew, he had to know Erica was doing something she loved as well. Just in case the worst should happen. Just in case he did end up on the wrong side of the grave.

"In front of the fireplace." She grabbed a small black remote from near her hip. The push of a button sent a gas log firing to life in the hearth behind him. "Perfect."

It felt perfect. Like the perfect atmosphere for sex. "Do you plan to work the fire into the sculpture?"

"No, just setting the mood. I need to be in a certain frame of mind. Considering how long it's been since I've done this, that's more important than ever."

She meant sketching in preparation of sculpting, Linc assured himself, even if it did sound like she was talking about preparing to fuck him. Even if she did fix her eyes on his chest as he undid the first button of his dress shirt.

Tackling the column of buttons in seconds, he shook the shirt off his arms and tossed it over the back of a bare wood rocking chair. Erica's eyes took on that sleepily sexy slant. Her mouth opened a quarter inch. A barely audible sigh escaped as her tongue darted out to dampen her lips for an excited millisecond.

The breath snagged in his throat. She looked like this back on the dance floor, back when he would have kissed her if she hadn't moved in a way that shocked his thoughts into awareness of their companions. Now they were alone. Now the risqué dress was gone. Now she could be wearing a potato sack and he would still be sucked in like a flame to tinder.

Hell, this was such a damned bad idea. He could never remain flaccid while she visually caressed every inch of his body. "Do I get a fig leaf?"

"Not unless you've changed your name to Adam."

Humor tinged her words, not lust. It gave Linc hope that she planned to be the professional. That hope rose as she diverted her attention back to the art board.

Quickly, he undressed the remainder of the way. If he got naked and posed while she was looking away, this was bound to feel less like a strip show. Only once he was standing there in the buff, the fire crackling at his back, heating his ass, calves, and spine, he didn't know how she wanted him to pose. "Sitting or standing?"

"Lying on your side, legs extended. Hand on your . . ." The words droned off as Erica looked up. Without a hint of subtlety, her gaze darted to his groin.

Setting the art board on the neighboring couch cushion, she came to her bare feet. Linc fought the urge to cup his hands over his cock, though he wasn't sure if the want stemmed from an unfathomable case of modesty or the fear he would shove inside her at the first opportunity.

If she advanced solely to grant him that opportunity, would he have the power to resist?

She crossed the ten feet that separated them. He held his breath as her hands extended toward him. "Let me move you."

If she only knew how much she did move him . . . to laughter, to frustration, to jealousy. To fighting off one big, swollen dick as she went down on her knees and took his hips in hand.

Erica's mouth hovered less than six inches from his shaft—too close for either comfort or a silent heart. The blood blistered through his veins. Sweat popped out on his brow. He focused on chilly thoughts. Frigid places. Frigid women.

Her lips parted. The warmth of her breath slammed into his rising flesh. His heart skipped a beat as he waited for her to lean forward, wrap those luscious lips around his cock, and suck him straight to heaven.

Tipping her head back, she frowned. "You're too tense."

Linc bit back an admittedly tense-as-hell laugh. How could any man in his situation not be on edge? "Maybe you should hire a professional."

"You already agreed to the job, so relax and let me work."

He let out a pent-up sigh. Levity was needed here, anything to get his mind off burying inside her for the next decade or two. "Yes, Mom. I promise to behave."

Erica's lips twisted in a way that said he'd missed the humor mark and moved right to grossing her out. The thought of standing naked in front of his mother had the intended effect for his shaft as well, talking it down from the ledge of erection.

Without words, she guided him to the plush beige carpet and positioned him on his side in front of the fireplace, head propped up slightly against the curve of one arm. Her fingers pressed against his outer thigh, rolling his hip forward a couple inches. His feet came next. Taking an ankle in hand, she rested one foot across the other.

She worked with utter precision, complete professionalism. To his amazement, Linc began to relax. He closed his eyes and let the fire snapping at his back and the familiar scent of the woman at his front soothe him further. Then he nearly shot off the floor when that woman captured his cock in her fingers.

His eyes slammed open on a ragged inhale. He half expected her to be seconds away from guiding him inside her mouth for a nice, long nibble. Erica was looking at his shaft, but from over a foot away and in a totally objective manner.

With infinite care, she arranged his member against his inner thigh. Her fingers speared through the thatch of dark, wiry curls at the base, arranging them as well and somehow still making the action seem professional.

"That's great." She stood. "Now try not to move much."

Resettled on the couch, legs extended on the footstool, she placed the art board on her lap and put pencil to paper. She worked without sound, without the hint of a smile, without even seeming to notice when a lock of curly, auburn hair came loose from her ponytail to fall softly across her cheek.

Her eyes held the emotion the rest of her face lacked: awareness, strength, and yet raw vulnerability.

Linc had never seen anything quite so exquisite. He'd never experienced such intimacy. It was like he was looking directly into her soul, playing voyeur to her greatest passion. It was a sensation he could quickly become addicted to, just as he found himself becoming more and more infatuated with Erica herself.

"I need you to move one of your hands," she said after several minutes had passed.

"Sure. Where do you want it?"

Her gaze lifted from his lower thighs. Sensuality merged with those other emotions. "Around your cock. Whenever I imagined sculpting a nude, the model was always erect."

Sweet mother of God. Nothing could have burst his reflection and killed his comfort so thoroughly. "You're pushing it."

"I'm being an artist."

He'd thought so, too, seconds ago. Maybe she still was. Her voice could reflect her fervor for the job, and aroused nude sculptures were hardly uncommon.

Taking the light approach, Linc sent her a teasing smile. "Just make sure I get credit where it's due."

She let go an amused laugh. "Got it. No teeny weenies."

Every ounce of mirth drained from Erica's face as he took his cock in hand. Her lips fell into a firm line. Dare he think a pensive one that suggested she was back to the professional?

Telling himself that was the case, he glided his fingers from corona to root. His shaft swelled to hardness in seconds, veins bulging with new life and hedonistic vitality. Pre-cum gelled at the red, throbbing tip. He used his thumb to brush the fluid away.

"No, don't wipe it away," she chastised. "I want this to look natural."

He just wanted it the hell over with, because there wasn't one single way he was returning to the easy intimacy of moments ago.

Linc's mind saturated with hard, carnal thoughts. His balls tightened with the want to explode. His cock leaked more fluid with each stroke of pencil against paper, each tight, tormenting pass of his fingers.

His thumbnail scraped against the tip of his cock with his next pass. A low growl erupted from his throat with the unintentional rub. Erica's hand jerked across the paper. She blinked twice, then a third time as he intentionally repeated the move. Clearly, he'd become a stupid bastard who couldn't resist a little taunting.

Pre-cum pearled up, thick and heavy. He circled his thumb in the gel. Pleasure skated over his every nerve ending as he traced the wet digit the length of his shaft. Firelight danced off the scarlet flesh, glistening his seed.

"Nice." The lone word purred from her lips.

Not nice. Naughty. Her eyes held one lone emotion now: lust, raw and electric. So damned erotic. So like nothing he ever believed he would witness in them.

Christ, how tempting it was to keep up the show. Masturbate to orgasm and see how she responded when he came with her name on his lips. Tempting, but not his purpose in agreeing to model for her. Not something Linc could allow in good faith when he still wasn't certain how she felt about Nathan. Not when he was nearly positive he belonged on Ladder 13 every bit as much as Erica belonged devoting her time to this art she clearly loved.

"Good." He released his shaft. "Then you don't need me to keep stroking."

She gasped disapprovingly. "Oh, no, you don't. Your hand stays on your cock. I don't want to risk you losing your erection just when I'm getting to the final touches."

"My fingers are starting to cramp."

Sympathy entered her eyes. "Sorry. I should have been more sensitive."

Setting the art board and pencil aside, Erica stood. Muscles corded in his shoulders and back, and his heart thundered into his throat as she started toward him. She once again went down on her knees before him. Last time he feared her mouth on his dick. This time he knew her hand was going around it even before she made contact.

"What are you doing?" he hissed.

Fisting his sex, she picked up the leisurely pace he'd set. "Giving you a break."

"Erica . . ." What he meant as a warning came out sounding like a plea.

But, shit, her hand was soft, warm, supple. A step away from losing himself in the damp sweetness of her mouth, the tight hotness of her pussy. Every one of his fantasies.

"I'm doing it for the sake of the sculpture."

"Are you?"

"Mostly." Her gaze lifted to his. Carnal need threatened to scorch him on the spot. "Is it such a crime if I stop for a lick or suck along the way?"

Swiping her finger in the gel at the head of his shaft, Erica brought the digit to her mouth. She sucked it inside on a blissful moan, and his cock bucked feverishly for an instant repeat followed by a dozen more. "I'm just human," she continued breathily. "Just a normal woman who hasn't had sex in over a year and a half. Not because I've been holding out in the hopes of Nathan's return, but because I've only wanted one man in that time."

And that man had turned her down, Linc acknowledged silently.

He should do so again. Get the hell off her carpet, away from her sexy-as-sin mouth, out of her house. If only because he'd come to understand why he couldn't get back to thinking of her as a friend, the way he'd done with every other woman he'd fooled around with. Those other women came and went from his life. Erica remained, burrowed deeper in his thoughts, wove her wants and desires around his own.

But had she?

Was she merely acting on her habit of seeing other's desires went fulfilled, or did she want him for her own reasons?

Moving onto her side, she mimicked his pose from six inches away. One arm tucked beneath her head, she stroked the fingers of her free hand along his cheek. "I had over eight years of serious relationship, Linc. Now, all I want is a fuck-and-run man to help me back on the sex wagon. One that I know will leave me satisfied. A friend I can trust. *You.*"

Relief cruised through him. She spoke the truth. He knew it with certainty, knew that she really was over Nathan. Knew that the soft caress of her fingers along his cheek warmed his blood better than any lover's salacious touch of the past.

Before desire clouded his brain entirely, he questioned, "What about your vow? I meant what I said earlier, about returning to the crew. Seeing the way you came to life tonight, when you were doing what you love, reminds me how much I do the same. I know now that I could never walk away from firefighting on a permanent basis."

A smugly entrancing grin curved Erica's lips. "It's about time you see things my way. As for my vow, I never meant it to apply to the short term." She lifted her fingers from his cheek to return them to his cock. "Now, quit thinking of all the reasons we shouldn't do this. We both know that you want me, and that you're not going to get over your frustration until you have me. Some things are inevitable."

She could have a point about his not getting over his hunger for her until he first gave in to it. Sleeping with her could also be best for her welfare. He could be her transition man. The trusted friend to reintroduce her to sex without her fearing he would push her past her limits.

If she had limits . . .

The ponytail, sweatshirt, and jeans-wearing Erica who Linc had known for years had always seemed the girl-next-door, do-it-in-the-dark type. The racy teddy, risqué dress, fuck-me stiletto-wearing Erica of the last week seemed a siren without sexual bounds. One who'd thrill in his penchant to play the dominant lover. One who'd squeal at the feel of his hand connecting with her backside. One who'd cream when he pinned her up against the wall and took her from behind.

His cock shoved hard in the circle of her fingers with the hedonistic thoughts. He ached to yank down her sweatpants and drive into the slick heat of her pussy. She would let him. He wouldn't let himself. Not yet. Not until she finished the sketches.

Losing his thoughts of a would-be lover to those of a caring friend, he nodded at her chest. "Are your breasts feeling better?"

She freed his shaft to lift her sweatshirt up past her bare breasts. Erotic invitation filled her eyes as she cupped the mounds in offering. "The bad pain's gone. Now they ache to feel your hands on them."

Linc had tried to lose his thoughts of a would-be lover, anyway. Erica wasn't letting that happen. He would have to be strong for both of them if she was to finish sketching what would become the blueprint for his sculpture. "I'll think about it on two conditions. You call me anything but baby, and you let me do the stroking while you finish drawing . . . in the buff."

After all, there was strong. And then there was one stunning view.

"Done." Erica set aside pencil and art board to work out the kink she hadn't realized had found its way into her neck.

How could she think about a neck kink when all her thoughts were channeled on getting kinky, period?

Setting each line, each groove, each powerful, rippling muscle of Linc's beautiful body to paper had her sex wet and throbbing in a way she'd never imagined possible. She'd wanted to rush through the sketches. But even more, she'd wanted to set his minutest feature down on paper so that her recreation in clay was nothing short of perfection.

Segueing into a stretch as she stood, she glimpsed the kitchen wall clock. "Oh, wow. I guess I got into it even more than I realized. It's after midnight."

"Does that mean you've changed your mind about sex?" Linc asked.

With her guidance, he'd altered his pose several times during her sketch. Now he was back to reclining on his side in front of the fireplace, both his stance and his tone oozing sexuality. And, now, Erica was back to remembering that she, too, was naked. Her nipples beaded and her pussy lubricated with fresh cream, lifting onto the air and racing her pulse.

No, she hadn't changed her mind. Not even close to it.

Feeling wicked and wanton and loving it, she slid her gaze from his feet to his calves to his thighs to his hands. His fingers returned to their earlier fondling, so strong, so deft, so knowing of exactly what a woman wanted.

Jolts of sensual delight stole through her sex as he caressed his thick cock. She moved toward him, slowly, sinuously, not bothering to stop her eager purr.

Oh, yeah, she was feeling like a tiger tonight, no encouragement needed.

"In case you've forgotten, I'm a big girl. I can get by on a few hours of sleep." Meeting his eyes, she flashed a taunting smile. "Presuming you can keep me entertained that long."

"I'd be more concerned about how sore you're going to be come morning," Linc responded with a touch of playful humor and a heaping of sexy arrogance.

And, God, what a combination.

Like their first kiss, the sensuality of his voice had her mind scattered to everything but her restless, consuming need to feel every part of him pressed up against every part of her.

Going down on her knees, this time at his feet, she took her aching breasts in hand. She rubbed her thumbs across their straining tips. "Are these the parts you had in mind?"

Hot, hungry appreciation flitted over his face only to be overtaken by sobriety. "Were you like this with him?"

No! Not talk of Nathan. Not now. But if she sidestepped the question, Linc was liable to take her silence the wrong way. She wouldn't risk chasing him off. "Like what?"

He reclined back on his elbows and spread his thighs. "Confident. Sexy. Impossible to resist."

Impossible to resist. Much like the ridged, glistening muscles of his chest and abdomen. The sinew that rippled in his brawny thighs as he bent his lightly furred legs. The engorged purple vein that throbbed along the underside of his cock and trailed down to his balls. While she was working, she'd forced herself to see his body as an art form alone. Now, all she could see was his potent masculinity.

Wicked heat balled in Erica's belly, vanquishing all thought of her ex. She shook her head on a hard swallow. "I've never felt the way you make me feel."

"How do you feel, Erica?"

"Like crawling between your knees and sucking your cock."

Unwilling—maybe unable—to restrain her desire a second longer, she pounced against him, knocking him farther back on his elbows. Settled blissfully in the cradle of his thighs, she took his shaft in hand. Pre-cum pearled from the eye as she nuzzled its hot, velvety softness. The rich, thick scent of his arousal rose up to tantalize her senses.

Finally, *finally* she was going to get what Erica wanted.

Quivering with anticipation, she flicked out her tongue and savored his heady, male taste. "Tonight, I feast."

7

"Is that what you want, just to feast?" Linc asked roughly.

It wasn't nearly enough for him. Erica's lips felt beyond incredible moving around his cock, as did the loose tendrils of hair escaping her ponytail to caress his groin. Still, he wanted—*needed*—to give her more. "Wouldn't you rather be cherished?"

Her gaze lifted to his, eyes sexily slanted and burning blue fire. The lush dampness of her mouth left his shaft, presumably to speak.

He didn't give her that chance.

Taking her by the shoulders, he flipped them over so that she lay sandwiched between his thighs on the carpet—trapped and mouthwatering. Firelight danced off the dark, erect tips of her nipples and shimmered against the damp, auburn curls at her mound. It was a blessing that she requested he be erect for her rendering. With her tantalizing curves on full display and her eyes hazed with worklust, there was no way he would have made it through in any other condition.

Erica's eyes were hazed now as well, but with an entirely

different sort of lust. The scaldingly wicked kind that had his heart hammering and his dick ready to split its skin.

Remembering her wild anticipation when he'd taken her wrists captive on his couch, Linc hauled her wrists into one hand and held them above her head. Dropping his mouth to a breast, he licked at the crown. A catching moan sounded from her throat. She wriggled beneath him, lifting her hips and rubbing her cunt brazenly against his cock as he took a second succulent lick. Feral hot heat rocked him to the core.

"Mmm . . . Linc," she sighed. "So good."

Exhilaration swelled in his chest. So much better than good was his name on her lips when passion painted her voice. He still wasn't convinced that giving in to their want was the smart thing to do, but he was damned well going to see it through.

"This is what you want, Erica. What you deserve." Cupping her breast in his free hand, he pressed his thumb against the pouting nipple. As fervently as her hips, the mound rose up to grind against his fingers. He gave the nipple a gentle pinch. "Every inch of your body worshipped."

He pinched her nipple again, harder. Eagerness gleamed in her eyes with her squeak. Arousal spiked her scent, making it more intoxicating than ever. He no longer questioned if she could handle his taste for playing the dominant lover. She could handle whatever he chose to dole out because he made her hot like no other.

The thought pitched Linc's own arousal higher. Made him ache like a horny teenager to forget about pleasuring her slowly to shove inside her immediately.

Biding his time, he kept his hold on her wrists with one hand and stroked his fingers down the smooth, sloped flesh of her belly with the other. "Every curve should be caressed." She trembled beneath his touch, and he moved to kneel next to her. Slipping his hand lower, he guided his fingers through her moist bush to pet the curve of her sex. "Every mound."

Erica's breath caught audibly with the contact. She bent her knees and separated her legs. Dewy folds parted in blissfully erotic invitation.

When he burned to sink his tongue inside her and bring her to instant climax, he kept to his knees. Allowing only his fingers to explore, he rode the crevice of her labia. Back and forth, back and forth, he led her in a slow, sensual dance much like the one they'd shared this evening in the fire hall.

Unlike that dance, this one ended with deliverance as he sank a finger into her passage. "Every hollow."

"Oh, God." Her breathy moan sounded in tandem with Linc's own. Tight muscles sucked greedily at his impaling, and his blood fired from hot to blistering.

Fuck, she was so wet, so ready.

"Yes," Erica panted, "that's what I want. All of it." Working her hips, she took his finger deeper, harder. Beyond his wettest, wildest dreams. "Cherish me."

As if he could do any less . . .

Firming his hold on her wrists, he resettled his thighs around hers. Her hips surged up. Biting down on her lower lip, she ground against his cock. He growled with the pressure, exquisite as hell and liable to bring him to a fast finish.

Readjusting his weight, he applied more pressure to her thighs, trapping her beneath him once again and stilling her actions.

Discontent flashed in her eyes. "I can't move when you do that."

"You don't need to. You're being cherished, remember?"

"Then can you do it a little faster?"

"I can." Linc moved down her legs. "But I won't." Taking the tender bud of her clit between thumb and forefinger, he turned whatever response she might have made into a sharp gasp of rapture.

Erica's eyelids fell closed. Long, dark lashes kissed her cheeks as he alternately fingered and squeezed the tender bud. With his mouth and lips and tongue, he loved every inch of her breasts. Nipping. Licking. Sucking. Feasting on her swollen nipples as she'd feasted on his solid cock. Moving lower, he repeated those same lascivious moves across the soft rise of her belly, down the smooth curves of her inner thighs. Back up again to nuzzle against the folds of her sex.

Without words, she wriggled in the binding of his hand. Insistently, she pressed her pussy against his mouth, showering his senses with her natural perfume. Impatience grew into a raging inferno that vibrated off her body to shudder through his.

Linc rewarded her endurance with his tongue. Or, rather, he was the rewarded one as he flicked the blade inside her and tasted sweet liquid honey. His cock pulsed with his groan of elation. "You're so tasty. I could eat you for days."

"Please fuck me instead."

Always her pleading had pushed his buttons. Never had it sounded so wickedly naughty and yet breathtakingly lovely. Never had he ached to fulfill a plea more.

Every muscle in his body drawn tight with the need to explode, he rose up over her. Erica lifted her head off the carpet and met him openmouthed. Eagerly, she took in the hot, carnal taste of her essence on his tongue. Joined him lick for starving lick, suck for fervent suck. Her hands released from his grasp to touch, stroke, caress every inch of his rock-solid body. He moved his own along each of her curves, each valley. Each gloriously generous mound.

Her ankles bumped against his spine as she roped her legs around his lower back. Her hands moved to the upper half. Short nails bit into his skin with the blatantly upward shove of her hips. The head of his cock glided past her thighs to nudge against her opening. Damp welcoming heat rose off her sex, beckoning him to move inside.

Christ, how he wanted to go there.

Before he lost his mind and accepted the offer, Linc retracted his mouth and body from hers. He pulled in cooling breaths as he came up on his knees.

Erica's expression went instantly stony. "Tell me you've changed your mind, and I swear I'll cover every hair on your body with two-way tape."

Caught between laughing and wincing, he crawled to the rocking chair. He pulled his wallet from his suit pants and took out a condom. "The only thing on my mind is putting on a condom so I can finally extinguish your burning pussy."

Stony look gone, she moved to her knees and extended a hand. "In that case, may I?"

She could do anything she pleased when she was dressed—make that undressed—that way. Newly freed of its ponytail, her hair framed her flushed face in wild, curly waves. Light from the fire framed the rest of her, casting a lustrous glow on the teasing triangle of her pubic hair and the tight tips of her nipples.

With effort, Linc pulled his mind from his dick to give her question real consideration. He'd always done the sheathing so that trusting a lover to do it right wouldn't be an issue. With Erica, the trust was already there. Still, would straying from the routine be wise?

Remembering this night was about seeing to her wants and happiness, first and foremost, he handed the foil-wrapped package over.

Her look became sheepish as she tore open the packet. "I've never done this before, so I'm sorry if I hurt you."

Never, as in never ever?

He couldn't stop his smug grin. It wasn't that he wanted to best Nathan in her eyes, but damn, did he love knowing that she'd never made the request of her ex. "You're not the only one who's big. I can handle a little pain."

A playfully naughty smile emerged. With an exaggerated wiggle of her eyebrows, she took his cock in hand and pumped. "Definitely plenty of 'big' credit to be given here." His shaft spasmed with her warm touch, and she asked, "How long has this been building?"

"Lately most every time you come within fifteen feet."

She gave a laugh rich with arousal. "I meant your want for me."

Linc hesitated with his response. Considering she was after the short term, would it worry her to know how long he'd wanted her? Should it worry him? "Right now it feels like forever," he improvised. "Reality beats fantasy by a landslide."

"I don't know when it started for me," Erica admitted.

Her expression turned to one of concentration as she focused on sheathing him. Mostly she did the job like a pro. Mostly, but for a couple minor pinches as she worked the condom up his length. Instead of hurting, those pinches sliced through his cock as sheer erotic tension nearly too intense to stop from bursting over.

What felt a lifetime later, she lifted her fingers from his shaft. She looked up to reveal her smile was back to brimming with naughty. Her lips parted, and the most beautiful words slipped out. "I feel like I'll explode if you don't fuck me soon."

Longing growled through Linc, low and hard. Sweet Jesus, the way it got to him when the girl next door played the vixen.

"Is this soon enough?" With his next thrashing heartbeat, he had her on her back on the carpet, his body held just above hers and her breasts pressed sinuously between them.

Bracing a hand on either side of her head, he nudged the tip of his cock against her opening. The condom masked her wetness. The ease with which he slipped inside those first incredible inches guaranteed she was dripping with arousal. After those inches she was tight like he hadn't experienced in ages. Hot like he would never forget.

Raw sensuality took over her face, and they gasped in unison when he pushed to the hilt. The urge to go fast slammed into him. Like the compulsion to play the dominant, he cast it aside for now. Loving her warm, silky mouth with the damp caress of his tongue, he moved above her in slow, deep strokes. She was using muscles she hadn't used in well over a year. Despite his promise to leave her sore, he didn't want that happening yet. Not when he had every intention of spending the rest of the night guiding her back onto the sex wagon.

Erica had no such qualms about taking it easy. She gripped his sides and drove her hips up hard into his. His mouth jerked free of hers as wild need chased through him with lightning-bolt intensity. Tension pulled razor sharp along his spine. Corralling both sensations, he ground his teeth together and concentrated on keeping the pace slow, even.

"No more waiting," she spoke in a hot, breathy whisper seconds later. "Make me come, Linc. *Now.*"

Ah, hell. As lost as he'd always felt to her pleading, her demand was even harder to deny.

His entire body trembled as the hunger for release smoldered through him. Retaking her mouth in a kiss of fervency, he gave in to her command, quickening the pace of his hips. Deep, deep, deeper he slid into the brilliant haze of sexual nirvana. Then deeper still, as she bucked her hips and met his with a potent thrust that snugged his balls tight.

The breath pushed from Linc's mouth into hers. Blood pulsed through his veins in a mad rush. His cock gave a savage throb of warning.

There would be no more holding back.

Bodies and tongues mating, sliding, fusing together, they settled into a frenetic pace of muffled moans and sighs. Near mindlessly, he slipped his hand between their bodies. Erica whimpered with the first stroke of his finger against her clit. A second caress had her sex tightening around his. The next had her falling from their set pace.

She writhed on the carpet in a wild erotic dance, the overwhelming scent of her arousal sweeping lusciously over his senses. Soft quakes shuddered through her sex and around his. A rush of heat surrounded his cock with his next deep plunge. Her cry was that of pure ecstasy as orgasm overtook her. His was that of relief as he gave into his own. Growling against her lips, he came fast, hard, and unforgettably.

Slowly, Linc emerged from a sensual daze like nothing he'd experienced in years, if ever. Erica lay beneath him, eyes closed, hair tossed about her head halo fashion, and a wide blissful smile spread across her puffy pink lips. His heart tightened with just how beautiful she looked, just how awesomely good she felt.

It was definitely going to take the rest of the night to guide her way back on the sex wagon, if not the rest of the year.

Linc's arms folded around Erica, and he changed their positions so that he lay beneath her in front of the faux fire. The move lifted her from what felt a fantastical dream as much as a carnal trance. She opened her eyes to find his closed. A satiated smile curved his lips that she knew matched her own.

God, she loved sex. Loved the aftershocks of orgasm still pinging through her. Loved the mingled scent of their sweat and arousal on the air.

How had she not known this part of her existed?

With Nathan sex had been okay, but something she could easily go without. With Linc, she was still basking in the glow of their first encounter, and she already wanted him again.

She was going to have him again. This time when more than a little wrist bondage and missionary-style loving was involved. Not that she was complaining about either. But the tiger in her was freed, and she wanted a taste of the Linc who took a woman hot and hard and drove her past the point of reason.

Squeezing her sex around his softening cock, Erica flicked

her tongue out to toy with his upper lip. He tasted of sweat and heat and masculine decadence. *Delicious.*

A low growl rumbled from his throat. "Careful, you're bound to get a repeat."

"That was the idea." Pushing off his chest, she sat back to straddle him. His eyes opened, and if she'd been expecting to see surprise there, what she got was pure predator.

His dark gaze seared into hers before moving down to give her breasts a nipple-throbbing ogling. This time the hug of her pussy around his cock was automatic.

Oh yeah, she was ready for a taste of his domineering side.

"Time to retreat to the bedroom." A trace of disappointment flashed in his eyes—clearly he thought she meant to sleep. Hiding her smile, she pushed to her feet and started toward her bedroom. She cast a taunting glance over her shoulder when she reached the hallway. "To get my handcuffs and flogger."

Erica wanted to look back a second time to see his response but made herself continue on to the bedroom. Like the risqué dress and shoes she'd worn tonight, the toys were recent purchases, easily located in her bottom dresser drawer. The muscles of her sex clenched expectantly as she gathered both items in hand, bliss-rendering supplements she'd never dared to experiment with in the past. The clenching became all-out spasming when a muscled arm snaked beneath hers and a large hand cupped the one holding the toys.

Shivers cascaded through her with the rub of Linc's cock along the rise of her butt. His already hardening cock. Her inner tiger preened with the knowledge she turned him on so completely.

Who knew she held such power? Who knew she could be an orgasm nympho?

Moving aside her hair, he feathered a damp kiss beneath her ear. Her pussy lubricated with the heady caress of his warm breath. There could be no doubt of her nympho status for the wanton way she panted out a moan and ground her ass against him.

Without words, he unfolded his hand from around hers. He relieved her of the fuzzy pink cuffs and flogger, and then turned her toward the bed. She'd long been a fan of pastels. Now her cloud white, baby blue, and sage green comforter seemed virginal in contrast to her lascivious thoughts. She *felt* suddenly virginal, about to engage in her first truly erotic encounter.

The tiger prowling inside Erica found a shade of nerves. What if Linc's dominant side was too much for her? Their sexual relationship was to be short term, but she didn't want that short term to consist of a single day.

The press of his erection left her butt. His hand came to her back, and he urged her forward with a little push. "Lie down." Quiet command centered his voice.

He wouldn't be too much for her, she knew with sudden conviction. He was her friend before anything else, one of her few, one of her closest. The moment he sensed he was pushing her past her comfort zone, he would back off, take her down to a point where she knew only rapture.

Part of her loved that she could trust him so implicitly. Part of her hated that he would allow himself less than total pleasure to ensure her bliss. All of her recognized that she'd do the exact same thing. The Erica of old would, anyway—the one who'd always put others first. The important thing was that she'd felt good about her actions back then, and so it stood to reason he would feel good about his now. Really, he was going to get an orgasm out of the deal no matter if the sex was sweet and tender or raw and dirty.

Relaxed in her ponderings, Erica crossed the rest of the way to the bed. She turned back when she reached the foot. Until now, Linc had been at her back and she hadn't been able to see his face. Now, she looked directly at him. At the wickedly wolfish smile curving his sexy lips. At his hungry, hazel eyes visually devouring the length of her naked body.

His gaze returned to her face, and he raised an eyebrow. "Do I need to repeat myself?"

He sounded arrogant, a trait she'd never cared for. But the touch of sexy arrogance he'd tossed her way in front of the fire had appealed to her on some baser level. Going by the salacious heat coiling in her belly and the anxious thrum of her pulse, the commanding arrogance he tossed her way now appealed equally as much.

"I don't know how you want me," she admitted. "Should I lay on my front or back?"

"Front," he responded without hesitation, without losing his feral smile.

Following his order, she climbed onto the bed and lay on her belly. She had only an instant to consider the vulnerability of the position before his weight was on her. Straddling her upper thighs, he straightened one of her arms and slipped a handcuff around the wrist. He attached the cuff to the headboard and then repeated the act with her other arm.

He'd restrained her wrists twice before and she'd loved it. She trusted him beyond words. Even knowing those two things, butterflies of tension fluttered in Erica's belly. Effecting a playful tone, she eyed her right arm. "Looks like I'm trapped."

Linc's chest hair tickled her back, easing her nerves a fraction, as he brought his mouth to her ear. Warm breath toyed with the lobe. A rough palm rubbed across her butt. "As much as I love looking at your gorgeous breasts, this way I can have my fill of your lovely ass."

The breath caught in her throat, and her sphincter muscles constricted. She'd never been taken from behind. Was that his intention?

"Relax, slave, and I'll promise to make this good for you."

"Slave?" Equal parts of shock and hesitation fueled the question.

With a short, rich laugh, he sat back again. "You know what you are. You also know you don't talk without my permission. You *know* what happens when you do."

She didn't, of course, but she found out less than two seconds later. When the flat of his palm connected with her backside. The smack wasn't hard, barely even registered a sound, and yet it came so suddenly and unexpectedly, Erica squeaked.

"Did I tell you to squeak?" he demanded.

Her belly tightened. He sounded sincere, like he was into this slave game to the point he could miss it if he pushed her beyond her comfort zone. He hadn't done that yet. The tightness of her belly was about want, the juices slickening her pussy anticipation. "Sorry," she muffled into the comforter. "Keep going. I promise to behave."

"Keep going *what*?" Linc's hand left her butt to push between her thighs. One finger nudged against the rear of her sex. "You'll call me Master."

Her legs parted instinctively. Juices leaked from her opening as his finger teased, probed, and then left her folds. Biting back a needy sigh, she assented, "Yes, Mast—"

Soft leather slapped against her ass, cutting her off short. Each of the flogger's dozen tails nipped into her tender flesh. A stinging throb whipped through her cheeks. Her sex clenched, unclenched, clenched again. Her hands fisted reflexively, opening and closing in the cuffs.

His finger returned between her thighs. No teasing play this time, but impaling her wet body with a knowing thrust. "Squeak again without permission and the next slap's against this hot little cunt."

"S-sorry," Erica mumbled. But she couldn't be less sorry. Her entire body felt alive with sexual tension, every nerve standing on end in wait of his next move. Every thought focused on this moment, on the two of them, on raw, consuming desire.

Her inner tiger reared its head with a "Squeak."

Linc released a sound between laughter and groan. His erection jerked against her thigh. "Some people never learn," he vowed in a voice wrought with lust.

His finger left her sex again. She anticipated the lash of the flogger this time, reveled in the bite of its tails. Harder this time. Pummeling into her ass. Raising a decadent sting that worked its way from her throbbing cheeks to her quaking sex. Writhing in her bindings, she prepared to squeak for more.

The flogger lifted from her butt. She thought she would get another swat without having to work for it. It wasn't the tails that met with her sensitized flesh next, though. He moved down her thighs and captured the portion of them nearest to her junction in his hands. His tongue swiped the aroused skin above one hand, and Erica's breath panted in while her juices leaked out.

Turning his tongue on the trickle of arousal, Linc feasted on her with long, languorous licks. "Such a tasty piece. I might have to keep you like this forever. Mine to use or abuse as I choose. To finger." He slipped a finger back inside her passage. "To fuck."

She whimpered as he fucked her, slowly in and out, with the lone digit. Then she confessed, "I'd like that."

The fingering ceased. "You would?" he asked, sounding surprised, hesitant.

Had it been too much to admit? Did it hint at more than the short term? Whatever the case, it was the truth. She no longer worried about her comfort zone. Wherever he took her, she was anxious to follow. "Yes, I'd let you do whatever you wanted. For however long you wanted."

"Erica . . ."

It was the warning again. The one she'd heard so many times before. The one she'd thought they moved past earlier tonight. Erica jerked at her bound wrists, wishing she could get free to see his face. "What, Linc? What is so wrong with liking the idea of being your sex slave?"

"You're playing with fire."

"Good. Burn me. I'm not afraid."

Silence followed, several long seconds of it where she thought her boldness had cost her dearly. That Linc was going to end things, here and now. Then he grabbed her around the waist and guided her to her knees.

His hand rubbed across her still tingling butt cheeks. "Such a pretty pink ass."

Relief poured through her with the words, spoken once more in the rough, arrogant tone. She gave into the urge to spread her thighs and wiggle her butt.

He tssked. "Such a shame it's so naughty."

"Teach it manners, Master. Please." She puckered her cheeks in wait of another swat. The flogger rewarded her, falling harder than before, the tails raining down upon her lower butt and the rear of her pussy. She winced at the flicker of pleasure pain, more incredible than she ever could have imagined. "Ahh . . . So, so good."

"Bad," he corrected, lifting the flogger and giving another whack. She cried out with the intensity. The heated need for release stabbed through her sex, pulsed through her veins. "You're pussy's dripping on the covers," he observed darkly. "Control your cum, slave."

"If I don't, will you punish me with your cock?" Erica dared. "Will you shove inside me and fuck me until I can't see straight?" She pulled her hips toward the bed and then reared them quickly, blatantly back up. "Will you give my famished ass something to play with too?"

Linc swore under his breath. Then again aloud. "You're too much. Too damned much to resist."

The flogger fell forgotten to the comforter, and tremors of anticipation shook through her. She grinned expectantly. Seconds passed. Ten, twenty. The bed creaked. She felt his weight leave the mattress, heard the rustle of what she assumed a condom wrapper. Then he was back on the bed, back behind her. His breathing came fast and loud as he took her hips in hand. The head of his cock nuzzled against the rear of her sex. As it had earlier, the condom masked the feel of his hot silky skin, the pre-cum that would otherwise be leaking out. For now, she would take it. For now, she craved to feel him inside her anyway she could get.

"And now for your famished ass," he said tightly.

The tremors gripped her again, this time with the thrill of the unfamiliar. Being unable to see his actions, only feel them, made that thrill all the greater. He lubricated a finger with the juices from her sex and brought it along her crack. She tightened her anus automatically. Then she forgot all about doing so as he thrust into her cunt and anal passage in tandem.

The breath hitched out of Erica with the rapid entry. Her fingers curled in the handcuffs, short nails nipping into her palms while her heart slammed wildly against her rib cage. Linc started to move then, finger and shaft, and her mind spun with erotic, exquisite sensation.

So much. So good. So intense it was, being taken in both orifices, she lost even her most basic abilities. Her eyes snapped shut of their own accord. She couldn't work her hips with his no matter her fierce want to do so. She let him do all the work, let him hold her up on her knees with one hand while he loved her ass with the other. Let him pummel into her pussy, again and again. Let him take her hot and hard, to the point where her inner tiger roared with her release.

Orgasm raged through her, blistered her blood, rendered her good and insensate, and completely captive to heady, blissful sensation. She was aware of Linc's powerful climax seconds later, the shout that accompanied it, and then his uncuffing her to pull her against him spoon fashion. Every other thought, sound, feeling evaded her.

When Erica finally surfaced from the euphoric fog, it was to turn in his arms and nip a kiss along the line of his mouth. Her groin rubbed unintentionally against his as she moved.

"More?" he asked, sounding incredulous.

She rubbed her groin against his a second time, purposefully this time. Awareness registered in her still moist sex, but she'd temporarily lost the stamina to respond to it. She sent him a ravenous smile all the same. "Yes, more. More, more, more." With a laugh, she added, "In a few hours. When I have the strength to move again."

They shared in the laughter this time. It droned off slowly, and they lay together, not talking, not moving aside from the subtle shifts caused by their breathing and the lazy rub of Linc's hand along her back. The silence stretched out, comfortably, intimately. The stroke of his palm felt as natural as breathing, as did his presence in her bed. As did her want for him.

Erica sighed contentedly. She could get used to this.

"Whatever's on your mind has to be pretty incredible for that smile."

Her lips lost the smile in mention. What was on her mind was purely dangerous stuff. She turned her thoughts on the night behind them. The last hours of sex aside, she hadn't felt so liberated in years as she had when she'd been sketching Linc's nude body. "Thanks for convincing me to give sculpting another try. I know I haven't done anything more than sketch so far, but even that much felt phenomenal."

"Why did you quit?"

"It's time-consuming, like I said before."

"And?" he prompted, his tone making it clear he knew there was more to it.

Erica had kept the rest of the reason from him to avoid talk of Nathan. Now she wanted to tell him. Having no secrets between them could only strengthen their friendship. "Supplies aren't cheap. After Nathan quit the crew and failed to hold down a job elsewhere, I couldn't rationalize spending money on a hobby."

"Not a hobby. A passion. One you're damned good at."

Warmth fanned through her with his complete faith in her abilities. Nathan had hinted at such a time or two, but he'd never come right out and said it. And he never acted like he cared when she packed up her supplies for what she believed would be forever. "Whatever. It wasn't making the house payment."

"It could. If you got your work into the hands of the right person. I'd be happy to help you locate those people."

The warmth grew. Emotions surfaced. Linc was just being friendly, yet it felt like so much more. Needing levity, Erica sent him a taunting grin. "Tell you what, as soon as I finish your nude, I promise to show it to anyone who'll look."

"Just so long as you uphold your end of the bargain and do me justice in the male anatomy department."

She'd spoken the words in jest. That he honestly wouldn't mind her showing off his naked resemblance to the masses said wonders about his self-esteem. Or the lengths he was willing to go to see her happy. Lengths no one in the past had even considered.

Calling out to levity a second time, she pushed her hand between their bodies and took his shaft into her fingers. No matter how tired she'd felt moments ago, the flex of his cock had her energy fast returning and her sex once again molten with desire.

Erica sighed. He truly had turned her, a woman who'd been convinced she didn't want for sex, into an orgasm nympho. "Mmm . . . I think I might need a reminder, just to be safe."

"What happened to taking a few hours off to recharge?"

"A few hours. A few minutes." Planting her palms on his chest, she pushed him onto his back and climbed on top. "Close enough."

8

Erica's doorbell rang followed by a merry sounding, "Trick or treat."

In the wake of a night ripe with fantasies come to the flesh, she'd forgotten today was Halloween. Shelby had saved her, giving Erica the candy she'd planned to pass out before learning she and her family would be spending the weekend up north at her parents' place. Erica had been invited along. She got on well with her one-time in-laws, and any other time would have accepted the invitation. This weekend she hoped to spend with Linc. Basking in his friendship, his warmth, his big sexy body.

Before her thoughts did wicked things to her panties, she opened the door. The smile she'd prepared to greet trick-or-treaters fell flat at the sight of her sister. The one who was notorious for only calling or showing up when she wanted something.

While her surprise settled, Erica took in Holly's beaming smile, perfect blond updo, and smart navy pantsuit. She looked great, well put together and better than Erica had ever seen her. Dare she think her sister had finally matured? Dare she hope this visit didn't come with the kind of strings that involved Erica setting aside her life to focus on Holly's happiness?

"What are you doing here?" Erica finally asked.

Holly chirped out a dry laugh. "It's good to see you, too, sis."

"Of course, it's good. Better than good." It was, for the most part. The part where she didn't feel like a leaden weight of responsibility had settled around her shoulders. "How are you?"

"Wonderful. I had a free weekend and thought it the perfect time to catch up."

"You're here for the whole weekend?"

"Unless that's a problem."

"Not at all." If this visit was truly to catch up. Even if it was just to visit, Holly's presence was going to put a serious damper on Erica's sex life. Presuming she had a sex life.

No discussion of further liaisons had taken place before Linc returned to his house early this morning. There had to be more sex in their future. He couldn't believe she'd meant a lone night by short term, or that she was already back on the sex wagon. Could he?

The thought of never again touching him as a lover twisted Erica's belly. As she'd done each time unwanted emotions rose up last night, she tuned out the sensation and tuned into a smile. "Have you eaten?"

"A burger and fries at the airport."

"The dinner of champions," Erica returned automatically, dryly, sounding just like the stand-in mother she no longer wanted her sister to regard her as. "Happen to bring me any?"

"Nope, but I did bring you this." Erica had been so caught up in her thoughts she hadn't noticed that Holly stood with her hands behind her back until she pulled one forward to offer a bottle of white wine. She retracted her other hand to reveal a second bottle. "And a matching one for yours truly. I know you don't drink much, but it's a special occasion."

Then this really was nothing more than a chance to catch

up? Erica warmed to the idea of Holly's company. Forty-eight hours of sisterly bonding; then she could worry about enticing Linc back into her arms. If he even needed enticing. "We haven't visited in a long time."

"Actually, I was talking about my engagement."

Engagement? Shock slammed into Erica twice as great as that she'd known upon opening her door to find Holly. She struggled to find her voice. "You're getting married? To whom?"

"Jayson Bani—"

"Trick or treat," a chorus of loud, little voices sang out behind Holly.

Erica stuck her first finger in the air. "Hold that thought. I want all the details."

Holly moved inside the house. While her head spun with her sister's announcement, Erica grabbed the candy bowl and greeted the assortment of miniature princesses, pirates, and one very lime dinosaur. Holly appeared in the doorway next to her as the kids said their thanks and started away from the house.

"God, they're adorable," her sister observed. "We plan to start trying to get pregnant right away on the honeymoon."

Holly was going to be a mother? Holly who'd always relied on Erica for everything short of chewing her food for her. To be fair, it *had* been a long time since they'd spent any quality time together. She'd already ascertained that Holly looked as though she'd matured. If Erica had always believed as the older sibling, she would be the first to have kids . . . things changed all the time. Holly was in a stable relationship and in the market to procreate. Erica was loving the single life and the freedom that came with not having children.

Her belly gave another nasty twist with the thought that didn't ring quite true. She shut out the sensation once again to share in her sister's joy. "So do you have a date set?"

"Christmas. I know that doesn't leave much preparation time. I also know you can get the details in place fast."

* * *

Sunday evening Linc sank down on his living room recliner, exhausted. He'd done what he'd sworn he was never going to do, and returned to Ladder 13. Today had been a dry run. He'd informed the captain he'd pulled his head out of his ass and wanted his old position back, part-time at first and then they would see. From there, he'd mostly sat around the firehouse and shot the bull with Trick and the rest of the crew. And thought of Erica.

His exhaustion came from the adrenaline rush that accompanied his return. The ceaseless thoughts of Erica were tiring in their own right. He hadn't seen her since leaving her asleep in her bedroom early Friday morning to head to work at the maintenance garage. He'd spotted her younger sister entering the house Friday evening and, knowing how little time the two spent together, figured Erica would value some distance.

Was Holly gone now? If she wasn't, would she mind him barging in and becoming a third party?

Damn, he was anxious to see Erica. To tell her how his day went. To see if she'd been serious when she said her no firefighter vow pertained only to the long run.

He'd wanted to believe once they'd slept together, he'd stop thinking of her and sex at every turn. He'd wanted to believe they could return to their platonic friendship, as he had with every friend-turned-lover before her. But now that he'd had her, now that he discovered she was the perfect balance of girl next door and sex goddess, he only wanted her more.

Shit.

Cursing a second time, with the idea he'd fucked up their friendship beyond repair when he'd instigated that kiss in his flowerbed, Linc stabbed the power button on the TV remote. He was surfing through the channels when someone knocked on the front door. He was hardly in the mood for visitors but went to the door anyway. Then he realized he was in the mood for visitors, after all, when he spotted Erica through the trio of window slats.

His heart and dick thrummed. Not bothering to cage his pleased smile, he opened the door. Thoughts of the night he opened his door to find her standing in the racy white teddy tripped through his mind and tightened his groin. His gaze slid downward. White stockings were visible beneath the knee-length hem of her black jacket. The same white stockings, make that thigh highs, she'd worn the night of the teddy?

A slow smile curved Erica's mouth. "Can I come in?"

"Always," Linc responded on rote, his gaze latched onto her lips. They were lined in fire engine red. A closer look at her eyes revealed the lids dusted in a smoky shade. Her hair lacked its traditional ponytail, instead styled in curly, shoulder-length waves. And her scent . . . Her familiar, intoxicating scent overlain with the musk of arousal was all it took to harden his cock.

She moved past him into the house. "I wanted to come over last night and wish you good luck today, but Holly showed up out of the blue on Friday and only just left. Did it go okay?"

"It was good." About to get better. Unless he'd only imagined her stimulation. Unless she didn't wear a sexy-as-hell teddy beneath her jacket. Unless she'd come over to tell him the sex was off now that he'd regained his firefighter status. He'd be one sorry bastard if that was the case. "Even with the guys giving me endless crap for quitting in the first place."

"I'm proud of you for going back, Linc. I'm sure a part of you still fears what might happen the next time you step foot on a fire scene, but a bigger part has to know you're where you belong, doing a job you love."

A part of him did still fear. It wasn't of becoming a victim to some rampant blaze, just as it had never been despite what he'd vowed to Trick the night of the benefit dinner and dance. It remained the fear of how it would affect Erica should he become that victim.

Linc's stomach turned with the thought of her losing another person close to her, this time to death. She was strong, more so for Nathan's leaving. Still, he couldn't dismiss how badly she'd taken that leaving. He couldn't forget all the tears she'd cried.

Her smile widened, gained a mischievous edge. He gladly turned his focus on it. As much as he was still infatuated with thoughts of her and sex, he was still equally infatuated with the lush curve of her lips. Still wanted to devour her mouth at every turn.

"Have you eaten?" he asked.

"Holly and I had an early dinner before I dropped her off at the airport."

Elation spiked through him. Her sister was gone. Erica was back to being all his. Maybe. Hopefully. At least for the short term. Fuck, he needed her kiss.

As if she suddenly knew that same fervent need, she eyed his mouth. Her tongue peeked from between her lips to dab at the lower one. "I could feed you."

The move was quick, and yet so hot, so suggestive. Or was he only reading into the action, seeing what he ached to see. "What do you have in mind?"

"Leftovers from the weekend. Lasagna or fettuccine—Holly's a huge pasta buff." Her fingers went to the throat of her jacket. A hissing tug of the zipper parted its sides. "Or I still have this left over from last weekend."

Linc's cock jerked hard against his fly. His pulse sped ecstatically. She wore the teddy. With its strategically cutaway nipple holes. With its sheer crotch that displayed the shimmering curls of her sex. With its tiny little white lace ass covering just waiting for him to tear it away.

In one fluid move, he pulled her into his arms and bent his

head to a breast. "Normally, I don't eat anything that's more than a few days old, but I feel an exception coming on."

"An exception," Erica sighed as his lips closed around her nipple, "or an erection?"

"Go away," Erica groaned into her pillow when her night-stand phone started to ring and refused to stop. It was Saturday for Pete's sake. A glance at her alarm clock revealed it a few minutes after seven, which meant she'd gotten a whopping three hours of sleep.

Last night, she'd happily traded sleep for good conversation with Linc while she worked on molding his likeness in clay, and then great sex while he worked on molding her body into a melting puddle of orgasmic bliss. This morning, her head ached from the lack of slumber. She wanted only to remain in bed, curled up next to his sleeping body. His sleeping, *snoring* body.

She smiled at the chainsaw sound ripping from his mouth. She was lucky to have gotten the few hours of sleep she had for the intensity of the sound. Nathan had never been a snorer. Nathan had never been a lot of things.

The continual shrill ring of the phone stopped the thought from taking shape. With a growl, she yanked up the cordless and barked into the mouthpiece, "What?"

"Can you come over for breakfast?" Shelby asked.

Erica's annoyance vanished. Her friend never called this early, which meant she had to have a good reason for doing so. "I can."

"But you don't want to because Linc's there," she guessed. "Is he sleeping?"

Another chainsaw snore left his lips. "Beyond a doubt."

"Then come over long enough for a cup of coffee. Leave a note telling him you ran out for donuts or something." Sudden tension coated Shelby's voice.

Erica forgot about sleeping and climbed from the bed. "What's the matter?" she asked as she pulled underwear, socks, jeans, and an oversized sweatshirt from her dresser.

"Nothing that has to be a big deal."

"Just big enough to wake me up at seven on a Saturday?"

Shelby paused a beat, then, "If you want to wait, you can."

Erica cast Linc a last look as she slipped out the bedroom door and closed it. She wanted to wait. There was no point in doing so, though, since she'd never get back to sleep for her wonder of what Shelby had to share. "I'll be there in ten minutes. I expect Danish."

Erica breezed through her friend's kitchen entrance less than ten minutes later. Shelby sipped hazelnut-scented coffee at the breakfast-nook-style table. Setting the mug down, she offered a smile that failed to warm her brown eyes. "Morning."

"Good morning." Erica took the seat across from her, where a second steaming cup of coffee waited. She swallowed back a long drink. "What's going on?"

Shelby nodded at the sliced Danish coffeecake in the center of the table. "Have some Danish first. It's blueberry cream cheese."

Erica's belly flip-flopped. Breaking out her favorite flavor could not be a good sign. It meant Shelby had traveled to the gourmet bakery in the next town, which meant forethought. And that meant Shelby had been planning this breakfast gathering since at least yesterday afternoon, given the bakery didn't open till seven.

Figuring she was going to need something to lift her spirits after Shelby shared her news, Erica selected a large piece of Danish dripping with blueberry sauce and cream cheese. She took a bite, murmuring over the decadent flavor, and then demanded, "Now spill."

"Nathan called."

"Oh." As in, *Oh, God, what a way to ruin an awesome bite*

of Danish. Nathan's long overdue call couldn't have been simply to say hello. Something major had to have been said or done to warrant this early-morning meeting. Something that involved Erica.

"He wants to come home for Thanksgiving."

"Oh." As in, *Oh, hell, she did not want to see him.*

But why not? She'd come to terms with their failed marriage months ago. She didn't blame him. She no longer blamed herself. If anything, she was thankful for the divorce. These last couple weeks with Linc had opened her eyes to precisely how wrong Nathan had been for her. They'd also opened her eyes to precisely how right Linc was for her, but that wasn't a subject she was allowed to explore, in her head or otherwise.

"I didn't say yes or no yet," Shelby advised. "I wanted to get your clearance first."

Erica frowned. "He's your brother. You don't need my permission to see him."

"You're my sister—maybe not on paper any longer, but always in heart—and you live less than a hundred feet away. I'd never have him come around here without getting your nod of approval." The warmth that had been missing from Shelby's eyes emerged. "He sounded good. Kind. Like the man we used to know. I know it's been over a year since he's bothered to call or make contact with anyone in the family, but I think he's ready to get back to his old life."

Erica's pulse quickened. How exactly did she mean that?

Shelby couldn't still believe Erica held out hope for Nathan's return so they could rekindle their love. Not after all the juicy details she'd shared about her sexcapades with Linc.

"I don't want Nathan back," she asserted as she'd done a gazillion times before. "I'm also not about to drop everything to help him should he ask. Yes, I agreed to essentially do that for the sake of Holly's wedding, but that's one very rare exception. From the grand standpoint, I've changed. I'm putting me first these days."

Shelby grinned. "Doing the horizontal mambo with Linc's been good for you. For once, I actually believe you when you say that."

"Does Nathan know about me and Linc?"

"Not unless he's become psychic." Shelby lost her smile. "I don't know that he wants everything the way it used to be. Or maybe he doesn't even want to come home for more than a few days and then never plans to call or visit again. I honestly don't have a problem telling him no to an initial visit. Like I said on the phone, it isn't a big deal."

And like Erica had known from the moment she'd identified Shelby as her early-morning caller, it was a damned big deal. "It's a *huge* deal, and you should say yes. I'll probably be out of town helping Holly with wedding stuff that week anyway. If I'm not and our paths cross, it will make for a good time to get the awkwardness out of the way."

Linc watched a frigid mix of gusting sleet and snow hammer Erica's bedroom window as he pulled on his jeans. Each day of the three weeks since they'd become lovers, he found it harder to leave her warm, rosy body behind. Mornings like this one, it was nearly impossible.

Without a sound to tell him she'd crawled from beneath the covers, the points of her nipples pressed against his bare back. Her arms wound around his torso. In a low, breathy tone, she noted, "There's no way a fire's going to stay burning in that mess."

Shivers rolled along his neck. He groaned under his breath. She still knew just what buttons to push to rile him. Or in this case, rile his testosterone.

Unwrapping her arms from around his middle settled a lead

weight of reality in Linc's gut. He shouldn't turn her down, no matter if accepting her advances would make him late for work. Any day now, she could decide they'd reached their short-term limits.

What then? He turned his unquenchable desire for her on some other woman? Fuck that woman while imagining Erica's sexy baby blues and entrancing scent?

The questions eating at him, Linc grabbed yesterday's sweat-shirt from the floor. He tugged it over his head. "Statistics say otherwise. More people lose their home to a total loss fire on a day like this than most any other time of the year. Besides, I'm only working at the firehouse two days a week. I can hardly miss one of those days."

"I know. I just had to try." Grabbing a throw blanket off the bed, she wrapped it around her nakedness and followed him out to the living room. Like a doting wife, she watched as he slipped into his boots. He pulled on his coat, and she moved into his arms for a good-bye kiss. It wasn't a passionate kiss, but a tender one that again reminded him of the way a wife might act.

It was a crazy thought, one he shouldn't be having. One that surfaced again when she sent a concerned look to the elements whipping about outside. "Be careful. It looks awful out there."

He considered making a "Yes, wife" crack like he would have done before they'd become lovers. For fear Erica would take it the wrong way, he offered up a reassuring smile instead. "I'm always careful. See you tonight?"

"Yeah, probably."

Linc frowned with the unexpected response as he stepped out into the wild weather. Why probably? Why not definitely? Did she have better plans? A better man to spend the night with?

It wasn't his business if she did. They hadn't agreed to be monogamous so long as they were sleeping together. The sound of a car starting drew his attention away from the irritation caused by his thoughts. Across the street, Shelby went to work on chipping away at a six-inch layer of snow frozen onto the windshield of her minivan. Seeing no sign of her husband, Linc grabbed the scraper from the cab of his truck and jogged across the street to join her.

"Where's Matt when you need him?" he asked, only half teasing.

From beneath a faux fur cap, Shelby gave him an exhausted look. "Sick in bed with the flu. The boys, too. The last thing I want to do is go out in this crap, but they're in dire need of medicine." She shoved a tangle of windblown hair from her face. "How've you been? I haven't seen much of you around the last couple weeks."

"Work and Erica have been keeping me busy. Particularly Erica. The girl's a sexaholic," It wasn't information he'd normally share, even jokingly, but he knew Erica told Shelby most everything that happened in her life.

"In that case, she must be perfect for you." Amusement shone in her eyes as they continued to work together to clear the windshield. With the heater on full blast and their joint chipping and scraping efforts, the job went quickly. Linc was about to head for his truck when Shelby sent him a serious look.

"What?" And did it have to do with her observation on how well he and Erica fit together? And if that observation were accurate, why the hell hadn't Erica said she'd definitely see him tonight?

"I asked Erica and she said it was okay, but now I'm thinking I should have asked your opinion on letting Nathan come home too."

Wonder over Erica's response evaporated as an ice-cold shiver skated along Linc's spine that had nothing to do with the wintry weather. Nathan was coming home? Erica knew and hadn't told him? Since it was clear Shelby thought she had, he shrugged. "He's allowed to live where he wants."

"Like I told Erica, I don't know that he wants to move back, just visit for a few days over Thanksgiving. I'm sure it's not going to be a big deal."

"I'm sure you're right." Only, he wasn't sure. Because it was a big deal, as was Erica's failure to share the news. A big damned deal that churned his gut in vicious circles.

The sound of her front door opening pulled Erica's attention from the paperback in her hands. She sat up from her reclined position on the couch to find Linc standing just inside the doorway. The snow/sleet mix had ended with the emergence of nightfall an hour before. Judging by the rosy shade of his cheeks, the bitterly fierce wind remained.

A naughty smile formed as she considered the many wicked ways she might warm him. Then she remembered he was supposed to be working. They wouldn't have him leave early when he worked only two days a week to begin with. Had he left on his own, suddenly decided he wasn't ready to return to the crew, after all, and walked out midshift?

Setting aside the paperback, she came to her feet. "Aren't you supposed to be on at the firehouse till noon tomorrow?"

"What are your plans for Thanksgiving?" Angry demand filled the question.

Erica recognized the anger in his eyes and rigid stance then, and a small pang of foreboding shot through her belly. "I don't know. Why?"

"I know you often spend it with Shelby and her family."

The observation was spoken hard, bitterly. The pang grew, clenching at her insides. He'd found out. Somehow Linc had to have found out that Nathan was coming home and believed the worst for not having heard it from her. She should have told him. Selfishness had kept her from doing so. She hadn't wanted friction between them when their days as lovers were numbered.

In case she was mistaken, she played ignorant. "Sometimes I do, but I don't plan on it this year."

A knowing smirk formed on his lips. "Going for a reunion with Nathan instead?" Betrayal clung to the words. "You told me he doesn't matter to you anymore. You said he couldn't come between us."

"He doesn't. He can't."

"Then why didn't you tell me?" he snapped.

"I didn't think it was a big deal." God, even now Erica couldn't get the depth of her reason out. No, she was afraid to get it out.

"You're lying. I know you better than that. You kept it from me for a reason." Linc's eyes narrowed, studied her face, and concluded the entirely inaccurate. "You still care about him, don't you? If he comes knocking on your door tomorrow, asking for help, you'll drop whatever you're doing to lend a hand. It's not your fault. It's just who you are."

Defensiveness nipped at her heels, growled through her belly. She shook her head. "You're wrong, Linc. It's not who I am. Not any longer."

"The way you jumped, like a faithful servant, to take on Holly's wedding planning says otherwise. The best thing you ever could have done for either of you was to tell her no."

"You're being an ass. One who has absolutely no say in what I do with my life." The instant the infuriated words left her mouth, Erica wanted to take them back. His accusation had just smarted so damned bad. Mainly because it was 100 percent on.

Hurt flashed through Linc's eyes. His expression went blank then, void, and the fight seemed to drain out of him. "You're right," he said quietly.

She blinked her shock. "I am?"

"I'm supposed to be working right now." Not bothering

with a good-bye, he yanked the door open and strode out of the house.

Erica swore as the blustery wind took hold of the door and slammed it shut. God, what a mess. One that was solely her fault. If she'd told Linc about Nathan coming home, the argument never would have happened. She wouldn't have suggested he meant nothing to her. She wouldn't be standing here, wondering if that callous lie had brought an end to more than their sex life.

Whatever the damage, they would move past it and be friends again, Erica assured herself. If she wanted more than that, if she was standing here with emotion clogging her throat, yearning for the long term, that was her all fault too. He'd agreed only to a temporary arrangement, and she hadn't planned on falling in love.

Heart heavy, she twisted the door lock and flicked off the porch light. It was barely after eight, far earlier than she'd consider going to bed on a normal night. This day had started frosty outside of the house and had ended frosty inside it, and she was mentally exhausted.

Feeling like she'd doze off instantly, Erica climbed into bed and snuggled beneath the weight and warmth of the covers. She shut her eyes, but they popped back open. Her mind raced with thought. She hated the idea that Linc was out in this wicked weather, his foul mood not suitable for driving. She hated knowing what a crappy friend she'd been.

Ten miserable minutes had passed when a knock carried down the hallway from the front door. Relief sighed through her. It had to be Linc, come back to apologize. To admit that he'd fallen victim to mistaken assumptions, even if she was to blame for them.

Erica climbed out of her bed and hurried to the front of the house. Her own apology on her lips, she twisted the lock and tugged open the door. "Please don't ever walk out on me—"

she started, then abruptly stalled as her eyes met those of the man on her doorstep.

They were intimately familiar, but they weren't Linc's. These ones were warm brown and, like the dishwater blond shade of his short hair, a dead match for his sister's. "Nathan?"

9

A soft smile tugged at the corners of Nathan's lips, revealing a hint of a dimple in his right cheek. "Hello, Erica."

"What are you doing . . . ?" There was no point in finishing the question. Unlike Linc, she'd been given plenty of advance notice of his visit. She'd assumed she would also get notice from Shelby once he actually arrived in town.

She tried at a smile of her own. It felt less than natural, so she let it slip away to ask, "How are you?"

"Good." He nodded to the inside of the house. "Can I come in?"

The frosty chill of the night registered. The stinging wind whipped at his coat and plastered his jeans around his legs. He wore neither a hat nor gloves. He was probably freezing, but did she really want him in her home?

A few more silent seconds passed, and Nathan's smile grew understanding. "Don't worry about it. I can come back tomorrow with Shelby."

"No, it's fine." This was her ex-husband. A man who'd

turned vocally cruel at the end of their marriage but had never laid a hand on her in anger. Never would. "Come in."

Nerves fluttered through Erica's belly as she stepped back from the doorway. What now? "I was about to make some coffee," she improvised. "Would you like a cup?" An instant laugh rolled out with the stupidity of the question. "Never mind. You don't drink coffee."

"Thanks anyway."

"I could get you something else."

"You don't have to take care of me, Erica."

He would never raise a hand to her in anger, but those words felt like a physical blow. Their meaning was also accurate. Without even realizing it, she was trying to play mother hen by seeing to his comfort.

"I just got into town and wanted to see you before you found out I was here from someone else," Nathan explained. He looked past her, into the living room, and his smile moved into his eyes. "You've been sculpting."

Erica followed his gaze to the full-body, erect nude of Linc on the fireplace mantel, and the heat of embarrassment pushed through. Even in small proportions, the statue's lifelikeness had turned out impeccable. Nathan couldn't miss the man behind the inspiration.

His gaze came back to hers. "How is Linc?"

She fought off her discomfort. "Better."

"Then he was after I left?"

"Shockingly, not everyone's life revolves around you." She flinched with the unexpected retort. Awkward tension was to blame. She honestly didn't harbor anger toward him anymore. At least, not that much. "Sorry, I didn't mean to snap. Linc temporarily lost his vision this summer following a flash burn exposure on the job. He quit the crew after that."

Sympathy entered his eyes. "He'll never be happy."

"That's what I told him. He finally came to terms with that fact and went back to work with the Ladder a couple weeks ago."

"You've done well for each other," Nathan observed.

"It's not like that."

"Like you make each other happy? That's not what your eyes are telling me. It's okay to admit that you care about him, Erica. I'm seeing someone too."

Erica's heart skipped a beat. And then it resumed a normal pace. More normal than she'd known since Linc had walked out. Despite her time and again claim she was over Nathan, a modicum of doubt had remained somewhere in the recesses of her mind. That last shred vanished as she accepted his moving on without a single tear or rise in her emotions.

"She reminds me a lot of you," he admitted. "Just not in the ways I can't handle."

Tension returned with the incredulous remark. "I made you feel incompetent?"

"Of course not. I made myself feel that way by trying to be the man you fell in love with when I knew that man died in the fire." His smile returned, became hopeful. "I'll always love you, Erica, just not as your husband. As a friend, that's up for you to decide."

"Why don't you do us all a favor and shove off early?" Trick suggested, sliding onto a mess room chair beside Linc.

"Thanks, but I'm good," Linc returned, knowing damned well he wasn't.

Erica's failure to tell him about Nathan's return had festered at him until he couldn't think about anything else and the fight that had resulted for her omission. He'd gone off the deep end a bit with his angry accusations, but he hadn't been able to help himself. The idea of their sex life reaching an end twisted at his gut. The idea of her loving another man burned a hole in it.

"No," Trick corrected, "you're pissy and not willing to spill your guts on the reason." His gaze narrowed in scrutiny. "Why did you quit the crew?"

"I told you before. Self-preservation."

"Bullshit. I trained you, man. I see the adrenaline rush in your eyes when you take on a blaze. You're not afraid of losing your life to one."

He was, though, just not in the way Trick meant. "I don't love the idea, either."

"Death is going to happen when it happens. We all know that. So what's the real story? Why did you quit?"

"I'd like to hear that answer too," a familiar male voice piped in from behind them. One from the past. One that turned Linc's frustration to all-out rage.

He met Nathan's eyes with a lethal glare. "You want to know why I quit? I did it for Erica. She deserves someone in her life who truly cares about her. Someone who's going to be there longer than five seconds after the going gets rough."

Erica answered her cubicle phone, expecting to hear a co-worker's or client's voice. Instead, it was Linc, getting right to the heart of the matter. "We need to talk."

Her heart gave a bump. She'd lain awake most the night, wanting to call him at the firehouse and plead his forgiveness, get their friendship, if not their sex life, back on track immediately. This morning, she'd considered calling in sick to work so she could meet him at his door whenever he arrived home. Since it was the day before Thanksgiving, she couldn't see her boss believing the excuse. "I'm sorry about last night. I—"

"In person," he cut her off. "I'll be off the clock in twenty minutes. Is there somewhere we can have privacy?"

"Shelby will lend us her office, I'm sure."

"All right. See you then."

Nausea roiled Erica's belly as she made her way down the

hall to Shelby's office. Her friend knew about last night's argument and greeted her with a warm smile. "How's it going?"

"Okay. Can I use your office over the lunch hour?"

"Conference call?"

"Linc's coming here." Erica's voice shook with the response. Her legs felt shaky now, too, a combination of lack of sleep and anxiety.

Shelby's smile widened. "Okay, but only if you promise to wipe everything down when you're done." She pushed back her wheeled chair. Crossing to the front of the office, she pulled closed the blinds that ran the length of two wide windows. "I'll assume you don't want voyeurs."

"Oh, Jesus," Erica gasped. "He's not coming for sex. He's coming to tell me he's through having it with me."

"Yeah, right. He's coming to apologize. You'll do the same. Lots of kissing and groping will ensue. Surfaces will get sweaty, sticky. Just wipe everything down when you're done." Shelby grabbed her purse from a bottom desk drawer and went to the door. "I'm going to head out for lunch. Go ahead and make yourself comfortable. I'll let Nancy know to bring Linc back when he gets here."

"Make myself comfortable?" Did she honestly believe relaxing was a possibility?

"Undo a few buttons. Show some cleavage. Remind him what he missed when he walked out on you last night."

Disbelief coursed through Erica with Shelby's meaning. "You're crazy."

Her friend lifted her left hand and wiggled her diamond-adorned ring finger. "Not to mention happily married for seven years."

Shelby uttered a "good-bye and good luck," then closed the office door.

Erica stared at the door. Seven years of marriage aside, Shelby *was* nuts. Out of her mind.

But what if she wasn't?

Linc *could* be coming over to apologize with the hopes that make-up sex would follow. Or he could be coming over to do as she feared, and bring an end to their sexcapades and any minute chance there was of their relationship becoming about more than sex and friendship on a permanent basis.

Even if it was the latter, why shouldn't she make herself comfortable? Why shouldn't she yank him inside Shelby's office and gift them both with an early Christmas present in the form of an unforgettable final screw?

She should, Erica thought as she flicked open the top button of her sweater. She would, she accepted as she made short work of the rest of the buttons and shook the sweater down her arms. Unleash the tiger one last time, she vowed as her slacks went the way of her sweater. Followed quickly by her socks, bra, and underwear.

"Thanks," Linc's voice came from the hallway outside Shelby's office a handful of minutes later.

Erica's breath caught. Feeling a hair too naked in such a public place, she'd borrowed the thigh-length, button-up sweater Shelby left in her office for those especially cold mornings. She took it off now and took herself to the door. The idea Nancy, the accounting firm's admin, might be standing outside had her snapping the light off. The door cracked open, then quickly closed.

A fraction of light seeped past the drawn miniblinds, lighting the room just enough for her to make out Linc's outline. The thick, dark hair she loved to lose her fingers in. The hard, muscled body she loved to lose the rest of herself in.

Damn, she didn't want this to be their last time as lovers. She never wanted that.

"Erica?" he questioned, sounding confused. "Are you in here?"

"I'm here." Without trying, her voice came out breathy, sexy, eager for his touch. The way he'd made her feel from that first kiss. "Come and get me, Linc."

"I came to talk." His hand snaked out and he felt blindly along the wall.

Before he could find the light switch, she darted a hand out, captured his wrist, and jerked hard. With a curse, he stumbled toward her. Their bodies collided and then propelled backward as one, until her back thudded against the wall.

Linc pressed his hands against the wall and attempted to push away from her. She slipped her arms around his middle, locked her fingers at his back, and stole any chance of escape.

"Erica . . ."

Her name came out with that old, familiar warning. She spoke his name in return, a hot, husky whisper that ended with the press of her lips to his.

Unable to see her advance, between their proximity and the darkness, he opened his mouth on a surprised gasp. Erica took total advantage. She slipped inside the warm, wet interior. Slipped her hands down to his luscious ass. Jerked hard again, this time his hips forward as she savored his taste on her tongue.

The bulge of his cock pressed into her naked mound. Her pussy lubricated. Sighing in carnal delight, she ground against that delicious bulge. For his part, he remained still, his tongue inert, his hands motionless on the wall at her back. Then all at once, that changed. His own sigh pushed hot and hungry into her mouth. His own tongue moved, licking, caressing, dampening her sex to the point juices leaked along her inner thighs.

One of Linc's hands lifted from the wall. It closed around her side, thumb extended to caress the nearby nipple. His surprise over her nudity came as the stilling of his tongue followed by a muffled gasp. His appreciation of the same as the hardening of his cock.

His tongue moved again, kissing her with a sudden urgency

that suggested he couldn't get enough of her. The shove of his knee between her thighs spoke of the same. Taking her breast into his hand, he kneaded the tingling mound with his palm.

Erotic sensation raced through her with his work-roughened touch. Whimpering against his lips, she arched into his palm. His knee pushed forward and then back again, taking her sex on a wanton ride along his solid thigh. The folds of her labia parted with the move. Her clit rubbed against the coarse material of his jeans. Wetness flooded her pussy, perfuming the office air. Made her desperate to feel him inside her, if for only one last time.

Erica tore her mouth from his. She freed her hand of his ass to grab the condom she'd planted on Shelby's desk. "Fuck me, Linc," she panted as she uncurled his fingers from her breast to fold the condom into them.

She expected a comment. He didn't say a word. The only sounds to light the darkness were those of their harried breathing and the crinkle of the condom wrapper. Then that of their joint cries as he took her butt in his hands, pressed the tip of his cock to her opening, and thrust inside.

Her pulse galloped. The hot need for release swarmed her. She didn't want to come so soon. Didn't want him to do so either. She wanted this to last forever. Emotion stormed through her with the knowledge it couldn't, wouldn't. Didn't.

Linc's mouth found her neck, latched on with a feral, claiming bite. Throwing her head back on a euphoric cry, she flooded around his cock. His fingers tightened on her ass, and his shaft pulsed inside her as he surrendered to his own powerful climax.

A lone second had passed when he freed her neck. He set her on her feet and stepped back, his outline nearly enveloped in the darkness.

Erica swayed with sudden light-headedness. Knowing she didn't dare reach out to Linc, now that the sex was over, she took hold of the edge of Shelby's nearby desk. The office light flickered on a moment later. She blinked at the intensity. Then at the gorgeous view of Linc standing with his jeans around his ankles, his shirt and hair sexily rumpled, and his softening condom-covered cock glistening with her cream.

"What was that for?" he asked.

He didn't sound upset, didn't sound happy either. His tone and expression were equally neutral.

Unable to have this conversation in her currently undressed state, she grabbed her underwear and pulled them on. "To end things on a happy note."

His eyes narrowed, then quickly regained that neutral air. As if he couldn't have the conversation half dressed either, he rolled off the condom and disposed of it in its wrapper. After pulling up his jeans, he asked, "This is it, then? Time's up. No more sex."

Erica finished dressing while she weighed his words. Lacking in emotion as they were, it was impossible to gauge his feelings. Her own feelings were tumultuous, and it was all she could do to keep them buried. "That's why you came here, isn't it? To end things?"

"I came here to talk. Not about ending things."

Unbelievable hope sailed through her. She'd kept her knowledge of Nathan's return from Linc out of the fear it would mean an end to their short-term arrangement. She wasn't making that same mistake twice. "Last night, after you left, Nathan came to the house. It was weird seeing him again. Weirder that I could have been married to him for years and feel absolutely nothing for him now, well, aside from a little discomfort when he saw your nude."

A hint of amusement sparked on his face. It passed with his next words. "He came to the firehouse this morning. After I got over the urge to beat the hell out of him, we had a pretty good talk. It made me realize some things." The touch of a smile curved his lips. Visible emotion shined his eyes. "Fighting fires is my passion, but you're my calling, Erica."

The air cruised out of Erica with the heart-thundering admission. She sank down on the edge of Shelby's desk, unable to find her voice.

"I told myself I'd quit the Ladder for your sake," Linc continued. "Because you deserved to have someone in your life you could count on to always be there. The truth is, I quit the Ladder for myself. I fell for you during those weeks you nursed me back to the seeing world, and I was afraid you'd never be able to feel the same so long as you knew I came attached with strings of the firefighter variety."

I fell for you.

The words repeated in her head, again and again. Beautiful. Wonderful. Everything she'd never realized she'd wanted until a few short days ago. Maybe, just maybe, she would give Holly a run in the first-to-have-a-baby department, after all.

Erica came to her feet. "You know why I swore off firefighters?" He shook his head, and she explained, "Not because I feared what might happen to them while on the job. But because I feared what might happen to them if they left the job behind. The thought of you not being you—nothing is worth that." She gave him a playfully naughty smile. "Not even knock-my-socks-off sex in Shelby's office."

Linc let out a short laugh. He sobered quickly to ask, "What about my love?"

Elation filled her with the all-out admission. She forced herself to stand her ground. "Not when it comes at the cost of giving up your passion."

A frown tugged at his lips that just about broke her heart. "Tell me how to win here, Erica. Is there a way I can get both the girl and the job?"

She couldn't stay away any longer. Closing the short distance between them, she slid her arms around his waist and tipped back her face to meet his eyes. For the first time, she allowed her love for him to come through in her expression. "You already have them, Linc. Just keep doing what you've been doing. Just keep loving us both. I can't speak for the fires, but I guarantee I'll keep on loving you back."

The frown left Linc's mouth. A slow, sexy smile took its place. He bent his head and pressed his lips to hers. The soft, tender kiss stirred her heart and arousal in turn. He made slow, sweet love to her mouth for one minute, two. More.

When he finally lifted his head, it was to flash an arrogant grin. "So I knocked your socks off, huh?"

Erica laughed, feeling truly happy for the first time in years. "Technically, I wasn't wearing any. But I'd be willing to put some on and let you try to knock them off again."